EVIL UPRIVER

Julia! I'm
still waiting on
or royalties or
my name!

EVIL UPRIVER

BLUE COLE

INDIE GYPSY BOOKS

9/15/17

IG
Indie Gypsy
847 Sumpter Road
#441
Belleville, MI 48111
http://www.indiegypsy.com

ISBN-13: 978-0998615103
ISBN-10: 0998615102

Library of Congress Control Number: 2017949963

For information on special discounts contact us at
orders@indiegypsy.com.

For Missy

PROLOGUE

It covered the raw land in a fog of death. Newly cooled rock was sterilized where it lay, and sulfur rain sizzled as it fell into the fog from above. Mindless, it floated, but great pleasure was found as it infected and destroyed even the simplest of life.

Eons passed, and eventually life–true life–developed. Then the fog rose again, floating, infecting, killing. Massive beasts ruled the earth, and it gorged. Six times the fog rose, and six times it floated until it was sated. Each time, it settled in a stupor, congealing among the bones and flesh it consumed into a black mass that pulsed on occasion.

At last, the time came when it rose and found a new master ruled the earth. Tiny compared to the previous beasts, these creatures possessed what the others did not: fear. All things feared something, but these! These could anticipate fear, could see the darkness in anything. They could learn to fear anything.

So again it feasted. Across the land it floated, infecting and killing. Until it was sated. And it slept.

CHAPTER 1

BOBBY PUFFED, CLIMBING THE HILL, trying to balance propane canisters gripped in each hand. Crossed with switchbacks, the high bluff had uneven footing, protruding roots, and loose rocks. Part of the reason they chose this spot, but damn, it could be easier. He'd heard his parents talk about driving up here as teenagers, but since the fifties, the path had deteriorated with disuse. A chill hit, covering his sweat-slicked body, and he trembled. Coming down sucked, but Mark should have a batch ready for testing.

A rock slid from under his foot, shifting him toward the edge. His heart jumped, and he wobbled, the drugs keeping him off balance. He whimpered as his other foot couldn't find purchase, and he involuntarily tried to get a better grip on the canister in his right hand. Slick from sweat, the handle slid out of his hand and dinged as it hit a rock. The weight in his left hand pulled him away from the edge, and his feet slid out from under him.

"Motherfuckermotherfuckermotherfucker," he whispered, as he sat down hard but quit sliding. He heard the tank bounce far below and tensed, fearful of an explosion.

"Oh god, that was close," he said, catching his breath. Below him and down river, Tanninville glowed, lights marking the patterns of streets. His heart jumped in his chest, an uncomfortable pressure building. He tried to breathe deep, but the pain spread, so he leaned to the side. After a moment the pain receded, and he groaned. That had happened too much lately. Mark was probably using too much muriatic acid in their mix. Bobby needed to say something to him; it wouldn't be good for business if the product killed people.

After a few minutes, he climbed to his feet, staying well away from the edge.

The opening on the high bluff faced away from the town, but they set up behind the first bend in the old mine, anyway. Their lanterns cast a pale glow, and paranoia was a meth cooker's closest friend. Bobby turned the rocky corner, the smell of chemicals getting stronger. Sweet nectar of the gods, hillbilly heroin, redneck racer. Whatever you called it, the smell made Bobby's mouth water. His roommate was carefully spooning the mixture into the glass pan set over the burner, and three other pans sat cooling on the table behind him.

"Where's the other canister?" Mark asked, his voice muffled by the mask he wore. A small fan blew the majority of fumes toward the back of the mine, and Bobby set the propane tank down as he examined their latest batch.

"Nice," Bobby said as he ignored the question. Almost clear, the thin layer of crystals on each pan was streaked with white. The clearer, the better, and Bobby reached for a metal putty knife they used for scraping. Before he could knock a chunk loose, Mark grabbed his arm. Focused on the meth, Bobby hadn't seen him finish and come his way.

"You've been doing too much," Mark said, his mask now off. Strap marks showed on his cheeks, disappearing into the thick beard he wore. "Man, fuck off. It's called testing," Bobby replied.

"No, you're a crack head," Mark said to his roommate; they shared a small shotgun house on the edge of town with another buddy.

Bobby lifted his lip in a snarl, but controlled his temper. Maybe he had been doing too much. He reached into his pocket. "Good thing I brought something to mellow us out," he said, tossing a bag of weed on the table.

Mark grunted and moved the propane canister to the shelf built into the wall. "Where's the other tank? I thought you took two with you."

"Man, I almost slipped on the way up. It slipped out of my hand, and I dropped it, man. It scared the shit out of me."

"That's fifty bucks for the canister! How will we exchange it now?" Mark demanded.

Bobby ignored Mark as he chipped a few crystals out of the newest pan and handed them to Mark, who had the bag of weed open. Staying upwind of the fan, Bobby studied the setup. He was looking for a leak in the condenser line when his foot squished into something, releasing a foul smell. "What the hell?"

Mark looked at him over the joint he was rolling. "Yeah, some nasty shit's coming out of the back. Mining chemicals or something. I wouldn't touch them. They stink worse than the shit we're cooking."

The hum of the fan blades carried Mark's words away as Bobby tried to scrape the gunk from the bottom of his shoe. When he disturbed the thick goo, a sour, thick smell rose to his nostrils. Bobby gagged, the fumes making his eyes water. He coughed as his eyes traced the trail of gunk, and then followed it as it disappeared into a crack closer to the entrance.

"Toldya," Mark said.

"The fuck is that?" Bobby asked, his eyes burning.

"Gotta be chemicals from the old mine." Mark lit the joint, holding in a breath and passing it to Bobby. They moved away from their makeshift lab and the strange liquid. A few plastic chairs and an old army cot were set up around a flimsy card table. Enough light washed down from the cooking area for Bobby to examine his shoes. The liquid stuck to the rubber, and Bobby grimaced.

A fast-food napkin fluttered on the table, and Bobby picked it up.

"Hey, wake up. I'm trying to pass you this," Mark said, poking Bobby in the shoulder.

"Jesus, fucker, quitit!" Bobby didn't hide the irritation in his voice. "I'm looking at my show." He took the joint from Mark's twitching fingers; the newest batch must kick ass.

"Show? You gotta show down there?" Mark cackled, ignoring the look Bobby gave him.

In response, Bobby took a huge hit off the doobie, giving Mark the finger, left leg crossed over the right, a smoker in repose. The weed and fresh-cooked meth hit him, and he leaned back into the rickety chair. He didn't hear the squeak of protesting, weather weakened plastic. Bobby's body relaxed, the fingers on his left

3

hand uncurled from around the joint, and his right arm twitched, causing his right hand to touch the side of his shoe and collect a smear of foul gunk. Bobby didn't notice; his eyes rolled back in his head.

"BROTHAS and SISTAS, the man is down!" Mark cawed as his friend relaxed in the chair. Leaning forward, he rescued the joint as Bobby's body continued to relax. Something popped in the joint as the crystal cooked off. "I guess you got the big ol' rock that was in the middle," Mark said to his friend. He took another hit, enjoying the combination. It wasn't good to get too geeked up while working, but there wasn't much left to do. The weed mellowed it out some, but Mark's body jumped as nerves fired off.

"Good shit, man, I'm telling you," he said to Bobby. Squinting at his friend, Mark leaned over to poke him again.

Bobby's mind swirled down the mine shaft. Something was on his hand, his right hand, crawling. Nope, now it was under his fingernail, working around his knuckle, finding a dozen small capillaries. The microscopic veins ran together, a bundle merging into a small vein no wider than the hair on his head. Bobby watched, fascinated, as the black bits pulled together again, forming a black drop that spun and tumbled.

Black wasn't the right word; black was just a color. This was the absence of light, or color, or life. It rotated slowly, as if trying to choose the right path. Fumes rolled from the surface, and Bobby knew they were also floating around the cave, collecting in his lungs, settling, putting out their own little tendrils. Bobby tried to shake his hand, tried to get the stuff off of him, but it was too late. From a great distance, Bobby heard a great, insignificant noise.

"BROTHAAS . . ."

Bobby tuned it out; Mark was saying something, but nothing important. He turned his attention to the thing that was happening inside of him. As he watched, the drop thinned, dispersing to find its way across his body. Bobby felt the buzz lifting, and something hard poked him in his shoulder, hitting a nerve and making pain tighten his hand. Fuckin' Mark.

"Yo, man, heads up. Your puff," Mark said. "Or toke. Or hit. Whatever."

When that didn't get a reaction, he reached over and poked his friend's shoulder again. Bobby moved slightly, mumbling something deep in his throat. A smell wafted past Mark's nose, something foul, reaching the smell receptors burned out by years of drug usage and chemically seared by cooking up said drugs. Mark shivered, leaning over to wake Bobby. He poked him in the shoulder again, harder, and the chair popped. Mark watched it twist and bend, popping along the back. Bobby was stumbling out of the seat, a snarl turning his face into a thin, grinning skull. Inside deep sockets, his eyes were small, black against the darkness, and Mark saw Bobby coming for his throat too late to block him.

Mark dropped the joint as Bobby's force carried him onto his back. Something massive hit the back of his head, jarring his hands loose from Bobby's wrists. Mark's eyes opened wide, the cavern around him brightening. He tried to gasp air into his lungs as Bobby straddled him, hands on his throat. The pressure was massive, and Mark opened his mouth, vainly searching for air. A snapping sound filled his ears, and the grip on his throat tightened until everything cracked and collapsed. His mouth closed involuntarily, bringing pain and wetness to his mouth, but it was inconsequential compared to the fire and pain in his throat.

"Gaaaaaaaaaaa," Bobby said above him.

Something on Bobby's hand burned him, and Mark felt something leave Bobby and worry its way under his skin. As his friend dwindled above him, Mark saw the cavern darken to a point around him, and something was there. Something had always been there. That something was coming back, awakening after these long years.

"Gaaaaaaaaaaa," Bobby felt himself saying. Mark was under him, blood frothing from his lips. Something small and pink tumbled from the bubbles of blood and landed on the floor of the cave with a wet plop. Bobby plainly heard it, just like he heard the snapping and popping of the small, delicate bones in Mark's throat. Bobby could hear everything: the low simmer of the meth in the cave; the roar of the fan, masking almost every other sound; the painful rush of blood and air in Mark's throat.

Something exhaled in the back of the cave. Mark let out a final explosive gasp, twitched, and lay still. Bobby stared at the still, purplish-blue face of his friend and moaned. In answer, another moan came from the cave behind him, a sound deeper than hearing, a sound from the stone that surrounded him. Bobby staggered to his feet, following the call.

CHAPTER 2

THE OUTSIDE OF THE HOTEL was dark. My coffee steamed in the night, the wisps lit by the single-arc sodium light from farther down the parking lot. I hadn't slept well in this tiny hotel somewhere north of Atlanta. Scenes kept replaying in my head: happy moments, romantic moments, stressful moments, and final moments. As I approached my car it sensed my presence, unlocking the door with a meaty *clump*. I smiled to myself. It was still new enough to show the sticker price glue in one window; I would stop somewhere and scrape it off.

I climbed in, settling into the smell of new-car leather. With a push of a button, the car purred to life, and I grinned again. This was my reward for years of toiling in the clubs, scratching out songs on napkins, and smelling stale beer breathed out by drunks and music hopefuls alike. There wasn't much difference, but one was definitely more desperate than the other. Sitting in my new car, three hundred miles from Nashville, I had a memory of those smells: the bar, the scent of my guitar as I pulled it from the case, and stage dust. Another memory intruded, again, and I let it roll over me as I sat in the dark.

I walked out of the small room, Andrea ahead of me. I could feel the shit-eating grin on my face, but I didn't care. I knew what had happened in there; it was the moon shot, the one-in-a-million thing every guy in Nashville was looking for. The memory left a raw, open pit inside of me; the embarrassment, the shame, and a bit of anger when the moment was ruined. I guided the car out of the parking lot onto the two-lane highway and put the rising sun to my left. I would use the dawn as my GPS; as long as I kept the sun to my left, it would put Nashville somewhere to the north and Atlanta to the west, and I would leave them both behind me. The car accelerated smoothly under me, the odometer still showing less than a thousand miles. I would drive in silence for a little longer; there was plenty of time for music, later. I deliberately focused on the road in front of me; I'd replayed the scene hundreds of times since it happened last week. I was tired of it.

The morning air held a bit of fog hovering over the roadway; the two lane highway I was on dipped and curved as it dropped toward the coast, but I had three quarters of Georgia to cross before I made it to my destination. I had no plan or finish line; I needed a break from the scene and wanted to celebrate my success. Part of it was the new car and part of it was me, driving the back-country roads to re-absorb the land I'd written about for the last five years. As a songwriter, my job was to take a few words and craft a memory, a sense of place, or an emotion. Everyone needed a chance to recharge the creative batteries, get a chance to relax, and let life and stress unwind. I also needed a break from Nicole, and the disastrous way the relationship ended.

Early in the afternoon, I crested a small rise. Since leaving the hotel, I had drifted east, as if I were going toward Athens, Georgia, but turned at the last opportunity and found the Oconee National Forest. I wandered through it, crossed Interstate 20 and kept heading south, the thoughts of a few nights at the beach slowly rising as a destination in my mind. The suburbs of densely packed cities turned into rolling farmland, which I followed to a nice-sized river. An hour after I found the river I pulled into an overlook cut into the side of the roadway, the river a few dozen feet below me.

I could see the start of a town on the distance; it crowded one side of a bridge, but the river turned, and I couldn't see the remainder of it. A lonely chimney stood guard further down the road, the remains of a burned-out building crumbling below it. Weeds covered a barren parking lot, and I could see through the roof to the ground below. Behind me a large bluff rose, blocking the view of the farmland behind me. I watched the river for a moment, leaning against the car. The geography of this place was odd, with the bluff towering over me on one side and the river channel to the left. It wasn't something you expected to see in the

Piedmont area of Georgia, but the view was nice. The only sounds I heard were the low hum of the car and a grasshopper in the weeds in front of me. The car was new, the seat was stiff, and the sun felt good after the forced-Freon air. I felt a tightening in my bladder; as I was debating relieving myself, a truck came around the curve behind me. I caught a flash of sunglasses and the pulled-back shape of a ponytail. A single finger drifted off the steering wheel in a greeting, a Southern salute of welcome. *Guess that's a sign*, I thought, and climbed into the car. The chimney I had seen in the distance were the remains of a burned-out structure; I tried to glimpse at it as I went by, but the river's road curved as I passed it, distracting me. A few trailers sat lonely alongside the road as it led into town, where a faded maroon and white sign proclaimed I'd arrived in "TANNINVILLE, City of Homecomings." Below that, in small letters it read, "Population 445"; some local wiseass had added a decimal between the four and the five, and I grunted in amusement. The road split in front of me, one fork into town and the other into the distance. I took my foot off the accelerator, and turned the car into the town, thinking of nothing but my bladder.

It was the kind of place you could sit outside for an hour or more and never notice the time passing. Occupying one corner of a four-way stop, the store offered iron cookware rattling against fiberglass fishing poles, late season vegetables, and faded tee shirts featuring a nearby tourist attraction. An archway above the sun-bleached front doors read "*Welcome to the Tanninville Traveler.*" Small gourds with holes drilled into them for birds hung on a wire stretched across the highway. Blue martins loved to eat insects, especially mosquitoes, and I'd helped my grandfather hang his own gourds.

The smell and sounds of crickets greeted me when I walked through the propped-open wooden doors. I bought a Dr. Pepper in a glass bottle and a cigarillo from the buxom and overly tanned girl behind the counter.

"Nice place," I said. "Good to see the old general stores haven't disappeared."

She smiled at me, showing a crooked tooth or two.

"Lots of people say that."

I thanked her and took my purchases outside. Pulling out my pocket knife, I cut my cigar in half. I'd been trying to quit for the last six months, but the breakup and my retreat from Nashville were testing my nerves.

My recent success had its own pitfall. I'd been playing and singing in the faux honky tonks and music clubs, generating a little buzz, and one of my songs was picked up by a megastar after his A&R rep heard one of my sets. The new car came after the first check, and my decision to drive south came after I couldn't convince my girlfriend Nicole that the A&R rep was only business; to the label's public relations department, artists were cattle. *At best.* At worst, we were issues to be dealt with.

I hoped another check would come soon. My sleek new Chrysler wouldn't run on empty promises or liquor-fueled curses. My song was currently holding at number one for a fifth week, and the megastar's tour was due to start in a few months.

I settled on a bench so old the wood was glassy to the touch. Stretching out my legs, I exhaled contentedly. For every milligram of cancer I was inhaling, I was shedding hours of stress. I tilted my head back, closing my eyes behind mirrored shades. If I'd had a drink in my hand, I could have happily spent the night in that position. The farther away I was from Nashville, the better I felt. Everyone needs a change of scenery now and then. I exhaled again, pinching the plastic tip between thumb and forefinger.

"What you smoking there, son?"

I jumped at the gravelly Southern drawl, almost upsetting the soda in my lap. I opened my eyes to see an older man dressed in a sheriff's uniform. He had the largest pot belly I'd ever seen, the buttons of his shirt barely holding in his girth. His patrol car was parked behind my sedan, long ways, and he was rolling a toothpick from side to side in his mouth.

"Nothing, sir," I said, regretting it immediately. It wasn't a response designed to inspire confidence. "I mean, just a cigar. I bought it inside a few minutes ago."

He nodded, looking me over and then glanced at my car. Dark grey slacks were at the top of my suitcase that morning. White shirt and my dark cowboy boots didn't seem like such a good choice now as he looked between me and my car.

"Where you headed?" he finally asked. When I didn't answer right away, he raised an eyebrow.

In a few sentences, I hit the high points. Nashville. Woman trouble. Songwriter. Road trip.

"Ayup," he said. "Sounds like a country song, all right." His accent made it sound like 'aye-ite,' but I had been born and raised in a town not much different from this one.

"I guess I need to see your license. Might as well do my job."

I dug into my back pocket and gave him my Tennessee driver's license.

"Go on and smoke it, but don't hold it funny," he said.

I relit it and puffed while he radioed in my information. I watched bemusedly as people slowed down as they drove by, and more than one made a sudden turn into the store's parking lot. The man ignored them all, alternately squinting at my I.D. and peering into my windows. My cigar was burning the plastic filter by the time he handed my license back to me.

"Where you heading tonight?" he asked. When I shrugged, he said, "Macon's 'bout two hours west of here, but there's not much south until Savannah." When I made a face, he grinned and thumbed his toothpick to the other side of his mouth. "We don't have much, but we got a small place right outside town. Real simple, but clean. Serve a little food, nice views. Might have a room if you hurry." He weighed me again with his eyes. "The lady that runs the place also has a bar, the only one in town. She might want you to play. But it's a simple place, like her boardin' house."

"Simple is good," I agreed. He gave me directions, and I shook his hand.

"It's a quiet place," he agreed. I wasn't sure if he meant the town or the boarding house. "Tell them Otis sent you, and you might not have to pay the deposit." It wasn't until much later I realized how happenstance everything was. What would have happened to the little town if I'd kept driving?

The yard of the boarding house was as quiet as the parking lot of the country store. Insects in the tall grass buzzed as the gravel dust cloud floated along the driveway, and the car door was loud when I shut it. The house in front of me was magnificent but showed its age in peeling paint and overgrown bushes. To my left was a parking area with three cars, but gaps showed me where others had been parked. One sat on two flats, and the others carried the dust of their travels.

A string of profanity came from the far side of the house, and I walked toward it. I got a good view of the porch, showing buckled boards and a line of rocking chairs. It was cooler in the shade, but I walked around a drive-through carport extending off the side of the house. There was a small outhouse at the back, and this was where the profanity was coming from. A woman's ass was propping the door open, and I hesitated.

"Piece of SHIT!" she said, backing out and catching sight of me.

"Well, it is an outhouse," I said. She was almost as tall as I was, dressed in jeans and a tank top. Dark hair, flashing eyes, and the frown the compressing her face didn't ruin her looks at all. She threw a wrench to the ground and swiped her hands across her face, flicking the sweat away. I saw a flash of grey behind one ear. A thin sheen moistened her chest, and I forced my eyes to stay on her face.

"Yeah, my husband had a sense of humor," she said, and I felt mild disappointment. "I'm Sonja. What can I do for you?"

"I ran into Otis in town, and he said you might have a room. I'm travelling through," I said.

She extended her hand, but I didn't see the flash of a wedding band on her opposite hand.

"Adam," I said, giving her hand a brief shake. No girly handshake for her; she took my hand and squeezed, and I felt an electric thrill run up my arm.

"Otis, huh?" She propped her hands on her hips as she studied me. *Definitely* no wedding band. "How long will you stay? A night? Or more?"

"It depends. I'm taking a road trip. Needed a new scene. Maybe a couple of days?" I said.

"Not running from anything, are you? Anyone chasing you?" she asked, a hint of challenge showing in her voice.

"No, she's definitely not chasing," I said, and then winced. "I meant no. No bad guys or hit men looking for me."

"Come on. I'll get you registered. We don't have water right now, but I should have it fixed soon. The damn well pump keeps giving up the ghost."

She turned toward the back door, pulling a rag from her back pocket. She walked with a smooth gait, long legs filling her jeans. I trailed behind her as she took the steps onto the porch, but moved around her to open the door. A cat sprang from the bushes, startling me, but she didn't pay it any notice. She smiled a brief thank you, and we went inside. The inside was in much better shape than the outside. Hardwood floors creaked agreeably, and fans moved above us in the tall ceilings, pushing cool air through the house. We moved down a hallway to the front of the house, and she stepped behind a counter with a pressed-tin front. She passed a registration card to me, and I started filling it out.

Turning back to me, she asked, "How long will you stay?"

I answered without thinking. "Three days, at least."

She named a rate I could live with, and I passed her my driver's license and bank card. She glanced at my information. "Nashville, huh?" she asked. "Hollywood with a touch of twang?" she said, quoting a minor hit a few years old.

"More than you know. Great place to live, but . . ." I let it trail off as she pushed a key across the counter at me.

"Your room's on the third floor. Bathrooms are community, a light dinner is served at noon, and supper is served at six. The menu is posted, and if you don't like what I fix, there's a few places in town. No obnoxious drinking and no loud parties. Any problems, just call from your room. Any questions?" She looked at me, and I felt the same electric thrill when our eyes met.

"No ma'am, not that I can think of."

She looked away and stepped toward the back door, and I went to the front to get some of my stuff from the car. She didn't say anything else, but I must admit I took a look as she walked down the dark hall.

What an interesting place.

CHAPTER 3

BOBBY FELT HIS WAY THROUGH the darkness, tripping over rocks, broken mining equipment, and the twisted rails that once carried ore carts. The darkness didn't scare him; it was his friend. Nothing was down here, of course, just Bobby and the thing growing inside him. It burned a little, but Bobby could ignore it. For now. Killing Mark sated it, gave it a little peace. But there was work to be done.

A small flicker of light ahead, unsteady; it was the cooking operation. Bobby came into the area he and Mark tried to foolishly claim as theirs, not knowing what they had awakened. Mark was sitting motionless at the table, his chin a dried-up river of red, his face purple. Bobby went to the burner where the last glass pan sat. His beautiful crystals had burned, scorched to the pan. Thankfully, the last container of propane had run dry. If not, they could have found out how much rock could burn. Bobby picked up the glass dish, feeling but not caring when the pads of his fingers sizzled and burned.

Behind him, Mark stood up and took a step. Bobby turned, putting the dish on the table, and watched his dead friend walk toward him.

"Stop," Bobby whispered. Mark stopped.

Bobby giggled, a high-pitched sound in the cave.

"Turn around."

Mark's opaque eyes didn't blink, didn't look around. He turned.

"When I say DANCE.... you best dance, motherfucker!" Bobby screamed, vocal cords straining against the sound. Mark began a stiff jig, and Bobby circled him, laughing. "Dance, BITCH!" he cawed, laughing even harder. He left Mark shuffling in place as the laughter faded away, an automaton whose springs were rusty and worn. Bobby chipped a wafer out of the unburned pans that lined the table. Placing it under his tongue, he tripped and twitched across to the cave.

The ribbon of foul liquid along the floor of the cave had grown longer, and a little wider, drifting away from the cavern's opening. Bobby studied it and retrieved a broken pickaxe, tossed to the side at the back of the cave. He and Mark discovered the pickaxe an eternity ago on their first excursion through the cave. The handle was cracked, but he thought it would still work; the earth at the entrance of the cave looked softer than the rock walls. Bobby dropped it where the goo ended, and walked into the daylight at the entrance. It hurt his eyes at first, but they responded, and he studied the river and the town below. Several boats floated, either with the current or anchored to fish a particular spot. One boat, red and white, would belong to Elias Cornwell. Looking over his shoulder, his eyes drew a line from the inky liquid to the entrance of the cave.

From the entrance of the cave, down the hill to the river.

Into the river and flowing toward the town below him.

CHAPTER 4

THE WINDOW IN MY ROOM faced north, catching the river as it flowed around a tall bluff. My room had an iron bed, a mismatched antique dresser and chest-of-drawers with peeling veneer, and no television. I looked at my phone; this high up, on the third floor, I gained another bar, for a grand total of one and a half. But that suited me just fine.

My room was at the end of the hallway, so I opened the door and the windows and turned the fan on high, pushing out the stale air and pulling in the fresh. Air moved around me, and I stretched out on the bed, not bothering to pull down the comforter. The gentle hum of the fan was soothing, and I dozed off, thinking of Nashville and wondering if I were far enough away.

I woke up several hours later to find the shadows in the corner of my room deeper and the air marginally cooler. I was no longer sweating; the fan and the cross-current of air through the windows and out the door and down the hallway kept me cool, despite the heat of the day. Older houses like Sonja's were designed to cool without air conditioning. I sat up, stretched, and looked around me. I wanted to brush my teeth; it felt like something shat in my mouth and died.

Most of my stuff was still in the car, so I slipped on my shoes and went downstairs. I caught a flash of Sonja, moving from what I assumed was the kitchen to the large, communal dining room. Several construction-looking types sat at the table, along with a teenage mother and her kid, who was strapped into a highchair. I nodded to those who looked up as I opened the screened door and went out onto the front porch, finding a few older chaps enjoying the shade.

"'Noon," I said, tipping my head and getting a nod in return. When I got close to the car, it flashed, sensing the keys in my pocket. I opened the trunk and pulled out my overnight bag, leaving the larger suitcase in the trunk. On a whim, I pulled out my guitar, a custom England acoustic. It had traveled many miles and many shows with me, and I didn't want to leave it overnight in the car. Slinging the bag over my shoulder, I walked back up the porch steps.

One of the old-timers said to me, "A picker? Sonja'll put you to work the second she sees it," and cackled.

I nodded with a small grin and said, "I'll sing for my supper, if she's not too picky," waiting to see if they'd pick up the pun. No one laughed, so I went inside. Sonja spied my guitar, but I went up the stairs before she could say anything. I might play, and I might not, but I didn't particularly feel like entertaining the dining room.

Dropping my bag and guitar on the bed, I brushed my teeth and smoothed my hair. When I reappeared downstairs, Sonja was nowhere to be found, but the food sat on a counter built into the pass-through window that linked the kitchen and the dining room. Several of the construction types had already moved to the front porch. I was alone except for a jackleg carpenter who introduced himself as Cliff.

"Adam," I said, scooping a chicken breast out of the pan and adding a scoop of green beans. Simple food, but it smelled good even cool.

"Ain't from here?" Cliff asked.

I shook my head. "You?" I asked between forkfuls.

He shook his head. "Naw, headed down to Savannah. Truck broke, so this cop . . ."

"Big guy? Stomach on sticks?" I asked.

He snorted laughter and nodded. "Nice fella, for a cop," Cliff agreed. "You play?" He mimed an air guitar.

"A little," I said.

"Girl that runs this place hire you?"

I shook my head. "Just like you; passing through. She never said anything about entertainment."

"Ain't much here," he said. "There's bingo hall, and this girl here has a honky tonk, but they say th'other one burned down a while back."

I paused, fork halfway to my mouth.

"The girl here? Owns a honky tonk?"

He nodded.

I grunted in surprise and finished my plate. I saw an empty pie plate and sighed. Cliff noticed my disappointment.

"Yup, it was as good as it looks. I 'spect some of those outside may have enjoyed your piece."

"Story of my life," I said, regretfully.

I picked up my plate and placed it in the old washtub sitting on a table by the door. Cliff and I walked outside, and while he sat in a rocker, I took a seat on the front step. He introduced me, and I collected about half of the names thrown at me. The house cat, a mix of grey, black and brown, came over and nosed me before settling on the step below; her purrs were audible.

"Adam here plays the git-tar," Cliff announced, and I groaned inside.

I had just gotten comfortable, and I knew the next question. When it came, I brushed it off. "I'll pull it out later, maybe. Been a long day," I said.

We swapped stories for a few minutes, and I found out most of them were like me: travelling through, looking for work, and in the case of the girl, looking for her husband.

"Sumbitch runned off, but I know where he's goin'. I just gotta find him." Several of the younger men looked like they wanted to help her forget about him, but right then, the baby yelled. She sighed and went back inside.

"Is the town as sleepy as it looks?" I asked.

I got several nods, and the guy in the squeaky rocker, Bert, said, "Only place 'round here is The Dive. Its Sonja's other place, but it ain't much. Since her music man ran off, she don't even have that. Just the jukebox."

"Some of the best stuff is on an old jukebox," I said. They nodded agreement.

"You said you're from Nashville?" Bert asked. When I nodded, he said, "You ever seen anybody famous up there?"

I nodded and rattled off a few names; it's always easier than explaining the reality. Nashville is a country music town, but it's a ladder. The ones you hear on the radio or see on television don't walk down Music Row. They live in the mansions on the hill. You'll see their buses going in and out, but never them. Your best bet is to scour the clubs and catch someone before they break. Their music is always more honest right before they take that final step out of obscurity.

"So why'd you leave? Tired of chasing the dream?" Cliff asked.

I shrugged. "Needed a new scene. Sold a couple of songs, got some spending money, so I decided to drive around," I answered.

Cliff nodded. The conversation flowed and ebbed on the porch, breaking around the usual topics: politics, war, social gossip. That peaceful evening showed me a side of the town I needed to see; otherwise, when the going got tough, I would have taken off. The homemade supper settled in my stomach and despite my earlier nap, I found my eyes getting heavy.

I must have closed my eyes for a minute, because when I blinked them open, one of the others said, "Good thing you didn't get a rocking chair, or we'd've left you for the night." Gentle laughter followed, and I grinned.

"I guess it's a sign. I never realized how much travelling can wear a man out."

"That means you haven't done enough of it," Cliff said wistfully. I rose to my feet, nodded good night to everyone, and went up to my room. Draped in shadows, the bed was a lump of white in the middle of the room. I shut the door and latched it, but left the windows wide open. Stripped down to my underwear, I stretched out on the bedspread and drifted off to sleep.

CHAPTER 5

SONJA EASED THE PORCH DOOR closed behind her, the lingering heat of the day mixing with the chill from the night air.

Gonna be fall soon, she thought. *We're toward the final part of the year already.* Usually, she could focus on the duty at hand and not worry overmuch about what was coming. When she looked ahead, either to the next season or year's end, she always felt the impending push of time's rush, shoving her along without regard. She sighed, settling into the rocker she always chose when she sat outside in the evening. *Nighttime,* she corrected. *It's well into nighttime; evening passed while I was in The Dive.* The house was quiet behind her, all of her boarders shuttered for the night.

For a Tuesday, the crowd at The Dive hadn't been bad. Her small bar was a friendly watering hole for the residents of town and those on the outlying farms. The latter part of the week, she'd have live music and run a special on a burger and a beer. *Mark should have called me tonight,* she thought. *He normally confirms a few days out.* As she realized how long it had been since she'd seen Mark, a sly voice in the back of her mind said, *The boarder upstairs is a music man . . . you could ask him.*

"Oh, no, I don't think so," she said aloud, and the cat raised a paw toward her. "That's the last thing we need," she said to the cat. Since she was talking to him, he rolled onto his back, exposing his belly for her to rub with a socked foot. She could feel the vibration of his purrs through her foot. A touch of sadness crept upon her; she and her husband had spent many nights on the porch. He would sit in the rocker beside her, and they'd talk about the day: he about the town and their farm on the outside of it, her about The Dive, and together about the days to come. She kept her eyes away from the empty rocking chair; instead, she forced herself to think about the last time she'd seen Mark.

"He picked up his check last week," she said to the cat. "Bobby was with him, and they looked like they were up to no good." The cat rolled away from her, and she pushed the chair into motion. The two kids—even though she was less than ten years their senior, Sonja still thought of Mark and Bobby as kids— had worked off and on for her at The Dive for the last few years. It was an informal relationship, but it had been a while.

If Mark doesn't call or show up, who's going to play music at The Dive? the voice insisted. *Will you turn on the radio?* it asked.

"Maybe," she answered, refusing to acknowledge the thought. The nocturnal insects buzzed and whirled in the bushes that surrounded the porch, and she heard a rumble in the distance. It sounded a bit like thunder over the horizon. The cat, who had moved over to the railing of the porch, looked up. In a blur, he darted off the porch, his tail raised and fluffed in an instant. The bugs fell silent, and a half second later her ears popped, as if she were in an elevator. She cracked a manufactured yawn to equalize the pressure.

"The hell got into you?" she asked the empty porch. "What was that?" she asked again, working her jaw to unstuff her ears. The weatherman hadn't said anything about a storm, and she didn't see any light on the horizon that could have signaled an explosion in town. The insects started up slowly, and the cat cautiously peered up from his hiding spot between the bushes.

Sonja rocked, her mind restless and wandering, feeling slightly off-kilter.

CHAPTER 6

THE BLACKENED SHELL PERCHED *by the river no longer produced a charred smell. Watched over by the slowly crumbling chimney the ruins remained, providing a home for rodents of the crawling and flying varieties. Grass grew in the poorly lined parking lot, exploiting cracks and finding tiny crevices to root. A stale wind stirred within the confines of the property, and the air grew thick with the smell of ozone. Flakes of char trembled and fell away as the pressure increased within the small area. The center of the ruined building swirled, a vortex appearing in the air. It consumed material, first attracting the loose particles, and as the pressure increased larger pieces were pulled to its center.*

Tiny flickers arced between unseen points, webs of pure light that obeyed no natural law. The light pulsed, connected, died, and pulsed again. As the ground cleared of human-made material, the web of light settled to the ground. Pulsing, it grew along the ground, maintaining a ghostly, illuminated shape. The light faded, revealing a building board by board. A long porch grew organically, ending in a tin roof, the faux-log wall broken by large doors and equally spaced windows. The building became more detailed, and tables and chairs appeared on a scarred wooden floor. Out by the road, light trembled as it formed a sign pole.

Chrome gleamed, and colored glass filled space along the back wall. Alive, it pulsed, beating like a human heart, the web of light pulsing to the heartbeats. A mechanical hum filled the air as electronic circuits were completed. Whirls and clicks sounded from inside as mechanical systems tested themselves and prepared for use. Finally, above the coin slot, a final light glowed to life: THREE PLAYS FOR A DIME.

Outside on the porch, the light gathered in a spot above the front steps. Streaming from all directions, it formed an intricate web that settled into a man shape. Above him, neon buzzed as the sign by the road flickered to life, throwing ribbons of light into the air. The neon flickered, then steadied, and the man who now stood on the front porch smiled. The sign began rotating even before the letters were formed, pale shapes lit by the glowing glass.

They slowly brightened as the sign revolved. . . . OCHET . . . RICO . . . RICOCHET . . . OCHET . . .

The ribbons of light gathered above the sign and pulsed one final time, gathering themselves. The sign paused, and the light exploded outward, producing a rumble that arched over the countryside. In houses across town, sleeping people stirred slightly and drifted back into their dreams.

The man shape on the porch adjusted a pair of half-rim glasses set in silver wire frames on his nose. He stepped toward the front doors, which opened at his approach. One by one, the lights inside came to life, and the newly created presence settled onto the land.

Another web of light coalesced, revealing a woman in a beaded dress, standing beside a long, polished bar. Around her others appeared, dressed in different styles and colors. The jukebox, which dominated the back wall, clacked and hummed to life. Turning to the man on the porch, the woman lifted her hand, beckoning him. The man felt the hum of energy around him and breathed deeply.

"Beautiful," he whispered.

CHAPTER 7

WHEN YOU'RE OUTSIDE of the city, there's something about the air that keeps you in touch with the world around you. If there's rain coming, it's the tang of the moisture getting ready to fall. If it's planting time, and the wind is right, you can smell the fresh dirt as it's turned in the field. When a drought holds the land, you can taste the dust and the dryness. There's nothing like stepping outside at nine in the morning and feeling eighty-five degrees grab you by the throat and the humidity try to drown you at your first step.

On that late summer morning, I woke up to the slight damp that comes from the morning dewfall, and I could smell the heat spell breaking on the wind. That morning's air was almost as perfect as perfect could get. Winter was coming, as it always does, but the air had a hint of the fall and a slight breeze to let everyone know. Wouldn't be fair for Mother Nature to keep the news to herself; the breeze let her share.

I sat up in my borrowed bed and yawned, looking around owlishly. I remember a time when I'd open my eyes and fly out of bed, never to slow down until nightfall, but those days were past. I'd learned to appreciate the mornings and savor waking up. I sat on the edge of the bed, listening to the house around me. Something scurried in the attic above, a pan banged or slammed downstairs, and the smell of coffee drifted up to my room. That got me moving.

I pulled socks and underwear from my travel bag and wandered my way to the bathroom. Yesterday's clothes would serve me fine until I could get to the car and my other suitcase. The bathrooms were large and tiled, and I gawked for a moment. Bathrooms like this didn't come standard in a plantation house built when this one was. Musing to myself, I made my way to the shower and welcomed the scalding water.

Most of the working men were gone; the salesman was out looking for leads, and I heard a baby squealing on the second floor, so I knew the young mother was still here. Voices floated up from the porch, and I pegged two more of the old timers outside. The dining room was empty, and the pass-through window into the kitchen was bare except for a coffee urn. When I walked over to get a cup, the cook saw me and lifted a covered plate from the table.

"Wasn't sure what you liked, so you got a scoop of everything," she said. Old smoker's lines on her face and a clean apron smiled at me. "Sonja wants you to find her, or she'll find you. Ain't you from Nashville?" As I nodded, she handed over the plate. "Silverware's inside."

I thanked her and took my plate to the porch. I maneuvered into a rocking chair, shooing away the house cat and setting my coffee on the porch floor.

"Somebody's special," the old man beside me grumbled. "Cook'll snatch away the last of the bacon, say bre'fust time has passed, but some folks git it saved."

Bert laughed.

"Woodie, if you wouldn't grumble so much, folks might save somepin' for you. It wouldn't hurt to smile at the ladies, either."

I shrugged and fell to the plate in front of me. The view from the porch was pretty in the morning light, but that wasn't quite fair. A few bluffs rose beside the river, and I could see some of the town. Mainly I could see crops getting ready for harvest, and a few already harvested to nubs. The river wasn't an especially large one, but large enough. In the distance to the north, I could see a tall bluff, taller than most. Even though the river took a bend in the middle of town, I could still see the tip of it.

A rattling pickup truck brought dust with it up the driveway. It was painted grey, with rust spots showing in places, and through the smudged windows I could barely see Sonja driving.

She looked at me and squealed the brakes before she circled the house. Rolling down her window, she said, "Will you be here a minute?" At my nod, she said, "I'll be in my office in the back. Will you find me?"

"I'm almost finished; I need to change and then I will."

She returned my nod and pulled through the carport, and we heard a door slam behind the big house.

"Now some folks git invited to the office. All others git is a cold stare and barely a 'how-ya doin'?'" Woodie muttered as he lit up a smoke.

Bert cackled, and I grinned.

I finished my plate and, after saving my coffee cup from the cat, gave my dishes to the cook, thanking her. "Which way is the office?" I asked, and got pointed directions. I had a good idea what Sonja wanted, and I was on the fence about it. But I was considering.

I went to the car to get my suitcase and heaved my bag up the stairs. I was out of breath by the time I reached the top, and a thin film of sweat decorated my forehead. Changing quickly, I balled up the dirty clothes and tossed them into the corner. I went back downstairs and navigated my way to the dining room, through the kitchen, and down a hallway to a doorway minus the door. It led into a corner room overflowing with books and pictures and a desk crammed into the corner. Sonja sat in a button-up blouse with her hair styled, studying a piece of paper with a bank's letterhead.

Seeing me, she set it down and moved it to the side.

"Have a seat," she offered, moving her purse and another bag out of the chair beside the desk. Jeans and low-heeled shoes completed her non-outhouse-repair outfit, and I must admit she pulled it off.

"I'm kinda surprised you didn't say anything about the bar when I checked in," I said. "Most business owners can't wait to tell you where to spend your money."

She grunted. "I can't tell if I own them or if they own me," she said. Now that I could see her sitting in the light, faint worry lines were etched around her eyes and mouth. They didn't detract from her looks, but they were a weight on her shoulders. "Besides, if I'd done that, you would have thought I was offering more than I wanted to," she said with a hint of directness. "I don't like it when that happens."

I nodded, taken aback, and she continued.

"So I have this bar, and it's got a small stage. Most of the time, I have a guy, Mark, who will come and play a couple hours a night. But he hasn't been around the last two nights or confirmed for this weekend. I need to know I have entertainment; I'll give you reduced room and board here if you'll play, say from seven to nine. I don't need you long; just to help nurse a few guys through a pitcher of beer or two. What do you say?"

"Why don't you give me free room and board, and I'll come from 7-10? Three nights a week?"

She frowned. "My other guy would play for beer. Why should I give you a free stay?" she asked.

"I guarantee you I'm better than the other guy. He probably knew a handful of songs; I've been playing the clubs in Nashville for the last five years. I know all the major hits from the last three, along with the classics. Alan Jackson, Johnny Cash, George Strait."

"What makes you think it's a country bar? We could be a Goth club. So your time in Nashville may not be as valuable as you thought."

When she laughed at my facial expression, the frown and worry lines eased. Her eyes almost sparkled, but I could still see a trace of her standoffishness in them.

I cleared my throat and shook my head, pointing out the window. "Pickups? Tractors? Red dirt? That's a song right there," I said.

She leaned back, drumming her fingertips.

"I'll give you back half of what you paid up front, and we'll see about the free stay. You may be worse than Mark, or he may come back."

"And if he does? And is pissed I'm there? What happens then?"

She blew out an exasperated breath. "I can't remember the last time we had a fight at The Dive," she said. "You'll finish your set, and I'll keep my word. Half back."

I nodded, holding out my hand, and saying, "Half back, three nights a week,"

A moment before we shook, she said, "From seven to ten."

When I tried to snatch back my hand, she gripped it and held on, letting out a delighted laugh.

"Deal," we said together, and our eyes met. For a half-second, there was a connection. She closed it down by looking away, but the delighted look lingered in her eye as she drew her hand back, and I settled in the chair.

"So tell me a little bit about Tanninville," I said.

Sonja shifted papers around and looked around the room. "Not much to tell. We're a farming community, and it's a friendly town. We have a festival twice a year," she trailed off, staring off into the distance.

"What about you? How did you end up here?"

That refocused her attention, and she looked sharply at me. "Actually, I need to get some work done on my books." She lifted a ledger book and opened it in front of her. I could tell it was a dismissal after I had asked a question I shouldn't have.

"Okay, sounds good." I wasn't going to show her the dismissal annoyed me; I smiled. "Do I start tonight?" I asked.

She was staring down at her ledger, frowning. "I'm sorry, what?"

"Do I start tonight?" I repeated, keeping the fake smile on my face.

"No, tomorrow. I only have music Thursday through Saturday."

I nodded and retreated out of her office. When I glanced over my shoulder, I saw her looking at me. I nodded and smiled, put off a little by the abrupt change. Finding my way back through the house, I headed for the car, determined to explore the little town.

CHAPTER 8

BOBBY WATCHED, FASCINATED, as the goo moved down the hill and stopped. Mark was looking the worse for wear; his greyish skin was cut and outright ripped in some places. A nasty tear of skin flapped at the elbow, bone showing through the wound. Bobby bounced a palm size rock in his hand and let it fall down the slope. It bounded down, gathering speed, and an especially hard bounce sent it airborne.

It sailed by Mark, barely missing his shoulder. Bobby laughed a bit to himself, imagining Mark turning ass over teakettle as he fell down the slope. Mark cleared another section, and the black substance pulsed, elongating and drawing closer to the river. Mark was moving methodically, using a spade in a steady motion, digging a trough down to the river. He'd been at it all night while Bobby ranged around exploring the bluff. Bobby leaned over and selected another rock to toss toward Mark. In the distance, across the water, he saw a small boat drift into view. Bobby froze, panic curling his insides. What if the man saw Mark out there, digging on the bluff? Bobby scrambled to the edge where Mark's head had disappeared.

"Get up here," Bobby said. Obediently, Mark dropped the spade in mid stroke, causing it to knock against his shin. Bobby winced needlessly. As Mark climbed to the top of the bluff, Bobby scampered back inside the cave. The darkness welcomed him, and he felt the presence inside him awaken.

Panic receded, and curiosity took its place. The fisherman was still there, with his boat anchored in the shade of trees that grew outward over the river. "He can't see me," Bobby said. Cautiously he edged toward the drop, looking at the distance between him and the riverbank. From his vantage point, there was only one place the fisherman could see him: where the second switchback crossed, a bare spot opened in the branches, exposing the river.

Bobby could probably crawl right to the edge where the water met the bluff.

Before he knew what he was doing, he reached into the trough beside him and scooped up a handful of the dark material. As he moved diagonally down the face of the bluff, he was surprised to find he moved . . . easier. His grip was stronger, even using one hand as the other tried to cradle the substance. It was alternately hot then cold, sticking together like a ball of . . . congealed . . . matter? Paint? Grease? The image that came to his mind was Jell-O, but an organic version of it. *Brains. Braaaains . . .* he thought, and giggled as he slid through the vegetation. His stomach growled at the thought of food; he couldn't remember the last time he ate. With a thump, he landed on the next-to-last switchback; remaining still for a moment, he made sure the fisherman hadn't moved. Bobby recognized the fisherman as Tom Watkins, who sat hunched over the gunwale, either watching the water or something beyond it. Bobby eased across the switchback and was hidden by the thin vegetation. The last few vertical feet weren't a problem; Bobby crept to the water's edge and reached his hand into the muck. Once his arm was extended the material released, falling into the water with barely a ripple. As soon as the material came into contact with the water it dissipated, growing thinner, but Bobby thought he saw it floating against the current, heading for Tom's aluminum jon boat. He slunk back through the reeds, slogging through the mud to scramble back up the bank.

His mission completed, Bobby felt a touch of panic being out of the cave; being outside seemed wrong, somehow. Bobby climbed the bluff, slow at first, but faster and faster as he imagined eyes staring at him from the river. When he looked over his shoulder, of course, no one was there. Panting, he made it to the top, scrambling over the lip and scurrying into the cave.

Catching his breath, he turned to face the front of the cave, and Mark stepped forward. Bobby's stomach growled, protesting his frenetic activity. He would need to leave soon for food; he hadn't eaten anything for three days. The meth he'd used kept the hunger at bay, but his body needed nourishment. He watched, fascinated, as the skin at Mark's elbow moved in the wind. He didn't know his mouth was watering until he realized he was imagining the texture of the skin; a little chewy, tasting of salt and the grime of the mine. Bobby looked away before the thought had time to settle in; his stomach gurgled, and he swallowed convulsively. Mark followed Bobby's every command, moving as an automaton now. He had no doubt Mark would remain still as he cut off the offending flap. Yes, it was time to leave. Soon.

CHAPTER 9

AFTER TALKING WITH SONJA, I spent the rest of the morning swapping tales with Bert and Woodie, rocking on the front porch and thinking over my conversation with Sonja. But I did it with my guitar in my hand, picking a few songs from memory and running through them. Each one had a small section that usually gave me trouble, and I wanted to make sure my fingers knew the steps.

"R'minds me of listening to my daddy pick," Bert said wistfully. Woodie grunted sourly. "He played a little, like you," he said motioning to me, "and he'd do the same thing from time to time. Sonja ask you about playing?"

When I nodded, he nodded in return.

"Figures. That Mark boy was awright, but . . ." Bert lapsed into a silence so long I thought he had lost his train of thought. "He played, but he didn't have no soul behind it. You touch the strings, and you strumming your soul. He was jest makin' noise."

I've been wooed by record executives, groupies, and conned by managers and promoters. No one ever paid me a compliment like Bert did that day. I thanked him, but he waved it off. It may have been experience, or his personality, but Bert was the kind of guy you felt comfortable around. No matter what was coming, he would weather it like a reed growing from a rock.

"Son, at my age, you learn it's the little things that count. A good meal, a good companion, good music. It's the simple things in life that make it complete. Good music is one of 'em."

For a moment, I saw the young man he once was. Tired from the farm, sitting with his daddy on the porch, enjoying the sunset. Bert was one of the old Southern throwbacks: a man of the land, confident with his hands and his place in life. The future might be uncertain, but he'd face it with a shrug and determination.

I worked on strumming my soul for the rest of the morning. Most music is a series of chord changes; most listeners can't distinguish a run up the frets from a good solid D to E to G. For most of the songs I played, I could swap out chords for the more intricate parts, and that's what I was practicing. Sonja came out right before lunch, hovering in the doorway. I knew she was there but didn't react. Partly because I was in the zone and partially because I didn't want her to know I was hoping she would hover. The little sparks between us couldn't be ignored, but two could play the ignoring-it game. I hit a final chord and let the strings sing as I flexed my hand. Despite the cool morning, I had worked up a sweat and my hand was protesting.

"I might have gotten the better end of the deal," she commented from the doorway. Woodie was dozing, but Bert nodded at her words.

"This is just a warm up. It might sound better or worse from the stage," I said, "but I'm willing to negotiate at the end of our current deal." There it was again. A flash of her green-hazel eyes, a little lift at the corner of her mouth. She relaxed and let her wall crumble just a little. We looked eye to eye, and I smiled back, and the lines on her face deepened just a touch. She looked away, and I felt the moment pass.

"Lunch is ready," she said, nudging the rocker holding Woodie. I was deflated, but expecting it. By the time I got inside to the dining room she was gone, presumably to her office. Instead of lunch I grabbed a couple pieces of fruit and a glass of sweet tea. I carried it upstairs, and as I was finishing the tart apple, I saw Sonja's truck pulling away. Lying back on the covers, I dozed, my hand aching pleasantly.

Afternoon naps in the fall are delightful. It's just comfortable enough to sleep with the windows open, and when you wake up you aren't sweating, the air is clear, and you still have enough hours to feel you haven't wasted time. I yawned, frowned at the taste in my mouth and my full bladder, and fixed both before I went downstairs.

Supper was soup, made with vegetables fresh from the harvest. My light lunch led to two and a half bowls, and I resumed my seat on the steps. There were rockers available, but I was a creature of habit. I commented on the empty chairs.

"Yeah, them young fellows running out to the bars. They were talking about this girl; as if one girl would be enough for all three, but they's smitten." A troubled look crossed his face.

"I don't think Sonja would let them all chase one girl, would she? That can cause trouble in a bar."

"Oh, no, it ain't there. It's out a' Ricochet. Millie, her name is. Girl can dance up a storm."

"Ricochet?" I asked. "I thought The Dive was the only place in town."

"No, nope," he replied. "Right 'fore you come into town, on East Riverside Drive, to the left. Right fancy place, great big ol' juke. They say it has the best music in town. The old Cauthon place." He glanced at me. "Present comp'ny excluded, of course."

I was confused. I remembered passing a burned-out shell on my way into town. It was the only place that remotely sounded like Bert's description, but it confused me. Bert snorted to himself, the troubled look passing from his face. As I replayed it in my mind, the conversation seemed disjointed, awkward, and I wondered if Bert wasn't suffering from a touch of the old timer's.

We talked while the sun went down; I found out he grew up in Tanninville, owned and managed a large farm until he sold out.

"It's nice and easy spending my time here. No grass t' keep up, no animals t' feed, and someone t' feed me." His face fell as he talked about losing his wife, and I told him a little about my time in Nashville. It sounded much more exciting when you can hit the high points, rather than being focused on the day-to-day struggle. When the sun was touching the trees to the west, I stood and asked him for directions to Sonja's.

"I thought you were playing tomorrow. She doesn't normally have music on a Wednesday," he said.

"No, I want to get a feel for the place before I perform. See the customers, hear how it sounds with a night-time crowd." I paused. I wanted to see if I could make her smile, but he didn't need to know that.

"Well, c'mon. If ya don't mind an old timer ridin' with ya, I'll show ya the way. Woodie won't mind; all he's gonna do is doze and bitch." He laughed to himself and I smiled. Something about Bert reminded me of my grandfather, who was a drinking man with a sense of humor and old country twang.

"Well, let's go. Nothing wrong with a couple of men about town, is there?" I asked, and we headed to the car.

We climbed into my car, and Bert peered at every surface. I'm not a car guy, but I loved my car. When I first came to Nashville, one of the first jobs I had was parking cars as a valet. I fell in love with a Chrysler 300, and when I got my first royalty check, I bought one. Mine was long and black, like the one Johnny Cash sang about, with every imaginable option. It rolled low and slow, with a ride so smooth you'd swear you were flying. I tapped the touch screen to bring up the air conditioning, then found a country station on the satellite radio.

Bert grunted. "It's almost like a damn spaceship. Wasn't there a television show where they tapped on screens to run the ship?" he asked.

I was backing up and didn't answer the question. We rolled down the driveway, sliding over the bumps in the gravel, and pulled onto the road.

Bert whistled. "Smooth ride," he said.

I nodded, loving the feel of the vehicle under my hands. Nicole said I loved the car more than her. She ended up being right, but it wasn't the car itself. It was the sense of accomplishment; it was something I'd earned. Something *nice* I'd earned.

Bert picked up his storytelling from the porch as he guided me to The Dive. Tanninville took up both sides of the Ogeechee River, with a bridge connecting the east and west ends of town. Bert laughed as he recounted the tale of the town's origin: two families founded settlements on either side of the river and feuded until their children ran away to Atlanta and eloped. Not just once, but twice.

"Back then, they didn't have no one else t' marry. So even though they was feudin', a brother 'n sister married a brother 'n sister." Bert laughed until tears came to his eyes, and I eventually pieced together that he was related to the family on the west side of the river.

Tanninville wasn't very big, and we arrived at Sonja's bar. Cracked asphalt parking lot, faded sign fronted with neon, cedar shingle roof; it could have substituted for any number of places I've played. I sighed, realizing I was a little let down.

"Ain't much to look at, is it?" Bert asked. I stopped myself from agreeing with him, and he sighed. "Ever since Billy died, it ain't been the same." At my questioning look, he said, "Sonja's husband. Died a coupl'a years ago."

We walked up, and I held back, staying close to Bert. He walked slowly, slightly hunched over, and I could tell he didn't have the best eyesight by the way he held his head and squinted. I opened the door for him.

The Dive was a cinderblock building, faded and grey from the outside, with a few tired plants. It had traces of having been landscaped once, in years before Sonja's husband died. Now it was overtaken by weeds and windblown trash. The front door needed a fresh coat of paint, but it matched everything else.

We walked in, and heads swiveled to check us out. Several farmer types clustered around the bar, dirty jeans and several pairs of overalls. Sonja was behind the bar, and I could see a cook moving in the kitchen behind her. The inside matched the outside; it wasn't dated, but several years had passed since it had been refreshed. Bert nodded and spoke to several customers, and I got a few nods. Sonja pulled down two glasses, and filled one, looking at me.

I ordered a draft beer and told her, "Put his on my tab."

She nodded and said, "Beer doesn't count in our deal." Her stern tone was marred by a quick smile, and the glint was back in her eye.

"But you haven't heard me play yet. It might be."

She rolled her eyes and didn't respond.

The conversation picked back up, punctuated by the sound of clicking pool balls from a table set up in the middle of the floor.

"So what do you think?" she asked, sliding the glass in front of me.

"Not bad," I said. "Better than most I've played in. At least there's no chicken wire protecting the stage."

"It's pretty calm. We're usually low key. The younger set knows I won't serve them, so we don't have much . . ." she trailed off.

"Testosterone?" I finished for her.

"Exactly."

The night manager, Donald, came up and introduced himself. Bert moved up to the stool beside me and sat down.

"That's what I call service," he said, smacking his lips and taking a slurp to pull the foam off the top of the beer. He looked around the bar top, and Sonja handed him a salt shaker. Squinting in the poor light, he managed to sprinkle some on top of his beer.

"That salt will kill you, Bert," she said. He pshaw'd her, and she wiped up the salt spilt on the bar. "And you made a mess."

"Just like a damn woman," he groused. "Fussing two times in one sentence. If I hadn't'a been married, I wouldn't be used to it."

I took another sip from my beer and looked at the stage.

Sonja saw me looking and nodded to it. "Go look at it, see what else you need. I've got some sound equipment in the back if you want it."

I took my beer and wandered over to the stage, eyes following me. A mismatched set of drums, guitar stands, and an acoustic guitar with a warped neck leaned against a scarred amplifier. A tangle of cords was to one side, and a battered mic stand completed the set-up. I clicked on the amp, listening for interference. It sounded fine, but the acoustic pickup on the guitar looked like shit. I had my own.

A cowboy saw me poking around. "Hey mister, you gonna play?"

I shook my head. "Tomorrow."

He saluted me with his glass and returned to his game of pool.

The front door opened, letting in fading daylight. I saw the shape of Otis, the sheriff, come in, and he reached the bar about the same time I did.

"Nashville," he greeted me, drawing looks from several of the barflies. "See you found a place to stay and a play to stay." He cackled at his own joke, pulling up a stool and accepting a glass from Sonja. Looking around the room, he said, "Customers are kinda slim tonight, ain't they, Sonja? You're gonna have to pick it up."

Sonja looked confused, but Bert spoke up. "The place upriver is taking your customers, girl. Maybe putting in some music will help. I've heard that place has a jukebox the size of Kansas in the back, will play anything you want."

Sonja's mouth formed a thin line.

"Otis, have you been out there?"

"A-yup," he said. "Right nice."

"And it's where the Cauthon place burned ten years ago? And somehow, it appeared overnight?" She slammed down the glass she was cleaning.

Otis and Bert shared a look. "What are you talking about?" Otis asked.

"I work a lot, but just last week I drove by there on my way to Macon. Nothing was there. And all of a sudden a brand new bar appears overnight, and no one says anything?"

Bert spoke up. "Now Sonja, he was just joking with you. You know you're local, and we like you just fine," he said in a calming tone.

"Is it that place tucked in the bend of the river? Past that big hill?" Eyes turned to me and everyone stiffened.

Sonja's eyes could have turned a tree into matchsticks. "What?"

"That's the old Jenkins Mine. Bad luck, that," Bert said, and Otis nodded.

Sonja found an invisible spot on the bar and rubbed it forlornly. She didn't see the look from Bert to Otis or the small shake of his head to me. I was mystified; I could understand Sonja not wanting competition in a small town, but why the headshake over a hill?

Sonja finished rubbing the invisible spot into oblivion and poured a refill for a table behind us. When she went to deliver it, Bert leaned over to me. "Her husband Billy died up on the hill.

The old Jenkins Mine has been bad luck for years, and never paid out a durn dime," he said.

I groaned to myself. *Smooth move, Ex-lax.* Otis leaned in as well.

"Never learned why he was there, either. He went missing, and they found him when they were searching along the river. A whole mess of stones had slid down with him. They followed the trail, and he was about halfway up to the old mining path when he slipped. Damn confusing time. Almost broke ol' Sonja's heart. Probably did, but she's a tough old bird," Otis said.

"Some kin of you'rn, ain't she?" Bert said. Otis nodded.

"My mama's cousin." He sighed. "We're the only ones left."

"Okay, I got that," I said. "What about this other bar? I thought you told me The Dive was the only place in town?" I asked Otis.

They were both quiet a minute before Otis said, "Nope, I don't recall that. Ricochet's been here a while. Hell of a nice feller runs it; can't remember his name."

"Lyles," Bert said.

"'At's right," Otis said, with satisfaction in his voice. "Lyles. Slipped my mind for a minute." Both Bert and Otis had a faraway look in their eyes, not looking at me or each other, just gazing toward an invisible horizon.

The front door opened, and a man entered, drawing Bert and Otis' attention. I was glad to let the subject drop. The conversation was disjointed and odd; opposite of what I'd experienced or remembered.

A thin man with a square-cut beard entered, and they both nodded to him, with Otis calling, "Tom, nice to see ya. How's Elaine feeling?" The man shot a glance at Otis that was rather unfriendly, and he moved stiffly to an empty table.

"Now, what the hell was that?" Otis muttered under his breath. He seemed more perplexed than mad. "Did you see that?" he said to Bert and me.

I nodded.

"Naw, can't see that far," Bert said. "I could tell it was Tom Watkins, though."

"He doesn't seem to think you two are on good terms," I said to Otis. We turned back to the bar.

"Don't see why. We go to church together, played ball as kids. Saw him just last week. Must've had a bad day fishing."

Sonja came back over to refill our glasses, but Otis turned it down. "I have more than two, Angie'll have my hide."

"You shouldn't drive the sheriff's car drunk," Sonja said. "Even if you are the sheriff."

Otis grunted. "The day two beers gets me drunk is the day you can have this badge, girly."

Sonja smiled, and I was glad to see it. She had to know I had no way of knowing where our conversation had gone, and I was relieved it was forgiven.

"So what's there to know about Tanninville?" I asked. I've always enjoyed the stories behind places; you never know when something you hear could turn into a song. Old-timers like these in a place like this always produced good stories.

"Well, you've seen most of it. It's a quiet place, thank the Lord, and most ev'ybody knows ev'ybody else. High school team does good, most years. As long as the jobs stay and food prices stay up, we do okay," Otis said.

"Great place to live," Sonja added. "Good folks, for the most part. Good bit of gossip, but nothing that cuts too deep."

Coming from a widow in a small town with a couple of businesses that was saying something. I'd heard of the rumor mill turning against young, pretty widows pretty fast. Liking the way the words rolled around in my head, I grabbed a napkin.

"What's that?" Sonja asked, peering at my chicken-scratch handwriting on the napkin.

"Song ideas," I said, hoping she couldn't read it upside down.

"Ol' Tanninville's gonna be famous," Bert laughed. "You can hang a sign in your boarding house, Sonja. "Adam spent the night here, wrote 'An Ode to Tanninville' in this very room."

A pair of drinkers down the bar motioned for more drinks, and Sonja moved to serve them.

"What else?" I said. "I know you're mostly farms, but what about the river? Did you get much river trade?"

"I remember my granddaddy talking about flatboats coming down. We had a gin out there at one time, they would pole cotton down the river. We'd gin it, then send it down the railroad." Bert said.

"Railroad coming through was big when they were boys," Otis said, motioning to Bert, who in turn nodded.

"We'd watch the train come in. Git one every two, three days for a while. Bringin' stuff in for the farmers, bringin' stuff ordered from the Sears 'n Roebuck catalog. Was a big thing for a time."

"We have a distillery one town over," Otis said. "They make rum."

"Rum?" I asked. "I thought..."

"Nope," Bert said. "I thought the same thing, when the fella came over. 'Rum?' I asked. 'That's what they make in the islands. We can't make that in Georgia.' Damn if I wasn't wrong."

"Not sure I'd like that," I said. "I had a rough time with that one night... It wasn't pretty."

"Hah," said Otis. "I said the same thing. Georgia rum is different, though."

I was skeptical. "Rum is rum. It's..." I started to say.

"Nope, hold on right there," Otis said. "I won't hold off if you have too much, but I'm going to tell you... Just try it."

Sonja came back over at Otis' wave, and he explained our discussion.

"Pour him a taste," he said.

She and I exchanged a glance, and I shrugged. Reaching under the bar, she pulled out a bottle and poured a shot, saying, "This came out of barrel number 124, and is bottle 261. It was filled in April, 2013."

The liquid was dark, and I held it up to the bar lights. "Isn't rum..."

"Not here," Otis said, and laughed. Bert joined him, and Sonja smiled at me, and nodded for me to try it. I tossed back the shot and was amazed.

"That's pretty good," I said. The warmth coursed down my throat, into my stomach. The warmth and heat of the liquor tasted as if I'd inhaled a combination of sun, earth, and sugar; Sonja smiled at me as I pushed the glass back to her.

"That's... wonderful," I said. "I never thought rum could taste like that."

"Made right here in our county," Bert said with pride. "I laughed at first, but damn if I wasn't proven wrong. If you'd asked me fifty years ago if we'd have all of this, I'd said no."

"If they hadn't moved the county seat to Jeffersonville, no telling how much bigger we would've gotten," Otis said. "But they can keep it. Big towns have big town problems. I like having small town problems."

As he said this, I glanced over my shoulder. The bearded man, Tom, was sitting alone at a table, an untouched drink in front of him. He was glaring at the pool players, and I felt a stirring of unease. He might be trouble. But it wasn't mine; I finished my beer and motioned for another one. Sonja came and pulled the tap, but Bert and Otis declined.

I sipped the froth off the top, and asked, "Sonja, what do you like about this place?"

She considered for a moment, and said, "The quiet. There are times I can open my window at night and hear the rumble strips from the intersection. I like most of the people. I like fixing things around the house and keeping busy." For a moment our eyes met, and I could see happiness in hers. They were unguarded, and it transformed her.

I started to speak, but a loud laugh from the pool players broke the moment. All of us looked up and found trouble.

Tom was no longer sitting in his chair; he was standing up facing the pool players. They hadn't noticed him, but he said something, and they looked up.

The three farmhands were a little dusty and full of beer. An empty pitcher sat on the table beside the pool table, and I knew it was at least their second. The one closest to Tom said something back, and Tom took a step toward him, despite the size difference. The farmhand had at least four inches and fifty pounds on Tom and was twenty years younger.

"Uh-oh," I muttered.

Laying his pool stick on the table, he took a step, halving the distance to Tom, whose face had gone a deep shade of red above the beard.

"Otis," I heard Bert say.

"You two, cut it out! Casey, Tom, we don't do that here!" Sonja called. Casey glanced at Sonja but didn't back down. A little of the aggression faded, but not from Tom. Tom took another step forward, and they were chest to chest.

"Dammit," Otis said, putting his beer down. To the young man's credit, he didn't make another move toward the older man. Otis moved across the floor and hooked Tom's arm to pull him back. Tom turned on Otis, breaking his grip and shoving him away. The move caught Otis by surprise, and I stood. I didn't need to; Casey reached over and locked both of his massive arms around Tom, who immediately bucked and tried to twist away. Otis recovered, and between the two of them, they got Tom to the floor, knocking tables away and spilling beer on the floor. I heard Sonja gasp behind me and Bert groan.

Tom thrashed, his face turning from red to a deep purple. Even with his hands cuffed, he still moved enough to wiggle, kicking his legs and drumming his feet on the floor. Otis was slightly out of breath and Casey was grinning.

"The hell's gotten into you, Tom?" Otis asked, pulling out a handkerchief and mopping his forehead. "Casey, do you want to press charges?" The young man shook his head.

"But you see how we took him down? Maybe you can keep me in mind if you need another deputy."

Otis grunted. On the floor, Tom finally lay still, panting.

"If I hired you as a deputy, would you quit growing weed in the middle of your daddy's corn patch?" Otis asked as he bent down to pick up Tom.

Casey's grin quivered, turning sickly, and his friends snickered.

The handcuffed man laid limp, and Otis drug him a few feet before motioning to Casey. "Well, c'mon now. Let's get him into the back of my truck. You've helped me so far." Casey took Tom's shoulders, and Otis grabbed his feet, and they carried him out between them.

Bert and I turned back to the bar. Sonja was standing there, surveying the damage, then with a sigh emerged from behind the bar with a bucket and mop, and everyone cleared out of her way. I got up and picked up chairs, shaking off the spilled beer. Two tables and several chairs were damaged, but I thought I could fix the tables and combine the broken chairs into several working units. As she mopped a few people headed out the door, and the crowd inside decreased dramatically.

"I promise you, this rarely happens. We're a bar, and sometimes the young guys get into it over a girl, but I haven't had a fight in here in at least a year," she said, her head down as she cleaned.

I shrugged. "As long as they don't come after me, I'm fine. I'm used to the bars, trust me. A little fight in the middle of it isn't going to scare me off."

"That's not it. I don't care if it bothers you; it bothers me. I don't think we've ever had furniture broken." She looked up as she slung the mop into the bucket. "My customers don't act like this."

"I think I can get you a few working chairs out of the mess, and probably fix the table, if you want me to," I said.

She nodded. "We can talk about it tomorrow." She rolled the mop bucket back into the kitchen, and I carried the damaged table and chairs to the back hallway, setting them beside the back door. When I got back to the bar, I could tell Bert was ready to go.

"Too much excitement for you?" he asked me when I asked him if he wanted to go.

We left Sonja with a forlorn look in her eyes and an almost empty bar.

CHAPTER 10

THE HOUSE WAS QUIET behind me, sleeping to the sounds of insects. The cat, who had started out rubbing my ankles, flicked her tail as Sonja's headlights cut across the porch. Sonja's truck turned into the driveway, startling a small herd of deer. She paused as they bounded away, tails white and upright. The truck rolled over the gravel, and it crunched and popped as the rocks rubbed together. Her headlights flashed across me on the porch, and I closed my eyes and lifted a hand.

I heard the door creak open and clunk shut, and she swished through the grass until her boot heel knocked on the step. I heard her steps hesitate as she saw me, and she turned and went inside.

Well then, I thought. *So much for that.* I closed my mouth; glad I hadn't said anything to embarrass myself. I liked Sonja. She was standoffish and independent, had great eyes, and was beautiful in her own way. But I was just drifting through. It was only in the lyrics I wrote that the drifting songwriter and the lonely bar owner found love and made it work.

I served her a song / She served me a beeeeer / Just a couple of lonely peanuts in the bowl of life . . .

I rolled my eyes in the dark and resumed rocking, not realizing I had stopped. I saw a light come on inside the house and then go off. She hipped the screen door open and caught it with a socked foot to keep it from slamming. She had two beers in her hand and something else tucked under her arm. I stood up and offered to help her, and she handed me a beer. The cat left me to welcome Sonja.

"Good evening," I said.

"I'm surprised to find you up," she said.

"It was an exciting night. I'm not used to those."

"I don't understand." I could hear the bitterness in her voice. "I haven't had a fight there in years. And Tom is usually quiet. I don't think I've ever heard him raise his voice."

I took a sip from my beer, and I heard the click of a lighter as it flared beside me. She lit a cigarette, and my will crumbled. It'd been a day and half—no, two days—since I'd had one. I slid one out of the pack.

"You smoke?" she asked, surprised.

"I've been quitting," I said, the same old song and dance running out of my mouth. "First one since I got here."

"When we were sitting at the bar, you said something about that new place," I said. Her face turned toward me in the dark, tensing. "You started to contradict Otis, but you stopped when he said it had been there forever. Which one is it?"

She inhaled in the dark, the ember flaring and coloring her face a pale orange. "Something's going on," she said finally. "If you think I'm crazy, or just a pissed off bar owner, scratch our deal and you can move on. But that bar wasn't there last week. I swear it wasn't. But if you talk to Bert, or Otis, or Johnny, or Richard, or . . ." she trailed off.

"I saw the place when I drove in on Tuesday afternoon. The ruins, I mean." In the dark, her hand reached over and grabbed mine, narrowly missing getting burned.

"You saw it? The Cauthon place?" Her hand was warm, callused, and her short nails dug into skin.

"I came in from the north, following the river. If you're talking about the burned-out place on the left back from the road, then, yes I saw it. Entire thing gutted, right side burned to the ground, left side just a corner? Still standing? Is that the Cauthon place?"

She gripped my hand, and then let go.

"Yes, that's it," she said quietly. "But I drove by there before I came here. Now it's a log cabin looking thing, with a great big front porch and tin overhang. Signs tacked up along the wall, the way they used to advertise things. Two windows above the porch that almost look like eyes. I swear they were staring at me."

"What's the name of the place?"

"It had a sign, rotating on a pole. 'Ricochet' it's called, the sign all dressed up in neon."

I grunted, and she turned toward me.

"What?" she asked.

"That's a good line," I said. And before I could stop myself, I thought *we danced all night / both of us dressed only in the neon light . . .*

"Oh, god, not for a song. Really?" she asked, exasperation touching her voice.

She smoked in silence for a minute, and I said,

"So why do people think it's been there forever?"

"I have no clue. The people here . . ." she paused then continued, "They may not be the brightest in book sense, but they've got hard headed practicality down to a science. They're tough. And they're hard workers who can smell bullshit a mile away. But every one of them didn't remember it being a burned-out hunk last week."

"I thought I was thinking of the wrong place," I admitted. "You just don't confuse something like that. At least I didn't think so."

She flicked her butt, and it arched over the porch railing and into the bushes. I let mine follow hers, and coughed, trying to clear my throat of the insult. But it felt damn good, especially with a beer in my hand.

"I've got too much on my mind to worry about them. I haven't been out that way in months; maybe someone bought it and fixed it up. But I would've thought someone would have mentioned it to me. You know, bar owner? Been here all my life?" She shook her head. "But that doesn't change what I need to focus on. The damn well pump is still giving me problems. I've got busted tables and chairs I need to replace. One of my cooks hasn't come in for the last two days, and neither has my music man."

She turned her head and looked at me, and the low light from somewhere inside illuminated half of her face. "But I've found a music man, I think. So that's one problem down."

I won't say my heart didn't do a flip at the look in her unguarded eyes, but I forced myself to chuckle. "Well, maybe. You might hear me tomorrow night and decide an old record player might be better. And the record player won't ask for free room and board."

"There is that." She stood up, stretching, and I didn't look away. "Goodnight, Adam."

"Goodnight, Sonja."

CHAPTER 11

BOBBY DROVE HIS BATTERED hatchback down the main drag in Tanninville, cruising at a steady pace. The morning was still, poised for the weekend, caught between solemn slumber and the awakening of the day. The streets were still empty, the sun barely pushing dawn upward by degrees. It was hunger that finally drove him down the mountain, forcing him to slip and slide down the switchbacks in the dark. During his trip down the bluff, over his panting and the rattle of gravel, he could hear the steady *tink tink tink* of Mark's pick. The wind had to be right, and he had to stand still to locate the noise, but he could hear it.

Even now, the thought of the forlorn sound brought chills dancing up and down Bobby's spine. At first, Mark's corpse had been amusing. A dead dude doing stuff for you was just *cool*. But as the days wore on, it became spooky, bordering on creepy and passing into weird. Mark never spoke, never blinked, the surfaces of his eyes drying up and becoming milky. His various wounds collected on him until he was more of a beat up piece of meat than a man. His beard grew dusty and matted. Despite all of that, the steady *tink tink tink* of Mark's pick followed him around the cave.

Bobby had his own project, deep in the dark reaches of the mine. That was where the source of the goo was, the source of the dark magic that brought Mark back to life and gave him his new strange hungers and dark memories. Bobby shivered in the cool air coming through his window, even though his skin burned with a heat from the inside. His stomach growled and the dark street in front of him wavered. Food. Real food, not the dreams of screaming and dying foods, thrashing against an angry red sky. Bobby pulled into his driveway and parked, his headlights flashing across the long-ago painted siding of the house they rented. Their roommate's low rider truck sat in the driveway, and Bobby felt a stirring within him. It competed with the hunger gnawing at him; a natural hunger of his body with the unnatural hunger of . . . this stuff.

"Food. Gotta have food first," he muttered, and looked down at his hand. As he watched, black dots extruded from beneath his finger nails, forming tiny dots on the tips of his fingers. He rubbed them on his filthy jeans, but they just flattened and reformed after he tried to wipe them off.

"No," he whimpered. "Food, please." Cradling his hands, he hooked the door open with his pinky, and climbed out. A wave of dizziness took him, and he wobbled up the driveway. The clunk of his door shutting brought a light on inside, even though it was almost daybreak. Chris worked the second shift at the lumber mill, so he might be up. Once again, Bobby's stomach growled. The creak of the porch steps followed him up, and he kicked a chair as he stumbled across the uneven wood floor. The porch light came on, blinding him, and he heard the front door open.

"What the hell?" he heard Chris say.

The black stuff on his fingernails was burning, and he walked into the smell of smoke, stale beer, and the aroma of fresh-cut pine.

"Where the fuck have you been?" Chris' hand grabbed his shoulder and spun him around. "Y'all been dipping into our shit, haven't you?" Chris' angry eyes caught him and drew him in.

Bobby's hunger was intense, but the sight of Chris' challenge was too much. Bobby reached for his throat, the black stuff inside him boiling up, giving him strength as he latched onto Chris' throat. Chris stumbled back; Bobby was far stronger than he thought. He rode Chris to the floor, the entire house shaking when they landed.

Bobby squeezed, feeling the warmth leave the tips of his fingers.

Bobby tried to cook the Spam first, but as the pink meat sizzled, he couldn't control himself. Picking up the uncut block, he took a huge bite, gagged, and swallowed, his stomach rejoicing.

Choking it down, his hands slippery with the yellow grease, he leaned over the sink, gulping water from the faucet until he thought he would burst. His stomach protested, but needed the food more than it needed to purge the insult and quantity of food crammed down his throat.

Chris sat on the couch, his eyes already glazed over. He tried to follow Bobby, bumping into stuff before Bobby told him to sit. The room swirled as Bobby tried to stand, and he had to hold on to the table. A large mirror was opposite the doorway leading out of the kitchen, and Bobby stared at the creature in its reflection. It had a thin, bony version of his face, covered in dirt and filth. A cut decorated his cheek, crusted blood leaking to his chin. The only clean spot on him was where the water from the faucet washed away the grime around his lips, leaving stark white skin exposed. Looking down at his clothes, Bobby saw they were equally filthy and shredded. He couldn't go to town like this. He had something to do, something to see for this thing inside of him, and if anyone saw him like this . . .

Bobby's legs didn't shake anymore. His stomach groaned once, and Bobby let out a massive belch. A little froth came up with it, and Bobby spit it into the sink. He could think again, now that his body was sated, and he needed things. A shower. Food. Stuff from town. Then he could go back upriver, back into the dark, back into the deep.

He walked out of the kitchen and said to Chris, "Gather up all the food, but stay inside. Put it in a box by the door." Chris sat still for a moment, and Bobby wondered if it would work like it did for Mark. Chris moved, standing up, and headed to the kitchen. Bobby smiled to himself and went to the bathroom.

The grime turned the bottom of the tub black, revealing far more cuts and bruises than Bobby remembered. He washed, and washed, and washed again until the water ran clear. Once he was clean, he watched the black dots form on his fingers and drop off, swirling down the drain like evil little seeds. When he climbed out of the water, he scrubbed the mirror clean of steam and looked at himself. Better, but he still looked too thin, with huge black circles under his eyes like twin bruises on a raccoon.

He padded out of the bathroom and saw Chris sitting on the couch again. All the foodstuff from the kitchen was piled up by the door, and under the pile, Bobby saw the corner of a small box. Chris looked at him with no expression.

Bobby stood there, dripping, and shook his head. "It's in a box by the door," he muttered. "*All* of it."

In his room, he pulled on some clean clothes and reemerged. Sorting through the pile of food, he filled the box with the useful food items and lugged it to the car. He called Chris, who had a wooden gait, like Frankenstein. Climbing in and sitting down, Bobby felt increased discomfort with Chris sitting beside him.

"Lie back," he said, and Chris obediently lowered his seat and reclined. His eyes stayed open, staring up at the car's ceiling. Bobby tried to drive, wanting to look around town, but Chris unnerved him.

"Close your eyes," he said, and Chris closed his eyes. This made him look dead, funeral parlor dead, and Bobby swore. "Sit up. Jesus Christ, I'm sorry. I didn't mean to kill you."

Chris sat up, moving awkwardly, and Bobby squirmed away from him to avoid touching shoulders. "I don't know what came over me. I just couldn't help it," he babbled. Chris sat, looking straight ahead. Faint purplish bruises showed on his neck. Bobby coasted to a stop at the red light in the center of town, feeling exposed.

"Put your head between your knees. Cross your arms." He watched Chris for a moment. "You only look drunk or something, now." Bobby saw the light turn green at the corner of his eye and took his foot off the brake. Before he could accelerate, another car honked behind him, and an automatic reaction took over. He slammed on the brake pedal, sending Chris's head into the dashboard with a solid *thump*, and the seatbelt dug into his shoulder. When he looked, Tom Watkins was standing in front of the car. Bobby tried to take a breath, but the shot of adrenaline made it hard to control. Tom stood there, in the middle of the street, and cars honked behind him. Looking in his rearview mirror, he saw the cottony head of Mrs. Sawyer, the aging wife of one of Tanninville's eternal citizens. Best known for her erratic driving and ill-behaved dogs, Bobby knew who she was at once. Bobby climbed out of the car, waving angrily at her while staring at the man in front of him.

"What the hell are you doing, old man?" he asked. "Gonna get your ass run over if you keep standing in the fucking street."

The man looked at him with blank eyes. Bobby blinked, realizing a moment later this was the same Tom he'd seen fishing the day before.

"Touch your nose," Bobby whispered.

Obediently, Tom's finger came up and touched his nose.

"Holy shit," he said. Mrs. Sawyer blared her horn again, and Bobby screamed, "Give me a fuckin' second, you old bag!"

Her mouth turned to a perfect "O" of surprise. Her dogs, two old cocker spaniels, barked when they sensed his rage was directed toward them. She reached for the horn again, but Bobby controlled his anger.

"Go to the old Jenkins Mine," he said to Tom. "Go there tonight, after dark. Walk." He turned and climbed back into the car.

Tom stood there.

Leaning out the window, Bobby called, "And get out of the fuckin' street!" Tom obediently turned and stepped back onto the curb, ignoring the people who stared and whispered. Bobby gunned the car around him and drove out of town.

CHAPTER 12

THE MORNING SUN WOKE ME, along with the smell of breakfast drifting up the stairs. I yawned, stretched, and did my morning thing. When I got downstairs, Sonja was setting the plates out. The girl and her baby weren't there; I assumed she'd moved on to find her wayward husband. Bert was there, a little red-eyed from the night before. Before I met Sonja on the porch, I made sure he was in his room.

The salesman and construction workers were quiet, and the conversation was lower than I remembered. Looking back, I guess that was the first sign I missed. I wasn't thinking about them; I wanted to grab a chance to talk with Sonja. So I shoveled down a few pieces of sausage, and was leaning by the back porch when she came out. Preoccupied, she didn't notice me at first and jumped when I stood up. On reflex, she raised the wrench she carried in her hand.

I snagged it before it could do any damage. She frowned at me, and I followed her to the well house.

"So what seems to be the trouble this morning?" I asked.

"Pressure is up and down," she said.

"I noticed the cold water was jumpy. Hot was fine, though."

"The hot water is held in a tank, but the cold water is in a small bladder. The pump keeps going in and out, so the bladder won't stay filled."

I nodded, even though I didn't know much about it. "So you need to figure why the pump isn't pulling it evenly."

She gave me a long look that said she saw through my ignorance. I tried again.

"Does the water come from river?"

She shook her head again.

"My well is separate from the river water. We drilled it two thousand feet down to get to the aquifer. The water we get is filtered by the limestone bedrock. The town gets its water from the river; it's collected right below the first bridge, treated, and pumped to the town."

She squatted by the housing, and I looked away quickly. She wore a V-neck tee shirt that gaped open as she leaned forward. As much as she attracted me, I still needed to treat her right. Staring down her shirt like an uneducated trailer park lout wasn't the way to go.

"I think it's the well head control that's out," she said. I moved to a position with a less distracting view. My movement brought me closer to her as she was reaching for a small yellow box with two wires dangling from it. My movement brought my right hand into her back, and I hastily backed up. The well house was small, and there was no room for me to dance around her.

"You know how to read a multi meter?" she asked, picking it up and offering me the box.

"No, electricity is something I stayed away from," I said. "My dad was a shade tree mechanic. I only know enough about electricity to be dangerous." I shuffled back away from her, and after giving me a strange look, she squatted back down, which restarted the original problem.

"You know, I think I'd better get started fixing the tables and chairs that got broken," I said. "Are they still in the back of your truck?"

She looked up right as I looked down, and I felt my face flush. I knew looking away quickly would confirm my guilt, so I made myself look her in the eyes until she responded.

"Sure. I might have some spares in the grey barn," she said, a little confused

I could actually feel the blood pounding in my ears as I acknowledged her and backed out of the well house.

"I'll go work on that, then," I said. *Idiot, idiot, idiot,* I thought.

"The keys are in the truck if you want to drive it around," she yelled to my retreating back.

Adam didn't see Sonja glance down at the front of her t-shirt, grin ruefully, and bend her head back to the multi meter. Nor did he see her small smile as she studied the readout.

I walked across the yard, mentally eviscerating myself. I've never been able to say the right thing at the right time when a woman is involved. I was the kind of guy who could say a compliment in a roundabout way and receive a furrowed brow instead of the smile I was expecting. Instead of being able to deftly handle a simple electrical problem, I got caught looking down her shirt when trying *not* to look down her shirt. I kicked at the damp grass as I crossed the yard, waving to Bert, who'd taken up his station on the porch. My unfortunate run of luck had started a few years ago in Nashville. After high school, I'd dated around. Following my move to Nashville, I'd had one serious relationship in almost a decade. Then I met Nicole.

Nicole was a redhead with killer eyes and the reason I left Nashville. We'd met in a city building as we were standing in line to pay our water bills. We dated for six months before deciding to move in together, and things went well for a year or so. She'd pull back a little from me, but I was so focused on pushing my songs to a few of my contacts I didn't notice. After my song was released Nicole and I had a blow-up fight in front of everyone at an industry event. It was pretty embarrassing, and I hit the road not long after that.

I climbed into Sonja's truck and sighed. I cranked it and put it into gear, shoving the gearshift into first, and caught the clutch neatly. I loved five-speeds, and had learned to drive on a truck just like hers. Navigating around the house to the barn, I backed it up to the rusted tin doors. Whatever was there with Sonja would sort itself out, given time. I'd play a few sets, let her get her music man back, and I'd hit the road. I had a couple ideas for some songs, and could circle back to Nashville. Scandals and gossip didn't last long; there was always too much going on. Not that they'd forget, but they'd have something else to talk about.

I surveyed the damaged chairs and cracked table top. Opening the sliding barn doors, I saw a work bench with tools scattered over the top of it. I pulled pieces of broken furniture off the truck after finding a drill.

I had both tables and all but one of the chairs put back together when Sonja came into the barn. She took a look at her refurbished chairs and repaired table and grunted, a slight frown on her face.

"What?" I asked. I was proud of what I'd done, only sacrificing one chair in the process.

"I guess it'll do." She frowned. I tried to keep the offended look off my face, but didn't succeed. She spun away from me, and I saw her shoulders shake. More of a twitch really, and I cocked my head to the side, watching her. A moment later, she peeked at me from under her eyelashes, and snickered under her breath.

"Very funny," I said, dropping the drill to the bench top. "I'll have you know I passed woodshop with all Bs, thank you very much." I grabbed two chairs and carried them to the back of her truck. She let out a laugh behind me, and when I turned after loading the chairs, she was grinning broadly.

"Just keeping you on your toes," she said. "Wouldn't want you to think you're too helpful, or anything."

"Of course not," I said, grabbing one side of the table and waiting for her to grab the other. "Are you taking these now?"

She nodded. "We open for prep at ten. I'll get the bar ready, and Donald will handle the kitchen."

We loaded the two tables, and I said, "If you don't mind, I'll ride with you. I'll bring my guitar and do a quick sound check."

She paused for the barest fraction of a second. "I'll come back when the server comes in, but it might not be until noon, or so; is that okay?"

I nodded and headed for the house to grab my guitar.

Inside, I quickly changed out of the clothes I had on; I wanted something fresh, and to be honest, something that looked a little better.

I grabbed my guitar, making sure I had extra cords. Good cords were hard to come by; I'd invested in a good guitar, and having a crappy cord took away the extra tone that all good instruments possessed. I had a small amp in the trunk of my car, but I'd wait until I saw how her system looked before pulling it out.

I debated taking my band box, but decided The Dive probably didn't need much more than my guitar. My band box was a small, DVD-sized unit that carried about a thousand tracks; you could select which instrument to play per track, and it allowed a single musician to have an entire band backing him. Select a play list, tell it which instrument you had, and it would do the rest. God bless technology.

I carried it all outside, waving to Bert on the porch. He waved back but didn't move. Tossing my case into the back, I climbed in.

"Going on a date?" she asked, seeing my new clothes.

"Never know who you'll meet in a bar. Gotta look my best," I said nonchalantly.

She put the truck in gear, and we rumbled down the driveway.

Tanninville's history was dominated by the river that divided it. Before it was consolidated into one town, each side had a main street later renamed for the side of the river it followed. Sonja's home place was on the east side of the river, a few miles out of town. We passed planted fields, and my eyes tracked the rows as they flashed past. She turned from the two-lane road leading to her boarding house and entered a residential area.

Some lots were overgrown, some lots were manicured, but each had a feeling of age around it. "Nice houses," I commented, breaking the silence.

She glanced to where I was looking and nodded. "Most of them were rebuilt after the war," she said. "Sherman came through here, tore the town up pretty bad. We were one of the few places he thought resisted, and he repaid the favor by burning almost everything."

"You can't really tell," I offered.

"It worked out in the end. He spent so much time in town he didn't get to the outlying farms. So when he left, he left the cotton fields. That allowed some folks to get money flowing, which saved the town in the long run. A few years ago, we found out we have the largest number of post-Civil War homes in the state."

"You know your stuff," I said.

"My daddy loved history," she said. "It was his hobby. He tried to get the town recognized for it, said we were 'The City of Homes.' But some other town near Atlanta was already using it, so he had to settle with 'The City of Homecomings.'"

I laughed, and we turned onto West Riverside Drive, heading to the bridge crossing the river. The main street was like other Southern main streets; modern signs stapled to old buildings, new construction edging up against brick and stone buildings that have seen a century or more. People were out, walking around in the early morning sunshine.

Sonja raised her hand every few minutes, and I found myself doing the same. A cluster of shop owners watched us pass, heads swiveling and following us.

"It seems pretty busy," I said.

"We never got a big box store, so we were able to keep most of our smaller places. There's one just on either side of the county line, so you can go twenty minutes in either direction and get just about anything you want."

"Who has the jobs here?" I asked.

"Mostly farming, but we have a lumber mill downstream. Lumber's big, and Macon's an hour away. So the high paying jobs are there. It's the perfect mix. I don't think Tanninville could happen anywhere else." She down-shifted at a red light idling while the single car in front of us puttered along.

"So where are you from?" she asked. "I know Nashville, but before that?"

I settled back in the seat, enjoying the morning sun. It was just right; enough of a breeze not to sweat, and just enough sun to keep you from being chilled. "Small town outside Atlanta. Just like this one, but not quite as big. Daddy worked at the plant, Mama at a local school. Originally he was from a family of farmers but when cotton went down, Daddy got sent to college. I went to Nashville after I graduated high school, and I've been working and playing there ever since."

"Why just sell your songs? Don't you want to be a performer?"

I shook my head emphatically. "I thought I did at first, but as I was playing clubs, I realized something. The people in the nicest cars were the ones who wrote the songs. Kinda like shop keepers during gold rush; the miners who struck it rich got all the attention, but the ones who were successful long term were the ones who sold the supplies."

"So you're just supplying songs? Writing them?"

"Pretty much. I still play the clubs, but getting seen by a music exec or record label is only part of it. I can preview songs and share them across town. Let the music do the talking." I mimed an air guitar riff.

"Interesting," she said as we crossed over the bridge. I could smell the river under us; a combination of water and mud. Several boats were out there, each with a person or two and a pole. She saw me looking. "The river runs into Lake Jefferson, which is popular with the lake-life crowd. They bring in their money, but don't stay," she said, satisfaction in her voice. "It's the best of both worlds."

"What about you?" I had asked as we turned into the broken asphalt parking lot in front of The Dive; she pulled around to a side door that faced away from the main street. We'd stopped for two cups of coffee once we crossed the bridge and sat, holding them and occasionally blowing on them to cool the liquid off. The morning was cool, and the warmth of the liquid just right. Neither one of us made a move to climb out of the truck and continue the day.

"Typical small town girl. Born here, raised here. Married here," she paused. "After Billy died, it seemed like everything would . . . slide away. The farm had been sold after my daddy died, and my mother passed away my second year in college. But when I lost Billy, I just got myself up the next morning. And I've been doing it ever since."

I didn't want to say how stark it all sounded, but I could hear it in her voice.

"I made myself get in the habit of not giving up," she continued. "In town, or any small town I guess, you're on stage. Everybody is watching for you to slip, fall, and land on your face. We've been here a while and my daddy was pretty active: on the town council, with the merchants, and at church. So when things went wrong, people were expecting us, me, to drop down a couple of pegs. But I've discovered that's the secret. You put your head down and keep going. You don't trip over what you see, you can step over it."

I mentally grabbed the last line, even if I didn't have paper in my hand. I could remember it until I got inside.

"Let's put Humpty Dumpty back together, shall we?" I didn't realize my words could have a double meaning until they were out of my mouth. I opened the truck door and swung my legs out, and she did the same a little slower. Setting my coffee cup down on the truck bed, I lifted out the chairs while she unlocked and opened the bar doors.

The smell that came out was like every other bar I've ever stepped in. Beer, grease, and industrial cleaner. I carried the chairs in with the awkward gait designed to save my shins and set them down inside. Sonja flipped the breakers to turn on the lights, and we carried the table to the empty spot on the floor. She directed me while I rearranged the tables and chairs, filling the void. Finally, she nodded her head in satisfaction. We both walked to the small stage.

"I had it wired, but I think Mark may have moved some things around," she said. "I don't mess with it unless I have to, so you'll have to figure it out on your own."

I set my guitar case down and stepped up to the stage. It seemed solid enough; I've been on some that have bent under the weight of the band. "It'll be fine. We're just looking for some background noise, a little bit of dancing music, right?"

She nodded. "Something to take their minds of their trouble," she said.

Our eyes met and did their thing; I'm glad I was up on the stage. If I had been closer to her, I might have made a move. "What music do you like?" I asked, smiling, trying to extend the moment.

Her face turned serious. "Public answer or private answer?" she replied. As she spoke, she set her hips and leaned back, almost in a defensive posture.

"Both," I said.

"In public, country. I'll sing along to Dolly, Faith, and even some Patsy Cline. But what I really like," she sighed, pretending to cover her eyes in embarrassment, "… are early 80's rock ballads. Journey. Meat Loaf. The Eagles."

I barked a laugh and said, "No, that's good stuff. Especially live. You can go from syrupy to rocking with a chord change. There's no shame in it. Unless you liked . . . Air Supply? Abba?"

Her defensive posture wilted further, and she nodded. "Guilty as charged. I guess you can say there are times I'm a hopeless romantic."

I shook my head ruefully. Turning my back to her, I said, "I'm not sure I want to talk to you anymore." I risked a glance over my shoulder, and I could tell she was trying to hold back a laugh. I turned back around. "But since you told me a secret, I'll tell you one: If you looked hard on my IPod, you might find Taylor Swift."

She smiled at me, and our eyes did that thing again. Tapping her chin, she took a step back, turned, and walked toward the kitchen. I hated to see her go, but I sure enjoyed watching her leave. As she moved behind the bar, I turned my attention back to the tangle of wires, sorting what I could and trying to straighten the jumble. No stage is ever clean, but you wanted it to be orderly. I spent about fifteen minutes organizing and pulled up a chair from the dining area. Plugging in, I tuned up my guitar, played a couple quick riffs, and then adjusted the volume of the amps behind me.

I pulled a microphone stand over, adjusted the height, and played the first few measures of a Johnny Cash song. I adjusted the mike volume, and continued, repeating the chorus a couple times, and launched into a steady Tom Petty rocker. Slowed down, with just a touch of twang, it served the setting well. I fell into my stage mind, blanking everything out around me, and concentrated on my left hand and my voice. I don't know if other performers did it, but I only saw the mike, my guitar neck, and felt my vocals. That's another reason I focused on song writing; other artists were also performers, but I just sat there and played.

I ran through a number of my favorites, *Long Cool Woman* by the Hollies, *Amarillo by Morning* by George Strait, and one more until my hands were sore and my throat dried up. I'd seen people moving around the dining area for a while, and when I stopped, applause came from Donald, dressed in his cook's whites, the day waitress, and Sonja. I smiled, nodding, a little embarrassed.

"Was the volume good enough back there?" I asked through the mike. I got three nods. Satisfied, I unplugged and put my guitar up. I swapped the chair for a barstool, one with a back, and climbed off the stage. I pulled my watch from my pocket and put it on, surprised to find it was almost eleven.

"I thought I was going to have to come up there and pull you off," Sonja said. "We're getting ready to open. Are you hungry?"

I nodded, and she handed me a menu and pointed me to a booth. I carried my guitar with me, but before I could get settled into the booth, the waitress came over.

"Ohmygod, you'rejustthebest! Myname'sDarlene," she said in a blur, holding her hand out. I tentatively reached for it, hoping her handshake wasn't as fast as her mouth. She almost vibrated in place, with constant moving and twitching. Her hands never remained still, bouncing between her waitress pad, her hair, and tugging at her shirt or jeans. I introduced myself, and ordered a light beer. Nothing heavy; I wasn't normally a day drinker, but it would suit my parched throat just right. The door opened, letting in light and a small work crew ready for lunch. Darlene winked at me and bounced over to them.

From where I was sitting, I could see the dull red light on the amplifier glowing, so I pulled myself out of the booth and climbed back up on stage, intending to cut it off. Older amps like this one could overheat if left on too long. Before I got halfway across the stage, a voice from the worker's table called out, "Hey, pretty boy! You gonna sing for us?"

Two of the other big chunkies with him laughed, and I said, "Not now, but come back tonight."

An older gentleman beside him frowned, and I assumed he was the supervisor of the crew.

"Nah, you're too pretty. I don't like that girly man music." He and his friends laughed again, and the super's frown deepened. I let the comment slide off; the big ugly couldn't know what I did or did not play.

Sonja came around the bar, carrying a tray loaded with beer, another drink, and a couple of plates. Her eyes tracked from me to the group, and as I slid back into the booth, she said, "Darryl, cut that out. I've seen you almost cry to a Patsy Cline song, so don't you talk about girly men." Her words were said with a smile, but his face drew into a grimace. His friends pulled back, and the supervisor put his hand on Darryl's shoulder and leaned in to whisper something to him. Sonja didn't react to his aggression, but she did slow her step slightly.

She brought the tray to my booth and unloaded it, setting out two hamburgers, our drinks, and a basket of fries. "I took the liberty of making you lunch," she said. "I hope you don't mind, but everyone loves our burgers. I never took you for a vegetarian." Sliding into the booth, she lowered her voice. "Did it come across wrong? Or did I have my bitch face on?"

I kept a smile on my face as I said, "No, I think he's just an asshole. He said something to me when I cut off the amp," I replied, my voice also low.

"Larry will keep him in line," she said, nodding to someone over my shoulder.

I turned my head to see the older man sitting with the workers sharing a 'What do you do?' look with Sonja. I took a big bite of my burger and made appropriate noises; it really was good. "So what's your secret?"

She shook her head. "Sorry, buddy, not yet. I'm not giving it up that easily."

I grunted around another mouthful, and we talked until the plates were empty and she took them to the kitchen. The lunch crowd seemed sparse, which didn't surprise me, but seemed to annoy Sonja. I had another beer and was thinking about Bert and his sun-drenched naps when she returned.

"Will you help me load something? After that, if you're ready, I'll take you back," she said.

I held in a yawn and nodded, grabbing my guitar from the bench beside me. She took a last, dissatisfied glance around the room and we went through the kitchen. Darlene bounced over, talking a mile a minute, and promising to come back tonight for my set. She gave me an enthusiastic hug, and I could smell sweat and beer on her. Sonja saw me disengage from her but made no comment. She led me to the storeroom and pointed to two large sacks of flour.

"Cook needs this at the house," she explained. I bent at my knees, picked up a bag, and waddled out to her truck. As I got to the door, she said, "I had a hand truck!"

I ignored her and laid the bag on the back of the truck. Going back inside, I handed her my guitar as I grabbed the other bag. Once it was loaded, we climbed in. I could feel the beer and the burger dragging me into afternoon nap mode. If I got an hour's sleep, I'd be good until midnight or more. I was contemplating this as we rode back in silence, each lost in our own thoughts.

"I enjoyed this morning," I said suddenly.

I saw Sonja jump out of the corner of my eye, and she said, "Not much too it."

We drove in silence and were heading through town when I dozed. The regular motion of the truck had almost done me in when Sonja halted, hard enough to lock up the brakes. I was relaxed, almost out, and was thrown against my seatbelt. My eyes came open and my arms shot out, catching my guitar.

A woman in a faded dress was shaking her fist at Sonja as she crossed the street.

"Gakk," I said, sweat breaking out on my forehead as a gallon of adrenaline dumped into my blood stream.

Sonja exhaled as she rolled down the window. "Dammit, Marsha, watch out. I could have killed you!" she said to the woman's back. Marsha hurried across the rest of the street without looking and scurried down the side walk, shooting poisonous glares at us.

"What the hell was that?" I said when I could speak.

"Crazy ass just walked out in front of me. If I hadn't been looking right at her . . ." Sonja let the words trail off as she put the truck in gear.

"I know what you've said about the people in this town, but I haven't seen the tiniest ounce of nice yet. The only nice thing I can think of so far is that Otis didn't run me in my first day in town," I said.

I caught Sonja with a funny look on her face, but she said, "No, I've never known anyone to be mean. I mean, we have our share of assholes – everybody does – but for the most part, everyone's agreeable."

"Even the last two days? Since I've been here?" I asked, awake now.

She thought a moment before conceding the point with a nod, saying, "It's just not like them."

We made it back to Sonja's safely, and I carried my guitar upstairs after waving to Bert. The day had grown warmer, and the cool of my room was more appealing. As I dozed off, I realized I was falling into my Nashville patterns; stay up late, get up early, take a recharge nap in the afternoons, and repeat. A breeze came through the window, feeling wonderful, and I was gone.

CHAPTER 13

I WOKE UP THAT EVENING feeling energized and ready to go. I put on some comfortable clothes – no stage outfit for me - grabbed my guitar, and was out the door when Bert waved me down.

"Headin' out?" Bert called.

"About to - you wanna come?"

He was out of his seat before I finished speaking, and I grinned to myself as he hurried down the steps and across the dusty parking lot. I patted my guitar as I placed it in the back seat. We'd been through many nights, and tonight promised to be a memorable one.

Bert and I climbed into the car, and with the push of a button the engine purred to life. Tonight would be one of those nights when I could feel the groove; everything was falling into a rhythm, from the songs on the radio to the slow rumble of the car.

When we pulled into The Dive I frowned. The parking lot only had a handful of cars in it, and I checked my watch. Seven o'clock on a Thursday night; the lull between the dinner eaters and the drinkers shouldn't be this low. Sonja had good food and a decent staff, and seemed to be the only place in town. It wasn't until I pushed open the door I thought about the new place in town everybody thought was an old place in town: Ricochet.

My set that night was as good as I hoped it would be. I took the stage to scattered applause, plugged in, and put together one of the best sets I've ever played. *I Walk the Line, Love Without End, Amen, Chattahoochee, Workin' Man Blues, Hotel California,* and *Gimmie Three Steps* were in my first set. When I stepped back from the mike, the applause was slightly louder, but it didn't matter. I *knew* how good it was and was shocked when I looked past the mike stand.

The crowd scattered around the dining area was smaller than the lunch crowd earlier that afternoon. I squinted past the stage lights, counting. Fourteen plus the servers, and the faces above the tables stood out, wan and emotionless. The loudest noise was the clink of silverware. Occasionally, I heard a murmur. The bar was empty of regulars, and only Bert occupied a stool.

I walked up to them. "Was it that bad?" I said, wondering if I was mistaken.

Sonja shook her head. "No, you're fine. It's not you." She looked down, her face stricken. Her bottom lip quivered, and my heart dropped for her. I reached across the bar. Her hand was cold, and wet from the rag she was holding.

I looked at her sympathetically, and said, "It's definitely not you. Know how many bars I've been in? Know how many *shitty* bars I've been in? Trust me, it's not you. Something else must be going on." I paused for a moment. "If it is me, I'll leave, I promise."

With her free hand, she wiped at the corners of her eyes.

I glanced at Bert, looking for some support. He was out woolgathering, staring off in to space. I nudged his stool, and he snapped back to attention. "Yes, I agree," Bert said.

Sonja laughed, the melancholy mood broken.

"What did I miss?" he asked.

"Sonja's upset at the turnout. She thinks it's her fault," I said.

"Oh, no," he said. "It's Ricochet." He blinked at us owlishly, and I realized he looked like the other diners. "I'm telling you, they have that jukebox. It will play anything you want." His eyes clouded back up, and he stared at the beer in front of him. Sonja and I looked at each other, and . . . It's hard to explain, but it's like we were waiting for that moment. I saw the hurt in her eyes, the doubt, and betrayal. This was her town, her people. I saw the strength in her that carried her through her husband's death and allowed her to pick up the pieces of her life.

"Ricochet?" she asked. "Maybe we need to pay them a visit."

"Together," I said, before I thought better of it.

I played a second, more subdued set. Before I began my encore for the night, I said into the microphone, "The final song for tonight is for the hopeless romantics out there. This song speaks to hope, to longing, and to realizing what you've got."

I picked the opening notes of a Journey song. Even though it was written for piano, I could do a passable job by picking the notes. I didn't have Steve Perry's vocal chops, but it was acceptable. Sonja was still down from our earlier conversation, and she turned toward me when I spoke to the crowd. When she realized what song I was playing, she broke into the first real smile of the night.

Lying beside you / Here in the dark / Feeling your heart beat with mine

I finished the first verse, inhaled to get the volume I needed, and belted out the second verse. Even though I didn't have the backing of a full band, I could convey the importance and emotion of the second verse.

The crowd stirred a little at the simple sounds, coming out of their stupor. Even though the song was for Sonja, they reacted, and the atmosphere cleared a bit. The crowd was even smaller than before, barely more than half a dozen. But it didn't matter; in that moment, she and I finally made a connection, and we gained a clue on how to defeat what was gripping her town, even if we didn't realize it.

CHAPTER 14

"WHAT DO YOU THINK it will be like?" Sonja asked me. We were pulling onto West Riverside Drive, leaving her place, and heading toward Ricochet.

"I have no idea." My voice was a little scratchy; I had strained to hit some notes in a few of the songs I sang the previous night. It was a good strain, but I could still feel it. Practice would take care of it; if I performed more, I'd strengthen my vocal cords and small sets like that wouldn't bother me. "Maybe they have dancers. That could explain where all the menfolk have gone."

There was no comment to my humor. Sonja shifted in the seat next to me. I was hyper-aware of her; she was stunning in a pair of jeans, boots, and a sheer green top that highlighted her eyes. I was in a short sleeve, button down shirt, also in jeans. As the bar was closing last night, we hatched our plan. She'd call in her assistant manager to close, and once supper was served at the boarding house, she and I would take a trip to Ricochet.

The car moved smoothly under us as we picked up speed. Her hands wandered over the center console, flipping through the menus of the touch screen. Her hands were well shaped, with long fingers. I drove easily with one hand, and occasionally her arm would brush mine. Her light touches against the hairs of my arm were strangely erotic, and the way she smelled . . . I had to force myself to pay attention to the road.

"So what was the place before it burned down?" I asked, trying to force myself not to make every tiny touch an unspoken promise.

"It was a junk store when I was a girl," she said, giving up her explorations of the car's technology. I was disappointed, but a little relieved. "The owner died, and his son turned it into a bar. This was before Billy and I opened The Dive, when I was in college." She paused. "It was even before we got married. I think

Billy would go hell-raising there." She looked out the window, and a few houses flashed past before she resumed talking. "It burned, oh, ten years ago or so. Rumor said it was arson, but when liquor burns, you can't tell. They said the fire started at the bar, and it just so happened he had a nice insurance policy. He and his mistress moved to Savannah not long after."

"Sounds like a champ," I said.

"His family tree grew a little crooked," she said. "Cross a couple of branches, and it starts producing nuts."

The river beside us was scenic, an occasional jonboat floating with a man or two holding poles. We passed over two large pipes jutting out into the river, and I must have grunted a question.

"Those are the intake pipes. The town takes in the river water, purifies it, and uses it for drinking water. We sell some to the neighboring towns when they need it. It's been a good year for rainfall."

We approached the North Bridge, and I could feel Sonja tense beside me. I debated for a minute, and laid my hand on her forearm. It was cool to the touch, and for a moment, her smell intensified.

"It will be okay. We'll go in, check it out, and see what you've got to deal with. At the worst, we'll enjoy a good dinner, and hopefully have a relaxing evening." We slowed to a stop at the red light leading to the North Bridge. She relaxed incrementally, and pulled her arm from under my hand. For a heart-stopping second she paused, then laid her hand over mine, giving me a half smile before looking away.

I pulled onto the bridge and I could feel my stomach clench. Even though we weren't planning to confront anyone, the anticipation was already seeping into my body. I cupped her hand loosely, finding calluses on one side and softness on the other. We turned from the bridge onto East Riverside, and the lay of the land gave us our first glimpse of Ricochet, several hills away and filtered by buildings and a few trees. Sonja gasped.

We eased into a near empty parking lot filled with a precise layer of gravel. The stones ground together beneath the tires, popping and snapping, the sound carrying through the bottom of the car.

"Oh my god," Sonja said. I wanted to echo her sentiment; when I drove past this location a few days ago, it was a weed-choked lot with small saplings sprouting up. I guess someone could have cleaned and graded the lot, but there was no evidence of one piece of dirt being moved. It was as if the gravel grew from the ground, covering up and consuming the weeds, trees, and trash. "It's Friday night. Where are . . ."

"We know where they *aren't*," I said. "They're not at The Dive."

But what grabbed our eyeballs and drew us to it like a lodestone was the building. Low and squat, it seemed to bulge from the hillside behind it. It was made of logs, as Otis had said, but no log cabin had ever been built with perfectly shaped logs requiring no chinking. A long porch extended down the front, and vintage signs were placed at regular intervals. Beside the porch, a bar sat atop two posts set in the ground, and it took me a minute to figure it out. It was a hitching post with nine brass rings gleaming in the sunlight. To the side of the hitching post was a post-modern Cadillac, or some type of hybrid automotive creation. It was long and multi-colored, with a beige hood, black front quarter-panel, grey door, and a white rear quarter panel. The back window had a Dead-Head sticker on one side, and a Black Flag sticker on the other. I looked at it, studied the creation, and then Sonja spoke.

"What the hell?" Sonja said, squinting just a bit to see under the shadows of the porch.

"No kidding. How did I miss this place?" I said aloud. I refused to acknowledge the musical icon I was parked beside.

"No, not that. That's a whole 'nother issue by itself. See those signs?" She pointed. "Bear Creek Farms is a peach and cattle farm. Well, it used to be. The family sold it to put a kid through college. But how did they get a sign? An original sign, no less?"

I pushed the button that turned the car off and said, "That's the least of our worries, I'm afraid." The car's engine ticked softly, and I added, "Are we ready to do this?"

"Yeah, we are. What the hell is this?"

We opened our doors at the same time. Even though the boarding house was less than ten minutes away, I felt like I'd been driving for hours. My back and legs were tight, and I stretched, and I saw Sonja doing the same. I'll admit she looked more attractive doing it, but my eyes were drawn to the massive neon sign placed at the roadside. As soon as our car doors clicked shut, a buzzing sound came from it, and it slowly turned. The buzzing came from the neon tubes as they flickered to life, a mix of white and red light. My eyes were fastened to it as it rotated, and the letters came into view between flashes.

RIC . . . RICOCH . . . RICOCHET. . .

Chills danced up my arms.

"What timing," I muttered under my breath, but anything else I was going to say stopped in my throat, because that's when the front door opened and a man stepped out. The front doors to the restaurant were oversized, with large frosted glass insets. Massive door hardware gleamed in the slanting sunlight, flashes of brass set against the dark wood.

"Welcome to Ricochet," he said from the doorway. I walked around the car and took Sonja's right hand, and pulled her slightly forward. We walked to the base of the steps leading up to the porch and stopped, trying to take in the view. I put one foot on the worn step, paused, and studied the man. He examined me openly and shifted his eyes to Sonja. I felt sweat pop out on her hand, and we stood there. My eyes wanted to drift over the porch and examine the exquisite detail, but they were drawn to the man in front of me.

Taller than me, and dressed in a three-piece grey suit. A dark tie—a *cravat*, my mind whispered—disappeared into his vest, and a silver chain held his vest and tie down. Thin, half-rim glasses perched on his nose. While he looked at us with kindly eyes, it was unsettling. Salt-and-pepper hair matched a neatly trimmed goatee, and his skin was the product of many hours inside. Great age seemed to emanate from him, a dustiness that spoke of time and wisdom. When he tilted his head to Sonja, I saw a small pearl earring in one ear.

"Adam and Sonja, as I live and breathe," he said, his hands working a spotless towel inside and around a glass, something I hadn't noticed before. "I've heard a lot about both of you. I am . . . Lyles, the proprietor of this establishment." To Sonja, he said, "We have that in common, do we not? It is something that is a part of us, yet . . . greater than we are." I felt my insides flutter at his words, and I took another step forward and tugged on Sonja's hand. She resisted for a moment, and then followed.

"What an amazing place," I heard myself say. My voice echoed in my throat, and I felt like I'd taken a huge hit of some high-grade cocaine; the sense of dislocation was so intense I felt like my legs and body were non-existent, and the only thing that was real was my face and mouth. Sonja still hadn't said a word but her hand was slippery with sweat.

"Please, come in. Ricochet is my labor of love. Three plays for a dime, all you need for a good time," he said in an incantation. Chill bumps worked along my back, and as he turned, the doors behind him swiveled open, exposing the interior. It was dim, but I could see a faint gleam on chrome.

"Is anyone here? I thought we'd come and find the place already full." Sonja's words were sharp, but the man barely blinked.

"My Regulars usually arrive after dark," he said, and I could hear the capital "R" in his words.

"You have regulars already?" Sonja asked. She didn't hide the disdain in her voice, and my eyes swiveled back to him. Once again, he showed no reaction, and my eyes went back to Sonja. "How long *have* you been here? I've lived here my whole life and a month ago, this place was a burned-out shack."

"We've been here forever," he said softly. "We've always been here."

The chills returned as I stepped into the space between them and entered the restaurant. I glanced back at the tableau behind me, seeing them framed within the doorway. Sonja, outside in the light; Lyles, partially obscured in the shadows of the doorway.

"Then explain why I've never seen you," Sonja demanded. I took another step inside, and I heard his response through the doorway.

"Do you always see what you're looking for?" Lyles asked.

The main dining area was recessed, sunken a step down from the entry way. The raised portion of the restaurant had tables and chairs spaced out between an ornate railing and the wall, which were covered with vintage items. A large dance floor filled the middle of the building, and I blinked and shook my head. The inside seemed larger than the building from the outside, but it had to be a trick of perception. There was also seating spread around the dance floor, and an oversized bar dominated the back left side of the dining room.

I heard steps behind me, and the bartender moved away from us, circling around the tables and chairs as he crossed the dance floor.

"Sonja," I said.

She ignored me; she neither responded nor followed me inside.

"Sonja, come here," I repeated. I wanted to look back, but I was afraid. If I took my eyes off of what I was looking at, I was afraid it would disappear. I was afraid if I blinked it would disappear.

Facing what I'd seen on the wall, I walked backward, reaching back with my hand. When my hand found Sonja on the porch, I pulled her in behind me. She resisted at first, but followed me inside, staying on the raised portion of the floor.

"What is this?" I demanded. "What do you see?"

"It's a record," she said. "A gold record. Don't they do that for . . ." her words trailed off. "It has your name on it. Did you record this?" she asked me.

I shook my head.

"Not yet. I've recorded the demo on my computer, but I haven't even cut the vocals." The reality of the plaque in front of me caused me to lift my hand and tentatively touch it. I wanted confirmation it wasn't a hallucination. It was real and cool to the touch. We walked along the outside of the room, examining the photographs and advertisements.

"This was a country store run by one of the founding families," Sonja said quietly.

"Look at the date," I said. "The 30s. And this one?"

She looked at the faded black and white photograph. "Another old company. They made railroad cars, boilers, thing like that after the Civil War. They're still in town. They were bought out in the 80s by some international company."

"I recognize this," I said. A rusting farm implement was mounted to the wall. "It's a threshing bar from a horse-drawn plow. My grandfather had one when I was growing up."

We heard a sound behind us and turned to find the bartender standing by a table on the dance floor, holding a tray with a pair of tall glasses on it.

"Please, come have a seat. I'm afraid we may have started our relationship off on the wrong foot." He placed the drinks on the table and motioned to us. "Will you allow me to start over? Please, have a seat. My name is Lyles, and I welcome you to Ricochet."

I blinked. Menus were sitting beside the drinks, and they hadn't been there when he set the drinks down. At least, I don't think they were.

Sonja lifted her head regally and turned on her heel. I shrugged at Lyles, who nodded in response. She walked to the opposite wall, and I picked up the drinks from the table. Behind me, I heard a gasp and saw Sonja staring at a faded newspaper pressed into a glass frame.

When I reached her, she ignored the glass I presented her, and when I saw the headline, I saw why. "THE DEVILS FOYER: JENKINS MINE CLAIMS 10 SOULS."

The news type below the headline was faded with age, but the date was clear: June of 1849. Something happened at the mine, and I knew Sonja was reliving the death of her husband. I nudged her shoulder, and when that didn't get a response, I set our drinks down and stepped in front of her, gripping her shoulders.

"Sonja, listen to me. Look at me." When her eyes finally moved to mine, I saw a tear tremble at the corner. She started to speak, but I pulled her close, and she buried her head against my shoulder.

"Adam, I want to go."

I stroked her hair, hoping to calm the sobs that were shaking her.

"Let's sit down for a minute, have a drink, and just see. There's something going on here, something strange, and I want to get to the bottom of it. Can we do that?"

Thankfully, she agreed, and I took her to the table for two with menus on it. She wiped her eyes after we sat down, and I looked over the menu. Instead of regular bar food, it listed items found in higher end restaurants.

"What do you want to do?" I asked quietly. "We can leave if you want. I've got cash to pay for the drinks."

She shook her head. "Like you said, I want to find out what's going on here. Something's just not right."

"You can say that again."

She smiled faintly. "If they are brand new, where did all the stuff from town come from? And your record?"

It was my turn to shake my head, and we saw Lyles drift around the bar and come toward us.

"Have you made a decision?"

Before I could answer, Sonja spoke up. "We'll have the Chef's special."

Lyles gave a brief nod and then said, "Excellent." Turning to me, he said, "Since you are the music man, would you like to look over our selections? We have a wide array of music to choose from. We also have live performances from time to time." Motioning with his hand, he gestured to the massive jukebox that filled the back wall to the right of the bar, and departed.

"Let's see what they've got," I said, standing up. When she stood, I took her hand, and we crossed the room.

To describe the monstrosity as a jukebox was wrong. It was . . . massive. Rising at least three feet over my head, it had at least twelve-inch subwoofers in a line along the bottom, with additional midrange and tweeters climbing either side. Most jukeboxes played compact discs now, but this one had full-sized vinyl records. A display area, the size of a car's windshield, showed the album covers in an accordion-style flip file. Jutting out was the selection board, with ornate letters and numbers. Looking closer, I saw the buttons were actually blocks, almost like an old typesetter would use, carved in a typeface to match the sign outside. Wrapping the entire thing was metal that spoke of great age. Looking closer, it may have been silver.

"How did they get this thing in here?" I asked, mostly to myself. In the center of the selection board was an impossibly small slot, and it had an inscription above it: *THREE PLAYS FOR A DIME* in elegant calligraphy. I dug into my pocket, hunting through my loose change. Pulling it out, I found a dime, and started to drop it in.

Instead of the bright coin I expected, it was a dull circle. Looking closer, I saw a woman's head on the coin. Wordlessly I showed it to Sonja.

"Where did you get a Mercury dime?" she asked. I shrugged my shoulders. It was the only dime I had, so I dropped it into the slot. The speakers activated, and the interior lights came on, displaying the album covers inside. I pushed the forward button, not surprised at what I saw: Kenny Loggins, George Strait, Hank Williams, T-Bone Watson, BB King, and Aerosmith all flashed before me.

"I owned every one of these," I whispered, my mouth drying out. "This is what I grew up on."

Sonja nudged me out of the way and pushed the forward button. The Bee Gees. Steppenwolf. Marvin Gaye. Grand Funk Railroad. The Doobie Brothers. "And these were mine." She pushed the back selection key, and even though she went well past where she took over, none of my albums reappeared. When she came to a Johnny Cash album, she stopped.

"Might as well," she said, pushing a few keys. The jukebox flashed, accepting her selection, but let out a slow buzz, as if a gear wasn't engaging. We exchanged a look.

"If you broke it . . ." I started, and she giggled. The release of finding something to laugh about infected me, and within a moment we were both laughing hysterically, trying to muffle our laughter and not spill our drinks. She leaned into me and I wrapped my one arm around her as she shook, trying to keep it in.

"Did I break it?" she choked out.

"I don't know. Let's get back to our table. Maybe he won't notice." She lifted her head, looking into my eyes. I felt the warmth coming off of her, and her scent filled my nose. I could almost taste her, sweet, with an undertone of sharp fear. I could feel every inch of her pressed against me, from her hand on the small of my back, to her breasts pressed into my chest. We stared at each other, faces an inch apart, and her eyes filled my vision. Deep, green pools they were, flecked with . . . hazel? Gold? I didn't care. We froze as the machine behind us burped again, and we heard the clap of a swinging door.

That sound broke the moment, and we looked up and gawked. Standing in the entrance was a tall, thin blond woman in a beaded dress that sparkled.

"Ooooh, I love to see love birds in the moment they realize how they feel," she said. The lights above the entrance way focused on her, highlighting every move. Sonja shifted away from me, breaking our spell, and the woman glided in. Behind her, dusk had fallen, the dropping sun's slanting rays creating pinks, purples, and blues. Sonja stared at her, and I tried to look away. The woman's high cheekbones and swan-like neck were stunning, and I felt a small stir of desire.

"Where's the music? Tonight is a night for dancing!" She stepped daintily beyond the entranceway and glided across the dance floor. Sonja and I took a step toward our table, and when Sonja tried to step away I kept my arm around her. Slowly, her hand came back up.

"I can't get the jukebox to work," I managed to say. A look of surprise crossed her face, and we all looked as Lyles came out of the door I assumed led to the kitchen. He carried two plates and set them down at the table as Sonja and I arrived.

"Mildred, dear," he greeted the woman, bussing her cheek.

"You know I prefer Millie," she said in mock severity. I couldn't keep my eyes off her; it was not only her carriage, but the way she projected her confidence and personality. She was dressed as a flapper from the 1920s, ready to step out to a gin-house speakeasy, and then stroll into our presence. A double-strand of pearls was draped around her pale, graceful neck. Her beaded dress shimmered in the overhead lighting, held up by two thin straps that exposed her shoulders and came to mid-thigh, showing the promise of great legs. The beads on her form-fitting cap matched her dress, and she had a silver mink stole draped over those exquisite, pale shoulders. I imagined the sensation of the fur as she wrapped it around herself, the tickling touch making me shiver. She gave me a coy smile as she extracted an ivory cigarette holder from her purse and held one out for Lyles to light.

"A man always greets a woman by her given name," he said. "It is only proper."

Blinking, I looked closer; Lyles held nothing in his hand, but a tiny flame danced from the tip of his thumb.

Turning to us, she said, "Enjoy your meal. We'll have dancing later, and maybe I can take your beau for a turn," she said to Sonja before she swayed away, walking to the bar.

Sonja and I sat down. Everything seemed to press down on me, and I picked up my fork. Before I took a bite, I found Lyles studying us.

"Something's wrong with the jukebox," I said through numb lips. Lyles blinked in what might have been surprise and turned to look at his machine. Even though it was mostly hidden by his body, I saw his hand make a small gesture, and a second clack came from the machine, and the opening piano riff came from the speakers. I looked at Sonja; she had selected "Open Arms," the song I'd played for her before.

"I like this song," I said, rather stupidly.

She gave me a vacant grin as well. "Me too," she replied, and picked up her fork. The meal on our plate was beautifully presented, a thin cut of pork in a light brown sauce. Long, steamed green beans were layered to one side, and a swirl of mashed potatoes balanced the other. We both dug in, and I found I was starving. Lyles was still studying us, and when he saw me looking, asked if the meal was satisfactory.

"Give my compliments to the chef," I said, and he left us to tend to the bar. We ate, our eyes roaming over the building around us.

Sonja's eyes drifted to the window, and she blinked. Looking at her wrist, she frowned. "What time is it?" she asked me.

I usually don't wear a watch, so I dug my phone out of my pocket to find the screen dark and unresponsive. "My phone's dead," I said, and she showed me her watch, which had stopped.

We both looked outside, and the darkness had deepened to full twilight.

"What time did we leave the boarding house?" I asked her.

"A few minutes before five," she answered.

"But it's full dark. How is it already dark? We haven't been here for three hours."

"Time change isn't until next week. It shouldn't be," she started, but whatever she was going to say was forgotten. The door opened again, and several people entered. They must have been people from town because they nodded to Sonja and smiled. She waved back, but her hand stopped in mid wave. Behind the townies came a family, dressed in older clothes. A middle aged, plump man, escorting an equally plump wife. Behind them trailed two younger women, dressed in gowns that flared out, and I saw a flash of petticoats. The man was dressed in a nineteenth century three-piece suit and carried a cane. With a top hat on his head, I wasn't surprised to see a pince-nez perched on his nose, a jeweled cord attached to his lapel. We watched as the door opened at regular intervals, admitting town people and others in unusual dress; a trio of young men in army fatigues; a black man in tattered clothing; a young boy, covered in dirt and grime; and a pair of hoods straight from Chicago gang-land, where they could have participated in the St. Valentine's Day massacre. They watched Millie as she moved around the room; one with a look of adoration, the other with a look of disdain.

Lyles came by and whisked the plates off our table but did not speak.

"Do you think we could just walk out?" I asked.

"I'm sure," Sonja answered. She stood up. "But I'm not ready to do that." Millie appeared by her side, sliding her hand onto Sonja's elbow.

"Darling," she drawled, inhaling on her cigarette holder, "I simply must ask you to allow me to dance with your friend."

Sonja glanced at me, an unreadable look in her eyes. Her eyes were darker, flat, and I wondered what thoughts were running behind them. "Sure," Sonja said, but I was uncomfortable with the way Sonja's eyes left me. They tracked across the dance floor, looking for something, and Millie glided over to me. Millie slipped her hand onto my elbow, her gloved hands cool. The jukebox thundered a big band song, and she slipped gracefully into my arms.

"So, do you come here. . ." The cheesy pickup line didn't leave my lips before a series of images filled my mind. *A crowded room with bodies pressed together in a small space. A sweating black man who worked a slide trombone, crammed against a drummer. The taste of unfiltered tobacco and bathtub gin. The joy of life, the thrill of winning the Great War. That thrill was fading, and the fight was now focusing on THE VOTE. She and her sisters needed THE VOTE, and it was coming.*

Millie smiled as she led us around the dance floor. My gaze went to her, taking me in a circle, and I felt the sensations come again.

The music swelled, shrilling against the backbeat of the conversation. Smoke hung from the ceiling, and a boom sounded from outside the club. Someone was coming, either cops or the revenuers. As everyone panicked around her, Millie raised her glass to the sky and laughed.

"There now, isn't that better?" she murmured against my ear. We moved across the dance floor, my plodding, staggering steps carried by her graceful leading. I went through a summer at Coney Island, hearing the screams from the roller coaster, and falling in love with a serviceman who didn't return.

As the next song started, I felt her light fingers in my mind.

"Why don't you share?" she whispered to me. Her eyes were the only thing I could see; unfocused, grey depths swam beneath me. She tickled through my life until she found something she liked.

"A music man!" she crowed happily, finding a memory she liked. I could dimly see what she saw; an early performance of mine in Nashville. She clung to me, and we danced.

Sonja watched as the flapper took Adam to the dance floor. She refused to be jealous, and she wouldn't watch his hands clutch at her hips. She looked away to find Lyles studying her.

"You won't be able to stay," he said, his words cut off as if he wanted to say more.

She met his gaze. "Why would I?" she countered. In response, he smiled slightly.

"There are advantages to becoming a Regular," he said, and moved away from the table. Sonja started to sit back down, but a man in a modern suit a few years out of date approached her.

"Would you mind if I had a dance?" he asked, in a slight New York accent. The smell of smoke and dust came from him, slight but enough to tickle her nose.

She wanted to decline, but saw Adam and the flapper girl – Millie? – spinning on the dance floor. She picked up her glass and took a gulp, the alcohol hitting her stomach. "Sure," she said, taking his offered hand.

A new song started up, something recent, but a flood of sensations mixed with the sounds. *She was in an elevator, a nondescript brown cube. The doors opened as the entire structure shook. Klaxons blared, and a rush of heat, dust, and a few tendrils of smoke were pushed from below to billow into the elevator. A woman screamed behind them, and they stumbled out. The man dropped the briefcase he was carrying and ran to the window. The tall glass was cracked, and Sonja looked out over Manhattan. The first window the man ran to had an unobstructed view, but the second was blocked by thick blanket of smoke.*

Then she understood. This man had died on September 11th, in one of the Twin Towers. Tears welled in her eyes as the narrative continued in her memory. *The shock of watching another plane hit the South Tower. The panicked calls to loved ones. He carefully gave his cell phone to the girl from the copy room; her boyfriend worked with a publisher on Broad Street. The man had no one to call. His mother passed a decade ago, and his father was in a nursing home. College was a series of trysts, and working for the firm didn't give him time to date.*

The floor filled with smoke until they managed to break a few windows. Relieved cries and shouts of joy came when someone got through to the fire department, but he knew. There would be no escaping.

Sonja felt tears coursing down her cheeks. "I'm sorry," she said. The man in her arms shrugged, and she closed her eyes, images flashing before them. *The slight trembles of the floor beneath his feet. The cries of alarm when the stairwells were discovered blocked. The temperature was climbing as the smoke thickened. He wondered how the girders below him were reacting to the intense heat. He looked at one of the*

90

shattered windows and the wide blue sky beyond it. The certainty as he approached the open window.

"Please stop," Sonja whispered, and the images faded away. The man looked a bit guilty, and she saw the flash of beads swinging closer. Business-Suit Man followed her eyes.

"Would you like to swap?" he asked, and she nodded her answer. When Adam and the flapper girl were an arm's length away, the man stepped away from her and tapped Millie's shoulder. Stepping neatly, Sonja caught Adam as Business-Suit Man and Millie swirled off.

"Adam?" she asked, looking into his shocked eyes. They cleared, and his hands tightened around her. She shivered, and he brought her closer.

"Well, at least I got to dance with you," he muttered. She lowered her head to his shoulder as a slow song started out of the jukebox.

"What is this place?" she asked the fabric of his shirt. When he didn't answer, she looked up. He stared at her, his hands grazing her back as they swayed in place.

"Right now I don't care," he said. Chills – the not unpleasant kind – broke out along her back and legs. The thrill of being close to him intensified, and she looked at up him. Their faces moved closer, and she felt her heartbeat speed up. A sweet taste flooded her mouth as she felt his warm breath on her, and she strained upward for the last quarter inch.

His mouth was warm, his lips cool and soft. She nuzzled them with soft brushes until they were moist. He kissed her a little harder, the tip of his tongue reaching out, and she shivered from head to toe.

Eventually they separated but moved slowly together as the music continued. A few whistles echoed across the dance floor, but they we were oblivious.

"Don't be getting any ideas," he said.

Sonja shook her head, but didn't say anything, her eyes looking around Ricochet. Lyles stood behind the bar, a worried look on his face. When she made eye contact with him, he nodded once, and turned away. Laying her head against his shirt, they rotated out of his sight.

CHAPTER 15

SHOUTS AND THE CRASH of furniture woke me the next morning. I sat up in bed, confused; wasn't I just . . . somewhere? With Sonja? A yell, distinct, and a scream brought me wide awake and scrambling out of bed. I pulled on the first thing I saw, a pair of jeans, and ran toward the stairs with my feet and chest bare. I pounded down the stairs as a few heads popped out of doors. Ignoring the questions, I jumped over the rail, dropping onto the first floor.

The shouts had moved from the dining room onto the front porch. Bert stood in the doorway, peering out with his near-sighted squint.

"What's happening?" I asked him, my hand on the door.

"What's happening?" Sonja echoed behind me. Her eyes were puffy with sleep, a worn robe around her. Bert's eyes went from me to her and back, and there was no nearsighted squint *there.*

"Cook's biscuits are in high demand," Bert said. The two men crashed into the rocking chairs Bert used during the day, turning them over with a loud bang. I felt Sonja touch my arm, and I pushed open the door and stepped out. Sonja followed me, turning left as I turned right.

"Alright boys, knock it off," I said. They ignored me, promptly rolling off the porch and onto the bushes. I winced at the thought of the holly bushes versus the thin t-shirts, but stood over them as they separated, growled at each other, and attacked. It wasn't a normal fight, in which they stood back and tried to throw punches, but a rolling, grabbing, growling wrestling grunt fest. I hopped over the bushes, avoiding the prickles, and stepped between them, grabbing one by the collar and pushing one back with my other hand.

"All right, guys, let's…" My words were cut off by two snarls, and they turned their anger on me.

Greg, the guy I had by the collar, grabbed my arm and pulled, and Jim, the one I pushed back, rushed me. Greg helped me because I could deflect Jim with my forearm and keep my balance. As Jim slid past my forearm, he snapped at it with his teeth. The blank, wild look in his eyes stunned me, and I gave a yell for help. When Jim tripped and went sprawling, I turned my attention to Greg. Staggering, I gave him a body shot to the ribs, but it didn't seem to faze him. He moved closer to me, and I closed my eyes, preparing myself for the blow. I've been in enough bar fights to realize you only had one weapon if your opponent stepped into you, inside your punch radius.

I pulled my head back and snapped it forward, head-butting Greg between the eyes. I was aiming for his nose, but he moved at the last second. There was a burst of light and a flash of pain in my head, but it didn't hurt that much. Neither of them knew the advantage I had.

Greg dropped like a puppet with snipped strings, and a growl from my right showed Jim coming at me on all fours. I was getting ready to kick at him, but my vision was doubling and I had at least two Jims to choose from. Behind me, I heard Sonja yell, and a stream of water shot past me, wetting my side, and catching Jim in the face. He gagged, retreated, and Sonja passed me, hosing both of them down.

A hand at my side, and Bert was steadying me. "Ain't seen a good head butt in years," he cackled.

I groaned and felt my forehead. "It hurts more than I remember," I said. Blinking my eyes, my vision came together, and I saw Sonja, in her bathrobe, still hosing down our two combatants. They were sitting in a fast growing puddle of mud, blinking, and looking confused.

"Had enough?" Sonja asked. She gave each of them another squirt of water, and they nodded.

"Explain to me what that was about, and maybe I won't kick both of you to the curb," she said.

"'At sumbitch," Jim started. He looked at Greg. "What was it? What'd you do?" he asked.

Greg frowned, dripping, and said, "Why, you shit, you . . ." and stopped. They looked at each other.

"Why did we go at it?" Jim asked.

"The biscuit?" Bert offered, standing outside the mud puddle.

"Yeah, I guess," Greg said. "I don't really remember it."

"You just pissed me off," Jim said.

"I don't care what it's about. One more cross look from either of you, and I'll have Otis toss you out on your ass. Am I clear?" Sonja said. She seemed to realize then all she had on was her robe, and whatever she slept in under it, and dropped the hose. "Roll this back up, and get cleaned up. You'll both be late for work."

She walked past me and eyed my bare chest and unbuttoned jeans.

"Thanks for your help," she said, laying her hand on my arm, and walking past me.

Bert chuckled behind me, and we both watched her climb the steps.

"Well, I guess you two had a good night last night," Bert murmured. He looked pleased.

"Not really," I said, then paused. "Dinner, and . . ." trying to recall the previous evening, I followed Sonja up the steps. Cook handed me a dry dish towel, eyeing me as well. I focused, trying to recall the night before. I remember us driving to Ricochet, eating dinner, and then . . . did we dance? Wasn't there something weird about the place?

"Um, Sonja?" I started to ask, and the glare she gave me cut me off.

"Thank you for your help," she said, planting her hands on her hips. "But I expect you to put on some clothes before you sit down at the table." She glared at everyone and then spun away from us, making her bathrobe flutter and float out. Cook smirked at me, Bert patted my back, and as I was walking up the stairs I tried to fill the gaps in my memory from the previous night.

When I rejoined the breakfast table, properly dressed, I found it silent, broken only by the clatter of silverware. The two combatants were nowhere to be seen, and Bert was the only one in his normal good cheer.

"Saved you a biscuit," he said.

I grunted my thanks.

95

"How's your head?" he asked, and a few people at the table looked at me.

"It's fine," I said, catching the undercurrent around me. I ate in silence, then joined Bert outside.

"Everybody sure is quiet this morning," I said as I sat in the rocker.

"It's better than it was before the fight started," Bert said. "Ev'ybody looking crossed at one another, actin' like they hadn't seen food in a month. How's your head?"

I touched my forehead. A little tender, but not bad. "It's fine. Guess I should have mentioned I have a steel plate in my forehead, huh?"

Bert stopped rocking, looked and me, and guffawed.

"Yeah, that boy looked cross-eyed for a few minutes, until he went upstairs. What'd you do to have it?"

I touched my forehead again, remembering the summer day I turned my bike down the steep driveway. Just as I reached the bottom, the bike wobbled, and I lost control. This was years before helmets were the fashionable thing to wear, and I was rushed to the hospital.

After I told Bert the story, he commented, "Damn lucky, sounds like." He scratched his chin for a moment. "You know, not that you need the encouragement, but I think Sonja had an accident like that too. I 'member she got kicked by her daddy's cart horse. Or was it his mule?" He shook his head. "Doesn't matter, I suppose. How did last night go?"

The sudden question interrupted my thoughts of the very same subject.

"It went ok," I started, but faltered. I had clear memories of driving there with Sonja, touching her arm, and walking inside. I remembered the look of the place; the jukebox, the decorations, the strange bartender. But things faded out once it got dark, which was weird; we had planned on going early and not staying out late.

"So why'd you think everybody is going there, 'stead of The Dive?" Bert prompted me.

Several reasons came to mind, but I chose the safest route. "It's a new place, new to discover, all that," I said.

Bert grunted, amused at my evasion.

"Well, while you're playing, I might mosey on out there myself. I'll see if Woodie wants to go." We glanced over; sure enough, Woodie was in his rocker, head thrown back, and thin bubble of drool gathering at the corner of his lips.

Sonja came out the front door and paused before going down the steps. She looked at me, uncertainty on her face, and I spoke, much calmer than I felt. "Need a hand?"

She nodded, and I said to Bert, "The boss calls. Stay out of trouble," and I stood up.

Quietly, so only I heard, he replied, "You too."

Sonja and I walked to her truck without speaking and climbed in. She nervously fiddled with the radio, the heater, and her seat belt as we rolled down the driveway.

When I get nervous, I get quiet, usually because I'm trying to keep the shakes out of my voice. "About last night," I said, and she froze.

"What about it?" she replied, looking straight ahead.

"Do you remember anything after we started eating?" I asked, praying it wasn't just me. She relaxed slightly, a little of the strain leaving her.

"I was afraid it was just me," she said.

"It wasn't," I said. "What do you remember?"

She recounted everything until the time we noticed our watches quit working. I added a few details, and then she said, "It seemed like someone came in, and . . . everything gets fuzzy. I think we may have danced, either with each other, or with someone else. But there is no doubt something strange about that place."

"Have you ever had a fight at your boarding house?" I asked. "Over a biscuit?"

She laughed, a little more relaxed.

"Never. We've had a few drunken fights over the years, but never anything like that."

"Good move with the hose," I said.

"Works with dogs and with men," she said lightly.

I prepared the question I really wanted to ask, turning it over in my mind, making sure it would come out the way I wanted.

"Do you think anything happened between us?" I asked. She guided the truck into The Dive's parking lot and took it out of gear.

"I hope not. That's something I'd want to remember." Her hand brushed mine as it came off the gear shift.

CHAPTER 16

BOBBY IGNORED THE TWITCHING jumble of bones that Mark had become. All things wear out, and Mark's decaying body could no longer support itself. Bobby had moved Mark to a rocky shelf in the cave where he could still see. Mark would occasionally snap his teeth when Bobby would walk by; he no longer knew Tom or Chris. Chris was holding up better than Mark had, but Mark had dug the trench leading to the river. The trench was now filled with a thin, sticky substance, a watered-down version of the thing infecting him and the others.

Tom appeared out of the cavern, carrying a basketball-sized rock. They were working to uncover more of whatever it was. The stuff in the river was a part of it. There was more, much more, but they had to reach it. Had to free it. Tom reached the edge of the cliff and dropped the rock, turning around with his shoulders slumped and trudging back into the cave. From Bobby's elevated position on the bluff, the sun was throwing shadows along both sides of the riverbank, cloaking the town in darkness.

Bobby flinched, feeling something tingle against his skin. It felt like a pinprick, something burrowing against it, trying to feed off of him. Below him, a flashing light rotated in the same spot it had for several previous nights. Seeing the lights come alive and feeling the annoyance, Bobby put the two together. The irritation had been growing over the last few days, but seeing the lights come to life below connected the dots. Bobby blinked, trying to trace the roads and discover the source of the irritating lights.

He saw East Riverside Drive leading north and out of town. If it occupied the bend of the river, was it the Cauthon place? Another memory tried to overlay his knowledge, something whispering a history and adding things to what he already knew. When the illusion touched his mind, it dissolved, and Bobby glimpsed the power behind the lights below. The conflicting thoughts recoiled from each other, Bobby snarling in the dark, the perceived history breaking up and drifting away.

Something else was strange in this town. Bobby listened to the faint sounds of hammer on rock and walked to the edge of the cavern. The thing inside him had been enclosed by the rock for eons, and Bobby spent more time feeling the sunlight and sensing the wind on his body because the Thing-in-the-Rock insisted. He entered the cavern, finding Tom working a rusted come-along, trying to pull the excavated rock to the surface.

"Come with me," Bobby said. Tom let the cart stop, and with bowed shoulders walked over to Bobby. He found he didn't have as much control over Tom, but enough. "We're going to town," Bobby said.

"What if I see my wife? Or kids?" Tom asked.

Bobby shrugged. "We'll bring them back here," Bobby replied. The Thing-in-the-Rock moved in the back of his mind, and Bobby felt his mouth water.

"N-n-n-no," Tom stuttered. "Not that. Why are you doing this?" Bobby ignored him as they walked out, arguing with the thing inside him. Bobby needed to clean up before he went out in public, but the thing inside him wanted to race down the mountain, find the interloper, and charge into battle. He needed to be more presentable before he went out, in case some saw him who couldn't be taken, but the Thing-in-the-Rock didn't understand. They walked down the path cut into the hillside, sliding now and again, not talking.

Above them, the stars shone in a sprawl across the dark sky. Bobby kept finding himself looking up, trying to pinpoint what looked different about them. He was growing confused until he realized the Thing-in-the-Rock sensed the change in the heavens; enough time had passed since its internment that the heavens had shifted above.

"What?" Tom asked beside him. Bobby didn't realize he had spoken aloud. He repeated what he'd figured out about the Thing-in-the-Rock.

"It's the demon in the mine," Tom said. "I can feel it in me. Why are you letting it do this?"

They drove the car back to Chris' house. His car was almost out of gas, so they stopped at the corner filling station. As he waved at the clerk to start the pump, he noticed Sam was alone in the store. Hanging up the pump handle, he walked inside.

Once he was in the back, by the drink coolers, he called up front. "Hey Sam, what's wrong with your cooler?" The clerk came down the aisle, rubbing sleep from his eyes.

"What is it, buddy?" he asked. He took another look at Bobby. "Wow, you been working hard. Finally got a job, huh?"

"Right here. What's that?" Bobby pointed to an imaginary spot, and Sam obligingly leaned over. Bobby wrapped his hands around Sam's neck, put a knee in his back, and rode him to the floor. Bobby had discovered it was much easier to choke someone to death if you were behind them.

"Real job, my ass," Bobby muttered. They needed more workers; the Thing-in-the-Rock was becoming more demanding and wanted to reach the surface.

As he showered, rinsing the grime and blood away, he was fascinated by the black goo that forced its way out of the pores of his body and ran down the drain. It pushed the dirt and grime away, making thin streams that drained away separately. The stuff inside him reacted to the water flowing over his skin; it absorbed it, making Bobby swell up, stretching his skin, bloating it. A small cut on his forearm stretched, spread, and then ripped. Bobby cried out, black stuff flowing out of his arm along with the blood. "Stop, please, you're gonna kill me!" he said, leaning against the shower wall. The growth in his forearm pulsed and slowly receded.

Now that he was naked, Bobby could see other changes that had taken place in his body. Small lumps protruded along his trunk and limbs and moved slowly under the skin. His hands seemed blockier, thicker. His fingernails curved downward, covering the tips on his fingers. As he watched, the cut on his forearm knit itself back together, the rip in his skin disappearing. Tiny black trails of the stuff leaked from the pores of his skin, making his body look almost grey in the light of the shower.

Bobby stepped out onto the porch, feeling clean for the first time in days. The wounds he'd taken over the last week had disappeared, not even leaving a scab or a scar. He'd found a few clothes that fit him, even though he'd lost even more weight. The meth was long gone, but the Thing-in-the-Rock kept the cravings at bay. Tom had refused a shower, but had changed out his filthy work clothing.

"Let's go," Bobby said, and they climbed back into the car. As they drove along Riverside Drive through town, Bobby felt the thing inside him grow more excited. Was it because they were about to challenge something for territory, or was it the exploration of something new? They passed from the lights of town to the unlighted section of roadway, but it was different; around the curve, Bobby could see lights where they hadn't existed for years. The illusion touched his mind again and this time, it was strong enough not to be easily dispelled.

He knew the old Cauthon place was there, knew it had burned before his birth, but at the same time, knew what the lights were. He knew the place – Ricochet – had been there almost a decade and was an integral part of the town. The thing inside his head recoiled at the intrusion, but Bobby soothed it with his acceptance. They pulled into the gravel parking lot, tires squeaking on gravel, and parked. Tom stared out the windshield, mouth hanging open.

"It's beautiful," he whispered, and Bobby didn't disagree. A few cars were in the parking lot, and shadows moved behind the windows. A horse was tied to a hitching post, and it shied away from them as they walked onto the porch. Someone was smoking at the far end, and Bobby recognized the silhouette of someone who'd graduated before he'd dropped out. The thing inside him was boiling; ready to fight for its territory. Bobby found his hands shaking; it was hard to control the impulses that pushed along his arms and legs.

They walked up to the doors and pushed their way inside. There was almost too much for Bobby to see at once, but the first thing he noticed was the number of people. They were dressed differently, and their numbers inside didn't match the vehicles outside. They stepped from the entranceway, down into the dining area and dance floor, and the music stopped.

Without the music, the silence pressed down on Bobby and Tom, and every head swiveled toward them. Not every head; Bobby saw the townspeople frozen in place, some laughing, some in the middle of taking a drink, all talking. A lady in fancy attire moved away from her suitor, ducking away from the kiss of a townie. The lights inside the bar sparkled off the beads of her dress, the reflections making Bobby squint.

"Why have you come?" she said into the silence. Hers was the only movement, but every eye watched them. A group of boys in army green, a man in a dusty business suit ten years or more out of style, a family of four in clothes popular in the last century. Someone else moved behind the bar, carefully setting down a glass and a rag. As Bobby tried to control the Thing-in-the-Rock and keep his arms by his side, the bartender moved out to the dance floor.

"ANSWER HER!" he said, his voice loud, reverberating around them. The sound moved glasses on the tables, shifting them ever so slightly. Somewhere, one fell with a crash, and the Thing-in-the-Rock went from rage at the intrusion to panic. Bobby was rooted to the floor, and couldn't pick up his feet to attack. Beside him, Tom whimpered, folding onto the floor.

The woman and the man approached them, weaving among the dancers, and everyone shifted, turning toward Bobby. At the bar, a grizzled man in buckskin clothing reached down and pulled out a razor-sharp tomahawk. The light flashed on the sharpened blade, hurting Bobby's eyes. Farther down the bar, a small brown and grey Yorkie growled. The long haired boy standing beside him reached down and picked up the axe that was leaning against the bar.

"Why have you come? You are unclean," the man declared, stopping at the edge of the crowd. "Do you seek to bring your evil into my place?"

Bobby shook, trying to fight his fear, and the fear of the thing inside of him. Never had he been challenged. Never had another living—or semi living—thing stopped the Thing-in-the-Rock from getting what it wanted. Bobby frothed, his head shook as his muscles compressed, trying to extrude the essence inside him.

The man smiled, lifting a hand, and the woman beside him dissolved into light. Bobby felt the touch of it, felt the burn, and screamed. Behind the pair, the others glowed, transforming into pillars of light, reaching from the ceiling to the floor.

"I would not test the strength of the vessel you possess. These humans are . . ." Lyles considered his words, then continued, "weak in some ways, but strong in others. The physical form is not a strength."

Beside him, Tom collapsed to the floor, and Bobby flinched at the thump. One of the Army boys dissolved into light, and moved toward Bobby. A heavy rumble of sound vibrated the floorboards, and at some point Bobby realized the jukebox was alive, pushing out sounds to defend its realm.

In desperation, Bobby reached out to a frozen townsperson. Elias Cornwell was a farmer north of town along the Ogeechee, and thus too far upriver to be affected. He got his hands on the man's shoulder, extruded his essence, and . . . some force moved him away from the farmer's body. As Bobby moved through the air, he watched the dark liquid evaporate and then met the floor with a jarring thump.

When he opened his eyes, Lyles was towering over him. "Begone," he said softly. "Foul not my place again," he said in a terrible voice.

Bobby's mind tried to equate it with crypts and moldy corpses, but the thing inside of him saw it for what it was. Despite the light, it was the end of existence, a force that could not be consumed because it had nothing physical to consume. Bobby needed no encouragement from the thing inside him to turn onto his belly and crawl toward the door.

When he reached the shadows of the entryway, the physical burning eased, but the fear remained. Bobby moved to push open the door, but it opened before him, and his forward momentum carried him outside to stumble down the steps and sprawl into the parking lot. Ignoring his car, Bobby crawled across the gravel, feeling the terror weaken.

The physical effects were gone by the time he reached the road, and Bobby stood. Staring hate at the structure before him, Bobby wobbled along the road, heading upriver toward the bluff.

CHAPTER 17

I PLAYED MY SET THAT NIGHT in a good mood, laughing between songs and talking to the crowd. Usually the performer can engage the audience, get them moving, dancing, something to show they are enjoying their time. But no matter how fast a song I played, or jokes I told, the crowd at The Dive just wouldn't come out of their shells.

"Is it me?" I asked Bert between sets. "I know I'm not the best, but jeez, at least tap on the table or something." Sonja served me a tall draft beer with a smile that went all the way to her eyes, and when I took it from her, our hands touched. She was looser since our conversation that morning, laughing more, and the wall around her seemed to crumble. I still couldn't remember what happened the night before, but that was a question for another time. I knew I had to just ride with the moment.

"Naw, it ain't you. These folks just ain't right tonight." He slurped the foam off the top of his beer and tried to add a dash of salt to the top. He couldn't see well in the dim light and covered the bar top with a sprinkling of salt.

"Bert, you're making a mess," Sonja said.

"You keep the lights down too low in here. A man can't see," he grumbled.

He added another dash, hitting the beer, and I asked, "Why do you put salt in it?"

"Just gives it more," he said. "My daddy did it, his daddy did it, and it's just a habit." He pushed the salt shaker over to me. "Try it."

I salted the rim and took a sip. Damn if he wasn't right; the salt was a nice counterpoint to the beer. I nodded to him.

"Just as long as you don't make a mess," Sonja said beside me. "I clean up enough after you as it is." Her smile took the sting out of her words.

Bert guffawed. "'At's what my wife said all those years. Would raise hell at me for drinking my beers, but when I found one she liked . . ." his voice trailed off. "She'd sit and drink with me," he said, remembering. A touch of sadness entered his voice. "We'd sit on the porch. I'd be parched, drink two or three in a row, just to get wet. She'd come out, and we'd watch the sun go down. Sometimes the grandkids would come over. . . ." he trailed off, lost in the memories, and Sonja leaned over and patted his back. I needed to change the conversation.

"What was it like growing up here?" I asked.

"It's a good life," he said automatically. He may have wiped his eyes for a moment as I looked away. "People worked hard, played hard at times, but you could always count on one 'nother. The town itself is like a character. She has 'er own quirks, 'er own sense of being. Some towns, like Macon, are pretty with a thin film of grit. This one was sweet through and through. It has good people, even today, and we all knew one another."

"I grew up in a place like this. Maybe it's the reason I like it so much," I said.

"Per'aps," Bert said, sneaking a glance at Sonja, and my face turned red.

"So what's happened to it?" I asked.

"Towns change all the time," Bert said. "Old people die off, new people come, and the towns grow."

"Maybe something has come that's not good for the town," Sonja said.

"Like your new competition?" Bert asked.

Sonja and I shared a glance.

"Something's not right about it," I said, and Sonja nodded.

"Is that an honest opinion, or the fact your place is half empty?" Bert asked. "I can't imagine something so nice being so bad."

"Bert, you don't get it. The people have changed. How many fights have we had? How many people wave at you from the streets? Will anyone talk to us anymore?" We looked across the room. The pool table was still, and all the customers sat huddled over their own tables staring into their drinks, not looking up.

Bert shook his head. "It's just a quiet night," Bert said.

Sonja snorted and threw her rag on the bar, stalking away.

"I guess I'll get my own beer next time," Bert said, watching her walk away.

"Let's go into town tomorrow," I said. "We'll get lunch downtown, or something. See if things are different there." I glanced at my watch. My next set was due to begin any minute.

"I s'pose. Be good to get out of the boarding house."

I clapped him on the shoulder, and he patted my forearm. I was growing fond of that quirky old man.

CHAPTER 18

SONJA STABBED THE MOP bucket with the mop, splashing greyish water up and over the edge. More than a few drops landed on her jean-clad leg, turning the fabric dark and soaking her to the skin. She grunted, sighed, and felt the frustration and anger bubbling up. It rose from the center of her stomach, grabbed her throat, and wanted to push the top of her head off. Taking in a deep breath, Sonja closed her eyes and held, waiting for her mental turbulence to settle. When she felt a little calmer, she opened her eyes and released her breath in a rush.

Step by step, she thought.

Step one. She glanced around her empty business. Why was she so slow? Could a new place really have done this to her, and if so, how could she not know it was coming?

Step two. She looked at the darkened stage. *I still haven't heard from Bobby or Mark.* "We had music tonight," she said. "Good music, so that can't be it." *...aaaaand a good looking man to play it, amiright?* The little voice spoke up. The frustration that had been welling internally all day subsided as she pushed the mop across the floor. Adam was . . . he *wasn't* all she'd thought the first night. At first, she'd suspected he was hiding from someone, but as the days passed, she wasn't so sure. Then she thought he would be gone one morning, with the room key on the dresser and an empty spot where that fancy car was parked.

Instead, she'd seen him grow closer to Bert, taking time with him, and she'd felt the kindness of their own unlikely friendship. He'd offered to play for her, at a reasonable rate, but she wasn't foolish enough to think he didn't have a little hope behind that offer. So if he wasn't all the negative things, and there were a few positive things . . .

You go for it, girl, her inner cheerleader spoke up again. Sonja dropped the mop into the bucket again, but moved her leg just in time. "Nope, nope, nope," she muttered under her breath. She didn't want to want him, even if it was for no other reason than to warm her bed for a night or two. The physical release would be momentary; she didn't want to have to deal with the emotional backlash. Her life was slowly moving downriver, time flowing gently around the shoals and sandbanks. She had her boarding house, The Dive, good neighbors . . . and she didn't need anyone to complicate it. She had gotten used to Billy's absence. He had been ripped from her, half of her gone in an instant. Their companionship, built over years, was what she missed the most. Adam couldn't replace that, unless she gave him years, and . . . *It could happen*, the little voice insisted. *If you weren't too chicken shit to take the first step.* She grunted in exasperation.

In the kitchen, pots banged and rang, Donald finishing up before he could leave. The money was counted and tucked away in the safe, waiting for her to deposit it in the morning. She rolled the mop bucket back to the floor sink and tipped it over.

"Donald, I'm done," she yelled, once the yellow bucket was tipped over and the mop hung to drip dry. An answering yell echoed back to her, and she walked through the dark dining area to the front door. Outside the air was cool, a clean smell coming with the breeze. She breathed deeply, trying to identify what made it different from the air inside The Dive. This air wasn't contained, she realized; it could drift or rise or fall as it wanted. Inside The Dive – inside anywhere – it could only go so far. As if to answer her, a breeze flowed across her skin, and she smiled. Nothing like a subtle sign to remind her of the direction she needed to go.

CHAPTER 19

FEAR WAS SOMETHING to be created, enjoyed, and savored. He wasn't meant to experience it because The Thing-in-the-Rock was the ultimate predator. The thing inside Bobby was ruthless, unstoppable, and insatiable. In earlier times, it fed until it felt like stopping, and then rested. Time was not a concern; time was a worn blanket that could be wrapped up and discarded as needed. The Thing-in-the-Rock, whatever its origins, was the deadliest thing on the history of the planet.

Bobby knew this as he ran down the road, tears and sweat mixing on his face, the thing inside him boiling in fear. Never had light burned. *He* was the thing that burned, the thing that consumed, that possessed. Bobby slowed, his heart stuttering in his chest, his muscles weakening and finally unable to carry him any longer. Collapsing, he scraped painfully along the asphalt and rolled into the cool grass. Stream rose from his sweat-slicked body, and the thing inside him subsided. It still raged, but for a time, the rage was spent.

Bobby stared at the stars overhead, points of light thrown across the heavens. How could they win? Bobby knew vaguely what the Thing-in-the-Rock knew, and knew this was a challenge it had never faced. But Bobby possessed something it didn't have: human cunning. In its previous existence, the Thing-in-the-Rock did not need cunning. It could simply be, consume, and be satisfied.

"More," he whispered, against a throat that was bone dry as the word came out in a croak. "We need more."

More of the essence, more bodies. More people to carry the Thing-in-the-Rock from its rocky prison into the light of day. The burning light could stop one of him, but a dozen? Two dozen? Could it stop the Thing-in-the-Rock, once it was totally free? Bobby sat up, sitting beside the empty road. He had the ability to move into town, among his people, and could recruit followers. He could *make* followers. He could make an army to lead against the light that burned.

The thing inside him was dormant. It rested, but Bobby could feel it listening, feeling what he was feeling. Perhaps it agreed. But the place they just left – ran from, to be honest – presented a challenge. It couldn't be consumed, it couldn't be killed like the others. It would have to be destroyed.

Bobby climbed first to his knees, and then stood. His legs held him, for now, and he walked back to town. He felt the Thing-in-the-Rock reach out to the bluff, calling the automatons, summoning then to Bobby. Maybe just one of them; it was hard to tell. Bobby knew of a place it could hide if daylight came, and the Thing-in-the-Rock passed on the information.

He needed to build an army, and his time was short.

The first building Bobby came to on the way back into town was an all-night dry cleaner. He vaguely knew the owner, Jimmy Fowler. Maybe he had gone to school with one of his kids? Bobby couldn't remember, but when he came outside for a smoke break, Bobby was waiting for him.

Bobby crept through the dark yard and stopped when he heard a growl coming from his left.

"Spike," he whispered. "C'm'ere, boy," he said, and the growl cut off. The yard dog trotted up and smelled him, recognizing his scent. At the last second, the dog realized something wasn't right, and tried to shy away with a small yip. Bobby grabbed the dog by the scruff of the neck, and felt some of the *stuff* push from under his fingers nails. The dog whined, scratching at his neck, and then shook on the ground.

Inside the house a light came on. Bobby trotted to the base of the porch step, and stood there as the porch light flared to life. The door cracked, and one eye peered out.

"Who the . . ." a voice said. "Bobby? What the fuck are you doing? It's three in the morning!"

"I need your help, man," Bobby said, putting a pleading look on his face. "Kyle, please," he said, climbing the steps. When the door opened, Bobby easily knocked the shotgun away, and got his hands on Kyle's throat.

The man and woman were walking a small dog together, moving through the pools of light decorating the sidewalk. Kyle's car was parked at a bank a few blocks away. Bobby had spotted the couple while cruising the streets, looking for recruits. The dog was old; it seemed to stop every few feet. The couple walked holding hands, and Bobby heard the low murmur of voices. She laughed, and the sound grated on Bobby's nerves. The night was taking its toll on Bobby; he'd visited quite a few people in the time since he'd fled . . . that place. He might have lost Tom to the light, but the night had been a success.

Bobby paused as the couple passed him on the opposite side of the street. The man glanced over, and Bobby nodded an early morning greeting. The man's eyes moved past, and Bobby let them gain a half block lead before crossing the street behind them. Trying to jog silently, he closed the distance between them.

Bobby tensed as a car passed them, but it kept going. Bobby looked ahead, trying to gauge the distance and the alternating pools of darkness. Bobby ghosted from street light to street light, closing toward his next victims. The man sensed something and paused to listen before they continued walking. Sprinting through the last splash of light, Bobby reached the couple before they could enter the next cone of light. Reaching out and grabbing the woman's head in one hand and the man's in his other, he brought their heads together with a solid *thunk*.

The woman dropped without a sound, but the man managed to turn his head at the last second, perhaps hearing the whisper of Bobby's steps. The dog paused, feeling the leash pull him back, and Bobby gave a halfhearted kick to chase it away. The man groaned, trying to struggle to his feet, and Bobby straddled him, hidden by the darkness.

"Come to me tomorrow night," he whispered to them.

The sun was filtering through the fog hanging over the river. Kyle sat in the passenger seat beside Bobby, staring straight ahead. They were almost finished for the night, and Bobby was exhausted, feeling the loss of the essence inside him. He didn't realize until now how much it was a part of him.

"Remember him? Mr. Davis?" Bobby asked the automaton Kyle. Bobby slowed down as the man walked to his car, balancing a cup of coffee with a box of doughnuts. His car was parked to the side of the bakery, much to his misfortune. "That scrawny motherfucker kicked me out of his class. Said I was 'dis-re-spect-ful'," he said, in a mocking falsetto. "Whatchoo think we should do?" Bobby drove past the bakery and parked the car. "Sit tight, buddyroo."

The automatons were great listeners, but couldn't carry their end of the conversation.

CHAPTER 20

BERT'S COLOGNE MET ME before I made it up the steps, making my eyes water and pulling out a cough. Sonja was outside as well, on the far side of the porch, and Bert waved at me from his rocker. He was dressed and ready for our trip to town, wearing clean jeans, suspenders, and a button up shirt. Sonja motioned me over as I looked in her direction, and I saw a list in her hand.

"Good morning," I said, walking toward her. I paused for a moment, unsure of the greeting; peck on the cheek? Side hug? We hadn't had any deliberate physical contact, but the air between our eyes was on fire. I should have kissed her, or at least tried, last night. The late night waitress hovered the entire time, yakking, and Sonja seemed distracted while we drove home. No one was around, yet I reached out a hand, but it wavered, unsure of where to go.

She put her hand on my chest. "Not out here, in front of everybody," she almost whispered, a slight blush creeping up her neck.

I reluctantly stepped back, grinning at her discomfort. "Well, perhaps I will come to call on you tonight, and ask you for a stroll under the moonlight," I said, and then heard my words. I was reaching into my pocket for a pen as she started laughing. I took the piece of paper she handed me and jotted the lyric down, then looked over it. "A shopping list?" I asked.

She nodded. "If you don't mind. I wish I could go with you," she said.

"You might not survive the drive into town. Think Bert would mind if I rolled the windows down?" I asked.

"He can't see how much he's putting in his hand. He's always liked his aftershave, but since Helen died . . ."

"Dear god," I muttered.

She patted my chest again. "Be good. He can't help it, and he likes you. You'll be that way one day," she said. "Now go, and quit staring at me. You'll make people talk."

"If I'm going to make them talk, it'll be for more than just staring at you," I quipped.

She laughed. "Go."

Bert's cologne wasn't that bad once we got into the car. He settled himself in, squinting at the dashboard, and finally leaned back. Much to my relief, he opened the window.

"I love this time of year," he said. "The air feels like winter's coming, but in the sun, it's just right for closing your eyes and taking a little nap."

"And there's the trees. Love looking at the color," I offered.

"Sonja seems to have taken a shine to you," Bert said, surprising me.

"There's something about her," I said.

"Must be, if she can give you a list," he cackled. "Never let my wife do that."

I pulled the list of out my pocket, driving with my knee for a second.

"Look out!" Bert squawked, and I looked up in time to see a short, round guy weaving along the side of the road walking toward us. I missed him in plenty of time, but Bert gasped and sucked in air like I'd missed the guy by inches.

"What the hell?" I asked, peering into the rearview mirror.

"That was Jimmy Fowler. Runs a cleaning service in town. What the hell is he doing walking out here?" Bert asked.

"Beats me," I said, my heart settling down. It wasn't that close of a call, but I wondered why the guy hadn't stepped out of the road when he saw us. I handed the list to Bert.

"Where do we need to go first?"

Bert peered at it. "She's got us going to two or three different places." He peered at the bottom of the list. "Here, I think this isn't for me." He handed me the list.

At the bottom of the note, written in a clean feminine hand, was a single sentence: *Let's see if we can remember what we forgot about the other night.* I cleared my throat, feeling my cheeks heat up.

Beside me, Bert stared straight ahead. "Adam, listen," he said, and the humor was gone from his voice. "Sonja's a good girl. You're just passing through. If you . . ." he trailed off. "Aww, hell," he muttered. "Be discreet. When Billy died, everyone expected her to up'n marry again. When she didn't, and she kept running the businesses, a few people whispered. Then they realized how much she loved Billy. She didn't *want* anybody else. So if it's time for her to move on, it's her choice. But be careful: with her, and with the town."

Bert frowned, and I studied the road in front of us. I knew what he meant; I grew up as part of a small town that whispered. Not from malice, but simple human nature. I knew how the town would react if Sonja and I carried on.

But I didn't care.

I cared about her, maybe more than I wanted to admit to myself. There was a spark in the air when we walked by each other. There was tension when she looked at me, and when I looked at her. When she brushed my arm, I felt it from the tips of my toes to the top of my head. I wanted to tell Bert all of this, but I knew how it would sound. So I'd have to think carefully.

"The last thing I want to do is . . ." I started, paused for the right word, and started again. "I know how these towns are. And I know it's only been a few days, but she's something special. The reason she stands out like she does in this town is because she's so special." Bert was looking at me out of the corner of his eye, and I fought down a grin. "Every time I look at her, I forget about Nashville."

"That's what I'm worried about," Bert muttered.

"No, not like that," I said, sitting up straighter. "Look, the last thing I want to do is make people talk. That would hurt her, right? Hurt her businesses?"

He nodded. "It could."

"So I'm going to do everything I can to keep her safe." I looked at the list again. "Where do we need to go first?"

"Turkey Creek General Store. On the left when we get to downtown," Bert said. I found a parking spot after driving in silence for a few minutes, and we pulled into the diagonal slot. We climbed out of the car, and as we waited to cross the street, Bert said, "You know why I said what I did, right?"

We waited for a hand-painted camo truck to pass us and then walked through the cloud of diesel exhaust. Bert ambled, and I glanced at the car coming up the street, hoping we'd make it across in time.

"Sure I do. I can tell how much you two think of each other," I said, restraining myself from pulling him across the street.

"Hang on, dammit, I'm coming," he muttered, and quickened his steps. The car was even closer, and I could see a shape through the sun-splattered windshield. "You're right, I do think a lot of her. She's basically taken me in," he said. Bert and I made it safely between two cars parked on the far side of the street, and the car accelerated in the street behind us. "Bastard," Bert muttered. He peered after the car. "Some people just don't have any cares but for 'emselves anymore."

Bert stepped onto the sidewalk, and I held out my arm for him to steady himself with. I clapped my hand over his and stopped him. When he looked at me, I said, "Bert, I promise, I won't do anything to hurt her. In town, or otherwise."

"I know you won't, son. I just had to let you know what the stakes were. Or what they could be," he said. He let go of my arm and pointed to the general store's sign I could clearly see.

"Come on, let's get this stuff. If we get done quick enough, we can get an ice cream on the way back." He smacked his lips, and I had to grin. As we walked in, I saw bulk packages of food and household items.

Bert walked up to the counter and motioned for the harried clerk.

After waiting on two other customers, he came over. "What can I do for you?" When he saw Bert, he greeted him and gave me a quick once-over.

Bert handed him the list.

He stood there, muttering, then turned his back to us and looked at the shelves. Scratching his head, he moved to the back of the store.

"That damn boy ain't never been right," Bert muttered. Looking over his shoulder, he said to me, "Even when he was a boy, he was peculiar. Couldn't abide a mask." At my confused look, he chuckled.

"When he was little, he was scairt of Halloween masks. Wouldn't even go into a store that sold 'em. When his mama could coax him inside, he refused to go near the aisle." Bert's silent laughter shook him, and I grinned. Small towns always had small stories. Bert wiped tears from the corners of eyes, and I nudged him as the clerk reappeared from the back.

"Got most of it," he said as three other shoppers entered. The clerk sighed.

"Chase, where's your help?" Bert asked.

"Didn't show up this morn'. Today's kids are shiftless, I'm telling you. Can't get an honest day's work out of 'em." His eyes shifted between us, and I wondered if he meant me as one of today's "kids."

"What do we owe?" I asked.

He waved me away. "Sonja runs an account. I'll send her the bill." Bert and I nodded our thanks, and we left the harried clerk to deal with the other customers.

"I remember being able to charge stuff," I said wistfully. "My parents had an account at the corner store. My brother and I would ride our bikes up the street in the summer, charge it, and ride home." We walked left out the door, heading up town, and I checked the list.

"Drug store. Need . . . Mercurochrome? Is that . . ." I trailed off.

"Cook swears by that stuff," Bert said.

"Is it the red stuff?" I asked. I remembered my grandmother using it on a variety of ills.

Bert nodded. "Don't ever tell her you have a sore throat."

I shuddered. I remembered my grandmother taking a cotton swab a mile long, coating it in the red stuff, and swabbing the back of my throat and tonsils, going all the way down to my toenails. If

I moved, I got a swat on the knee or a pinch to the soft part of the triceps. "At least it worked," I said.

"Anything that bad had to kill whatever it came into contact with," Bert said.

I agreed.

We made it to the drug store, and Bert grunted when he pulled on the door which didn't move. The inside was dark, and Bert and I stepped to the window and cupped a hand to the glass.

"He ain't in," a gruff voice turned us around. I was surprised to see Otis behind us.

"Did you check on him?" Bert asked.

"Why would I do that? Do I look like his mama?" Otis said, and Bert and I exchanged a glance.

"I think he was asking because you're the Sheriff," I said, my defensiveness surprising me. "Bert was just asking a logical question."

Otis glared at me, and said, "Nashville, I'd keep your out-of-town trap shut. You telling me how to run my department?" he demanded, stepping up to me.

I took a step back.

"Otis," Bert said, putting a hand on his arm, which was promptly shaken off.

"I got too much other stuff to do than worry about old man Lee. We've had a dozen domestics over the last few days. I've got half a dozen missing person's reports . . ." he trailed off, realizing what he said.

"Then isn't that a reason--" I began, but Otis interrupted.

"One more damn word and I'm running you in, boy. I'm warning you," Otis snapped, his face turning red. "A man can have a vacation, can't he? Since you're asking, both of them and their dog is gone. There, you happy? Now that you know? Think you have all the answers, Nashville?" Otis glared at both of us, then stepped back, taking a deep breath.

"Come on, Adam, let's get the rest of the list," Bert said. "The hardware store is right up here." He took a step up the street, and I dropped my eyes from Otis'. Before I looked away, I recognized the look. It was hate. Was it because I questioned him? Or thought I knew more about his town than he did? I followed

Bert, breaking contact with Otis. As we walked down the street, Bert said, "Don't look back. Let's jus' get on with our business."

Before we entered the hardware store, Bert glanced back up the street.

When we were inside, I asked, "Was he still there?"

Bert nodded. "Surprised he didn't drill a hole in our heads with them beady eyes of his."

A man in an apron called to us from the front of the store. The general store was filled to the rafters with assorted junk, everything with a handwritten price tag.

"Howdy, Malcolm. Got to have a pump part." Bert described the part we needed, and the man nodded.

"Yep, sold Billy 'n her the well pump myself. I got plenty of spares. How long ago did they put it in?" The man scratched his chin, thinking. "Fifteen years? 'bout that?" Nodding to himself, Malcom said, "Yeah, 'bout time for it to give out." To me, he said, "Malcolm, nice tameetcha," as he gave me the up'n'down look I was used to.

"Adam," I replied, thankful to escape the glares I'd started getting.

"You must be the music man," he said. "My son saw you at The Dive, said you were purty good."

"Thank you," I said. "I've worked hard at it."

"Got anything on the radio? Or online?"

I told him about the megastar's single, and he seemed pretty impressed.

"Music today ain't what it used to be. All about trucks and girls. 'At song, though, is good. It's more like what I was raised on."

"I like the old stuff. You need to know where you come from," I said. "Plus, it's a little different. That's why it's so successful, I think. People want something different."

We were leaning on the counter, having an honest-to-god pleasant conversation. Bert broke in, "Malcolm and his clan live outside of town, on a compound. Got his whole family around him."

"It's good, most of the time," Malcolm said, in a way that told me he'd used the line a thousand times. "But sometimes, it gets hairy. We're family, and we try not to forget it."

"Family doing okay?" Bert asked.

"Yeah, pretty good. Mama fell the other day, but she's just fine. Scared her though, roughed up her elbow."

"That's a woman you can't slow down. Kids good?"

Malcolm nodded a yes, and a tall kid stuck his head around the doorway leading to what I assumed was a warehouse.

"Daddy, Mrs. Foxie needs some fertilizer! Can you send Jep over?"

Malcolm waved a hand over his shoulder, and the head disappeared. "Old Foxie puts so much fertilizer on her stuff she damn near kills it," he confided to us. "I keep trying to tell her--"

Bert interrupted, "But it'd be bad for business." They laughed together, and I grinned.

Before he could walk away, I asked him, "Has everybody showed up for work today?"

He gave me a funny glance, but said,

"Sure. Had to drag my oldest out of bed, though, which is unlike him. I guess he went out to the old Cauthon place last night. Been spending a lot of time out there."

"Chasing girls," I said.

"Chasing a girl," Malcolm replied. "Tried to tell him. They'll let you buy a drink, but if you can't get her out of the bar, she ain't the one for you, no matter how sparkly the dress."

The comment made a memory stir in my mind, but it was gone like dandelion fluff in the wind.

"I'll fix up this order and send Jep out with it. He sure likes your song. Just wait 'til I tell him." We shook hands and spent a few minutes in the store before we went back outside.

As we were walking to the car, enjoying the day, Bert spoke to a middle-aged lady waiting outside the florist shop. "Martha, how are you?"

"I'd be better if Mr. Rooks would open up. My sister's at the hospital in Macon, and I'd like to get her some flowers. I guess I could stop at the supermarket on the way out of town, but it's such a hassle to park the car and get out. Then you have to go inside, find a cart, and I bet I'd find ten other things I don't need. And some of them would be cold, and I'd have to bring them home, and don't you know that would be a hassle? Little Rocco would want out, and it takes him forever to go potty. He's an old dog, you know, and . . ."

"We need to get going, Martha. He'll open soon." Bert started back up the sidewalk, pulling me along, and the lady turned to watch us leave.

"Christ, I forgot how much she talks. Would have kept us there an hour, talking about nothing," he muttered.

"I could have gotten Sonja some flowers," I mused. "I wonder if Rooks is on vacation as well."

Bert started to say something, but closed his mouth without speaking.

We walked the rest of the way without being accosted by any more talkative seniors. We climbed in, backed out of our parking spot, cruised through the rest of the morning, and headed to The Dive.

Sonja was prepping the bar when we arrived, and her smile was all for me. My mind flashed to Bert's conversation in the car, and I felt a touch of guilt; where did I expect this to go?

"Did you get the pump part?" she asked us as we sat down. The lunch crowd was filled in around us, and it looked busier that I'd seen it before. Darlene, the daytime waitress, was hustling from table to table, and a line of food was waiting to be carried to the patrons.

"Of course," Bert said. "Ol' Malcom knew right where it was. Even said it was about time to replace it." Sonja passed a pair of baskets to Deloris, who zoomed off to deliver them. "His stock boy didn't show up, and Rook's was closed. Malcolm and his boys were there, and said hello. Said he'd send Jep by with the order."

The murmur of voices spiked, one man's voice rising above it. We all turned to look and saw the same work crew from earlier in the week. Two of the workers were staring at each other, fists clenched around silverware, red faced and scowling. The supervisor looked between them, said something, and was promptly ignored. One threw a punch, the other knocked it aside, and the table boiled with movement. The other diners scrambled away from them, but before the fight could really get going, the other crew members hooked arms and contained the two combatants.

The supervisor, now red faced, pointed to the door, and they were carried out. He came over to Sonja. "Ms. Sonja, I'm sure sorry about that. I don't know what's happened to my boys. Ev'y one of 'em's been grouchy and touchy all week. I made them all promise to behave before we came in today, and look at what happened." He turned and surveyed the mess.

"Well, nothing got broken, and you know how boys can be," Sonja said.

"It ain't right," he said.

"I've seen more and more of this," Sonja said, sighing. "Don't worry about it, Clyde. We'll get it fixed up. Come back tonight; you're always welcome."

He nodded, relieved, and paid for his meals.

Bert and Sonja and I exchanged glances.

"Three fights in a week?" I asked. "Maybe we should put some chicken wire over the stage. Will I start getting hazard pay?" I was joking, but it fell flat.

"These people are tiring me out. I feel my chair calling," Bert said. "Adam, can you run me back to the house?"

I patted Sonja's hand before I got up, and she squeezed mine in return. "Do you want me to come back?" I asked her.

She shook her head. "I'll be done early tonight. Donald is coming in and closing up."

"Meet on the front porch?" I asked, smiling. I thought she nodded a little happier than when I came in, and I was pleased.

CHAPTER 21

I SET TWO BEERS on the table between the rockers. Cocking my head sideways, I examined the table, and decided it was missing . . . something. November in Georgia wasn't the best time for roses, but Sonja had some pansies growing in a flower pot near the front steps. Finding one, I picked it and laid it beside the bottles. Jumping on the table, the cat sniffed it, investigating until I shooed her away.

The porch was dark, lit only by the hall light from inside the house. The kitchen and dining room were both closed down with the lights off, and I was hoping we could talk without being interrupted. I glanced at my watch, my stomach tightening. I was actually nervous for this, hoping I wasn't making a fool of myself. I forced myself to sit in the rocker, and the chair and porch squeaked in time as I let the motion sooth my nerves and order my mind.

A flash of light came from the road and turned up the driveway. The crack and pop of gravel turned into Sonja's truck, and I stood as she pulled around the side. I planned on waiting for her on the porch, to present the flower and beer, but I was moving before I thought it out. I saw her silhouette in front of the truck's interior light, and it went off with the clunk of the door being shut.

"Good evening, my lady," I whispered.

She froze, perhaps startled, and then said, "Adam?"

"Of course." I walked to her, and she slid naturally into my arms, wrapping her arms around my back, placing a warm hand behind my neck. She looked up at me, her eyes reflecting light from somewhere, and I fell into them. With my arms around her and her head tilted up to me, I could smell the bar on her, her perfume, and I lowered my lips to hers. Our kiss was gentle at first, breath tickling as it danced across our lips and cheeks. Full and warm, her mouth settled over mine, and I felt her touch throughout my body.

However long we stood there, I don't know. The air was cold around us, but we were creating warmth. I was surprised steam didn't come from between us when we separated, and I realized I was holding my breath. We moved apart, but held onto each other.

"*That* was a first kiss," I said to the air above her head.

"No kidding," she said, her words muffled against my shirt.

I didn't want to move, but we both stepped away from the truck and to the porch. She kept her arm looped through mine, her head against my shoulder. When we walked up the steps, she moved slightly away from me, and I regretted the loss of her touch.

"Beer? For me?" She caught sight of the flower, lying limp and despondent between the two bottles. "You picked my flower!" she said, looking over at the flower pot. "I've been trying to get them to bloom for months! That was the first or second bloom!"

"Well, it looked better in my head," I admitted. "It didn't look so wimpy."

"I guess it's the thought that counts," she said. Looking up and me, she smiled, and her hand found mine. I wanted to kiss her again but knew if I moved in, she'd step back.

"I'll be right back," she said.

I sat down, opened the bottles, and took a sip of mine.

She came back onto the porch a few minutes later, her hair pulled back and wearing a sweater. To my delight, she had her smokes with her, and lit one for both of us. We inhaled together, content not to speak for a moment. As she put her beer on the table, I reached over and caught her hand before it could disappear into her lap.

"I'll be careful," I said. "I know what small towns can be like."

She smoked in silence, then said, "I'm not as worried about that as I am . . ." she paused. "About you moving on."

"I can write songs from anywhere," I said.

"That's way too soon," she said.

I felt a bit of annoyance creep up. "I know. But you brought it up. But I like this weird little town. If I could find a gig somewhere, you know, singing, or something . . ."

She choked out a laugh. "It's definitely gotten weirder, that's for sure."

"Did anything happen after I left?"

She nodded in the dark. Her hand was warm in mine. "Otis came in, but he was grumpy. Didn't talk much."

I told her about Bert's and my trip into town, and the way Otis acted.

"That's not like him. Sure, he's a cop, but he's not an asshole cop. He's more like . . ."

"A stern uncle," I supplied.

"Exactly."

"Then why is he different all of a sudden?"

We heard movement inside, and a light came on in the kitchen. Sonja looked over her shoulder, then said, "It's just Bert." She considered my question. "He may be feeling some pressure about some of the people who disappeared. I know I've asked him about Bobby."

The door behind us moved, and she slid her hand out of mine.

"Thought I smelled them old cancer sticks," Bert said. I got up and dragged a rocker over. "Did Otis have any answers about that?" he asked Sonja.

She shook her head. "I wasn't going to ask. Especially after Don Hutchins came in this afternoon," she said, and Bert nodded.

"Who's Don Hutchins?" I asked in a low voice.

"Town council man," Bert supplied as Sonja said, "He was telling me Otis pulled over Johnny Wilson – remember him? And during the traffic stop, Johnny popped off to Otis. Johnny is maybe ninety-eight pounds with his boots on. Has a club foot from when his daddy ran it over with a tractor."

"They live one farm over from Don," Bert said to me as Sonja continued.

"Well, Otis told Johnny to get out of the car. Johnny gets along fine on his foot, if he's walking, but Johnny refused. So Otis opens the door, pulls him out, and Johnny falls over. It's natural, if you think about it, but Johnny resisted, or something, and it got worse. Otis beat him up pretty bad. May have cracked a rib or two."

Bert hissed in the chair beside me.

"When did this happen?" I asked.

"Around lunchtime. Don said Johnny put up a fight, but . . ."

"Ain't like him," Bert said. "Gawdamighty, what's this place coming to? Did Adam tell you about our trip to town?" Bert asked her. At her nod, he said, "He's feeling the pressure from somewhere."

"I think it's connected to the old Cauthon place," Sonja said.

I nodded as Bert snorted in derision.

Before he could speak, Sonja continued. "Think about it. People started vanishing at the same time it appeared." She held up a hand before Bert could speak. "Bert, I know you and everybody else thinks they've been here 'forever,' but let me ask you: have you ever seen them out and about in town? Over the last ten years?"

Bert opened his mouth to argue, but I had a moment when two thoughts connected. "I've got one better. Bert, you told me Sonja and I had something in common. After the fight on the porch. Do you remember?"

"Damn," he grumbled. "Man just wants some good comp'ny, and it turns into an interrogation." He thought for a moment. "You both had head injuries."

Sonja's head whipped around to mine, and I told her in a few sentences what I went through as a kid. Halfway through, she nodded.

"It makes sense. Our brains got scrambled," Sonja said. Beside her, Bert grunted in amusement. "So whatever magic the place has, it doesn't affect us."

"How many people have vanished or acted strange since it came?" Between the three of us, we came up with over a dozen names.

Sonja and I batted theories back and forth while Bert sat there, silent. He finally spoke up. "Another theory," he said, "is that it could be you, Adam." Sonja started to laugh, but I put a hand on her arm. "This all started happening after you got here.

Now," he paused and waggled a finger at me. "I don't think much of it, but it could be said."

"What about me?" Sonja challenged.

"Why, he has feelings for you, of course. So you're immune."

We glanced at each other in the dark. There was just enough light I could see a gleam of humor in her eye. Sonja snorted. "Why, that's just crazy," she started to say, but Bert spoke over her.

"Just as crazy as a mysterious bar that appears overnight? And that everybody remembers except you two? That's making people mean, or making them disappear? Yup, that's crazy, all right."

We sat in silence, digesting the conversation. Sonja lit another smoke, but I declined.

"Both theories sound crazy," I admitted, and got two nods, "but something is happening to the town, and we need to keep thinking about it. Maybe there's something we can do, and maybe not, but I want to make sure the people I care about stay safe."

That was the last sentence for a while between the three of us as we listened to the fall night around us.

CHAPTER 22

"COME ON, CAN'T YOU?" Mills called out. His brother Jep always took extra-long getting ready. "Worse 'n a damn woman," Mills muttered under his breath.

"I heard that," his brother called from the bathroom they shared.

"I meant for you to," Mills replied.

"You try moving fifty bags of charcoal by yourself. See if you come out clean." Their family owned the brick hardware store in downtown Tanninville, which meant they both worked there around their college schedules.

"Where do you want to go? The Dive, or the new place?" Jep asked.

"I saw the guy from Nashville yesterday," Mills said. "He came into buy a part with Mr. Bert . . . you know, the one that boards with the Turner lady."

"I'd rather go to Ricochet," Jep said.

"You want to go to the blond in the sparkly dress," Mills said.

"Shut up."

"You know it's true." His older brother stood up. "I'm going downstairs. Hurry up –I'm ready to go.

Mills found his dad sitting outside, rocking on the front porch. Supper was finished, and his father had a drink in a tall glass jar. The yard dog, an ancient dachshund, thumped the porch with his tail.

"Heading into town?" Malcolm asked.

"Eventually, if Jep ever gets finished making himself pretty," Mills said as he squatted down to rub the dog's ears.

His father snorted as he said, "He just has more work to do."
On the tail of their laughter, Jep walked out.

"What?" he asked those on the porch.

"Nothing," Mills said to him. "We'll be back later," he said.

"Y'all be careful," Malcolm said, raising his drink in their
direction.

"Think they'll be okay?" he asked the dog as their boys
climbed into one of the farm trucks.

The parking lot was half full when they arrived, the sign over
the pole already flashing and rotating.

"How much rock you think they have here?" Jep asked his
brother. "I bet at least a dozen tons."

"No . . . this is at least three loads. And you're talking a dozen
tons per load. So . . . thirty-six tons? At least?"

"That much?" Jep asked as they opened the doors and
climbed out.

"Look." Mills kicked at some of the rock, digging a hole with
the toe of his boot. "There's at least six inches of rock here. And
the parking lot is at least half an acre. So that's . . ." As they
walked in, Jep could see his brother trying to do the math in his
head.

"Forget it. All I know is it's a shitload of rock."

"That it is," his brother agreed. They climbed the steps to
enter the wide log building in front of them.

Behind them, hidden between the cars, the rocks trembled
around the hole Mills had created. A rock fell to the bottom of it,
followed by a second. The ridges of misplaced stones flowed,
smoothing out, and in a few seconds, the surface of the gravel
parking lot was level once again. Above it all, the sign continued
to revolve, beckoning the community inward.

Inside, the chrome jukebox shimmered with the glow of the
neon lights surrounding it. Jep's eyes swept over the crowd, not

registering the variety of clothing inside the building. To him, the man with top hat and coat tails matched perfectly with the gnarled trapper hunched over the bar. The boy with long hair, a backpack, and a small dog his feet seemed to be a natural part of the bar, and was as unremarkable as the massive jukebox along the rear wall. He was searching for one particular person, one particular dress, and when he found it, he sighed. His brother picked it up.

"What?" he asked.

"She's with those Army boys again," Jep said. "Dammit."

"So? Why would that stop you? Just join them. Didn't you talk to one of them the other night? Pick up where you left off," Mills said. From across the bar, Jep saw the bartender slide a drink to a town kid. Even from that distance the man's eyes locked on his, and a solemn nod nudged him on.

"Yeah," Jep muttered to himself. "I got this. Go big or go home." Stepping down into the recessed dance floor, he squared his shoulders and headed to the table, his eyes fastened on the group ahead of him.

"My daddy had peanuts," the private said, slurring his words. "I hated them. Dusty, nasty things." He looked across the table, his eyes having trouble focusing on Jep. "What'd you say your family did around here?" he asked, for at least the second time. Jep had taken the seat beside Mildred, even though she'd been deep in conversation with the other man in green fatigues.

"We have the hardware store here in town," Jep said.

"The worst thing? It had to be the bugs. You see, in the South Pacific . . ." The man beside Mildred started talking about his deployment. To Jep, it was a litany of complaints; the bugs, the beds, the battles. As he drained the last of his drink, Jep found himself wondering if the fellow shot complaints at his enemies instead of bullets. Beside him, Mildred giggled, a high-pitched awkward sound.

Damn, now I'll never get a chance to talk with her, he thought. With a sigh, he put his empty glass down on the table.

Without looking over at him, Mildred's hand came up and covered his, giving it a quick pat. Jep jumped, not expecting the physical contact. She glanced over at his movement, and noticed his empty glass. Glancing around the table, she said to her companion, "Steve, it looks like we're all about ready for another. Would you mind moseying over to the bar and picking us up another round?"

Steve nodded and pushed back his chair. While the smile on his face was easy, his eyes lingered on Jep, and then moved to Mildred, who had turned to Jep.

The smell of her perfume intensified around Jep as she turned to face him. "Jepson," she said, and the noise around them was reduced to a low hum. "I know they call you Jep, but isn't it . . ." she paused for a moment, her brow wrinkling. "Jepson? Your full name?"

For a few seconds, Jep's mind couldn't unstick itself. His mouth was dry, her eyes were locked on his, and his body hummed, a reaction that his mind couldn't seem to process. "Yes. It was my great-grandfather's . . . maybe a great-great, I can't remember. We tend to pass names down. I didn't have any say in it, but that's where it came from."

Mildred's laugh seemed to smooth everything out.

His brain started working as his body relaxed, and Jep smiled at her. "What about you? Mildred? We both seem to have old-school names."

"Yes, my family prefers them as well. From an aunt on my mother's side. Deplorable woman; had a house on the south side of Chicago. Always had to have everything in its place and a place for everything."

"Life's like that."

"I know! She insisted on paying for finishing school, and talked Mother into sending me to secretary school."

"Did you want to be a secretary?" Jep asked.

"That's what I like about you," Mildred said, reaching over and patting his face. "Not many men back then – or now, for that matter – ever asked me that question."

Jep's words were thick, but managed to come out. "Would you like to dance?" he asked.

"I was just about to ask you the same thing," she said, and they stood up. Mildred took his hand and led him to the massive jukebox that squatted along the back wall. Mildred trailed a hand along it and it pulsed, the lights moving from yellow to red and then to green, pale luminescence that seemed to flow like water. Mildred was light in his arms as he reached around her waist.

"Millie, please," she said as the music changed to a slow beat. "Mildred is . . . so old fashioned." Her words were quiet as their bodies moved closer. She laid her head on his shoulder, and Jep's mind seemed to white out, overcome with the sensations; her body, molded to his; the smell of her, sweet with a tang of sweat, but not unpleasant; the feel of her hand in his. The temperature around him dropped, and . . . *She stepped out of the school, pulling her coat around her. The wind barreling down Jackson Boulevard caused her to stumble, and she felt her hat trying to lift off her head. Her fingertips were sore, having typed three pages of correspondence, and her wrists ached from the positioning her teacher, Mrs. Butler, forced upon her. "Old bag," she said out loud, the wind whipping her words away from her. She didn't mind the work; she wanted to work, to provide for herself, but her options were limited. By her sex, her time, and . . .that of others. She was a woman, and only that... but she was also more than that.*

"It's cold," Jep said, and shivered. Millie clutched him as they moved. "Why can't you . . . did you have to . . ." he started to ask, but the dance floor dissolved again.

The hotel was bursting with revelers. It was New Year's Eve, 1924, and Millie giggled as she walked through the doorway, arm-in-arm with her girlfriends. The hours with shorthand and dictation turned into a job clerking for a ferry operator on Lake Michigan. Millie suspected there was much more to the operation than simply a ferry service, but she'd vowed to keep her head down and her mouth shut. Even though they'd won the vote, an outspoken woman was still frowned upon. Her backside was more appreciated than her mind, she often mused. Which is why she jumped when she felt a hand cup it as she was chatting with Sarah and Rachael in the ballroom, excitedly watching the clock. She jumped and saw a short man wearing an expensive overcoat. His face was fleshy, with lips that were plump. He reeked of garlic, and a sheen of sweat coated his face.

"Hello, doll. Haven't I seen you working at Waters Ferry? You're in the office back there, I could swear. And if not, I can get you a job there. Or

137

anywhere in town. How about it? You'd make any office look better." Behind him stood two other men who looked completely sober, despite the holiday.

"Get your filthy hand off me," she said, knocking his arm away. Behind her, she felt Sarah and Rachael step back. She could feel their shock, but they'd talked about this very thing. Hadn't Sarah been the one to slap the newsboy when he'd made a lewd comment? Where was she now?

"Now, lady, listen," the man started to say, but Millie stepped toward him.

"I'm not a doll, or a baby, or anything you can grab," she said, the gin making her braver than she normally was. "I'm a lady, and I expect to be treated as such."

The three men shared a glance; the two who hovered had become more alert as Millie stepped forward.

"Well, now, I can see that. My apologies," said the fleshy one. "You want to the opera? I can do that. Want to go to the museum? I'll let you in to see those paintings by . . . what's his name, Geo? The guy with no ears. Or one ear?"

"Pablo," one of the body guards answered; the other said, "Picasso."

"Yeah, whatever. You wanna go? Wanna meet him? I'll take you to dinner afterwards. I can treat a lady."

Millie glanced over her shoulder, seeing her friends several steps away, shock still on their faces. Their abandonment hurt, feeding her irritation.

"I don't care if you knew Pablo Picasso. I wouldn't go anywhere with you. I'm looking for more of a man than one who's short and has fishy lips. And I like garlic, just not on a man." She turned away from the trio of men and strode across the ballroom. When she looked behind her, the men were departing the room, and her friends were hurrying to catch up.

"Do you know who that was?" Rachael said.

"No, and I don't care. Why didn't you . . . do something? We've always talked about how we're treated. And when it came down to it, you just . . . stood there."

"Millie, that's what we're trying to say. That was Al Capone. Didn't you recognize him?" Sarah asked.

Millie shook her head. "I don't care. It doesn't matter . . ." she trailed off. It did matter, at least in Chicago in 1924. "He won't bother with anyone like me. I'm just a girl," she said.

"A brave one," Jep said as the dance ended.

"And you?" she asked him. Even though the dance was over, she stayed close, swaying against him, her face tilted up. Her eyes were huge, magnetic under her beaded cap.

"Me?" he asked

"What is your time like?" she whispered. Jep's memories surfaced, and she sighed.

The smell of fresh turned dirt mixed with the sour smell of diesel exhaust. It's cold outside, early March, time to turn the dirt in preparation for planting. The tractor below him sends up a steady warmth, so his legs and feet stay warm, but his upper body is huddled in a thick coat. Once this pass is made, he can go to the truck, and . . .

The smell of dressing filled the house, accented by the wood smoke. Daddy and his brother have been up all night as they tended the smoker, and it's almost time to bring the turkey in. His cousins will be here soon . . . is that them? Jep jumped up, hearing the front door close. The dog barked, and is immediately shushed. The holidays are here, and . . .

The crowd roared as the football player, clad in purple and gold, broke from the scrum and raced away. Jep was standing in the stands and screamed with the others as the player crossed the goal line and was mobbed by his teammates. Jep picked up the yellow milk jug and shook it, causing the handful of coins inside it to rattle. Around him, the other spectators raised their noisemakers, and the resulting sound was a cacophony...

The smell of the general store, just as it opened: Leather, seeds, and fertilizer. The sweetness of the wheat straw...

The warmth of the hand in his as he walked a girl to the door. The anticipation as she turned to him, her face tilted up...

Millie sighed, the satisfaction of Jep's memories settling in.

"It's so beautiful," she said.

"What?" Jep asked, nuzzling her ear with his nose. She had dabbed her perfume behind her ear, and this close to the scent made his knees weak.

"Life. The simplicity. The sweetness. The . . ."

January's wind howled, pushing February's snow into drifts as she wandered through the streets. Mildred kept a nervous eye over her shoulder for the first few weeks, but as the months passed she relaxed. It was easy to dismiss the interaction, the anxiety, the fear; as it receded in her memory, so did her wariness.

As she stepped from the sheltered doorway of the ferry service, she adjusted her collar and braced herself for the gust of wind that would push her as soon as she stepped out onto the sidewalk. The wind stilled, and she smiled to herself, pleased at the break in the buffeting force. Behind her a car started, but she didn't notice. A headscarf kept her hair off her face and warmed her ears. A heavy coat muffled her body, and thick boots kept her feet warm and her footing secure. The wind started back up, making her eyes water, and she lowered her head against the onslaught.

The crunch of snow and ice came from behind her, and with her head ducked she glanced back. The black car was a dozen feet behind her, and she could see two large shapes hunched in the front seat. Panic rose inside her as one of the two shapes grinned at her through the punishing wind. She looked away and tried to run. Her boots had thick soles, perfect for warmth, but less so for escape. She heard the rumble of the car behind her, and the ice and snow groaned as it caught up to her and stopped. She swerved away from the street, closer to the line of buildings standing shoulder-to-shoulder. The man climbing out of the passenger seat was still grinning, and he said something to her that was lost to the wind as it went by. The street ahead of her was covered in gloom; early afternoon in the dead of winter lay heavy over the land, and lights were coming on in nearby houses and offices.

The men were out of the car and sauntering up the street behind her. In her panic, she considered dashing across the street, and then looked to her right. Down an alleyway, a neon light flickered and pulsed. She turned toward it. The wind was cut off by the squat shapes of the buildings, and she heard a surprised shout behind her. The stench of the alley assaulted her and then faded away. The sight of rubbish piled to the side, awaiting pickup, skimmed off her mind. She saw the doorway ahead of her, the beckoning light, and felt the warmth. As she pushed through the door, she sounds of the city faded behind her, the cold replaced with safety.

140

"Oh, thank god," she said to the man behind the bar. "Please, help me."

Behind her, the door crashed open again as the two men followed her inside. At the bar, a man stepped off his stool. He had a long, tangled beard and his clothes were filthy. A pair of boys in grey clothing were sitting at a table, and as they stood up Millie recognized the military uniforms, even if she couldn't place the army they belonged to.

"Bitch, you're gonna regret running," one of Capone's goons said. "The boss wants to see you."

"Gentlemen, no need to be rude to the lady," the bartender said. He stepped gracefully around the bar as Millie heard the hum of speakers from somewhere in the back.

"Well, this lady is spoken for," the other said. "We'll take her with us and be out of your way."

"You're not in my way, but I'm not sure the lady wants to go with you," the bartender said. He stepped between Millie and the men.

"It doesn't matter what she wants. Our boss wants to speak with her – a matter of some unfinished business – and it's our job to escort her to the conversation." The man reached out, perhaps to give an affable pat on the bartender's shoulder, or perhaps to push him aside. Either way, as soon as he made contact with the bartender's shoulder, the hood froze. His eyes rolled and swam in his sockets, and he let out a low groan that quickly increased in pitch and panic, but he froze. His partner jumped back, frantically reaching deep into the pockets of his overcoat, trying to find his gun.

"Who the hell are you, mister?"

"I'm the keeper of this establishment, and I don't particularly care for those who harass my patrons." He stepped away from the frozen man, who was now quivering against the force that held him stock-still. "You can eat, you can drink, you can dance. Three plays for a dime are all you need for a good time."

Millie shuddered in Jep's arms, partially from fear, partially from excitement. "You should have seen it," she whispered. "It was . . . something else." She and Jep turned from the dance floor, but she stayed tucked between his arm and side.

"This place . . . is always here, isn't it? Is it somewhere I can stay?" Jep asked.

"Of course. But live your life. Have a family, a wife. There's so much more out there than the little you've seen.

"What about you? Do you do all of that?"

Mildred trembled against him as they arrived at the table. She didn't answer, but Jep felt the longing through their bond.

CHAPTER 23

BOBBY SAT, WATCHING A TENDRIL of The-Thing-in-the-Rock pulse and flow. It moved in little waves, constricting, expanding, and pushing its way through the trough Mark dug during the first days. Mark's body still moved at times, but it was decaying fast. His skin was sloughed off in places, and even the muscle was breaking down. White bone, turned dark by the cave dust, showed through in places.

The essence could propel itself short distances, moving in spurts and starts. More automatons had come to him during the night, making the journey along the roads and in some cases through the woods. Bobby had been explicit in his instructions: *Come to me. Hide from sight. Hide from the light. Come in the night.*

After his second killing, he realized the questions that could be asked if the newly made automatons were seen staggering on the outskirts of town toward the high bluff in plain sight. In another couple of days it wouldn't matter, but the time wasn't right for anyone to come investigating. Still, he realized too late with Jimmy that he still needed to protect his secret for a few more days.

Bobby thought again about the goo; it traveled from the pit of the mine, down the trough, and into the river. The essence of The-Thing-in-the-Rock was already affecting the town; Bobby could sense it, a low groundswell of irritation, aggression, and the beginning of hate. But it wasn't quite enough. One or two curious people could unravel everything he'd done.

He glanced again at the cave mouth and walked inside. Mark's body lay on a rocky shelf, almost still, the automatic movements now nothing more than slight tremors.

"Jimmy," Bobby called into the mine. The steady *chip-chip-chip* paused, and Bobby heard the shuffle of footsteps. Faintly, he could hear the digging continue as Chris and the others kept working. Space was tight down at the bottom, and only one automaton could work at a time. Earlier, Bobby had set them to expanding the crack where the essence came from. This was where The-Thing-in-the-Rock was, where it lived, and where it needed to be freed.

Jimmy stopped beside him, waiting patiently.

Bobby motioned to Mark. "Pick him up."

Jimmy obediently stepped over the goo and leaned over the rocky shelf. Bobby had learned short, simple commands were best. Jimmy's touch brought a little more response from Mark, but not much.

"Bring him over here."

Jimmy stepped back across the goo and stood beside Bobby, who took a step back.

"Lay him down right here," Bobby said indicating.

Jimmy squatted, his knees grinding in their sockets. Mark tumbled from his arms with a looseness that made Bobby wince. Jimmy stood up and stepped back.

"Do you still have a boat tied up to your dock?"

The Jimmy-thing paused, as he accessed the information and gave a stiff nod.

"Give me your keys," Bobby said.

After the command processed, Jimmy reached into his pocket and dug out a set of keys.

Glancing at the key ring, Bobby found what he was looking for. "Go back to digging."

Jimmy shuffled off as Bobby stood looking at the body on the cave floor. Hopefully no one came in; the body was visible if someone walked more than five feet into the cave. Marks's body lay parallel to the goo and Bobby grimaced as he picked up Mark's arm, positioning his hand directly into the ichor. The goo retreated, then pulsed forward, covering Mark's fingers to the exposed knuckles. Mark's fingernails had been ripped off within the first day by the harsh rock, and the goo covered the raw wounds.

Bobby shuddered as he saw the goo begin to enter his friend's body.

Bobby parked Chris' car along an old logging road on the back side of Jimmy's property. From there it was a short trek through the woods to the dock where Jimmy's small boat was tied up. Bobby felt it was best not to take chances; even though Jimmy was divorced, Bobby didn't want anyone to notice a strange car in the area. He walked through the woods pausing at the tree line. Watching the house for a few minutes, and scanning the neighbor's yard, he waited. Satisfied no one was around; he walked out of the woods to the dock. The boat had a small motor, which Bobby gassed up, stowing an extra gas can. He'd finish his business later that night, bring the boat back, and pick up the car. Time was running short; The-Thing-in-the-Rock was getting impatient as it could sense its rocky layer of imprisonment grow thinner.

Bobby was also impatient; he was ready to be done hiding, sleeping and living in a cave, and sulking around at night like a furtive dog. Bobby stepped into the boat and untied it from the dock. The motor caught on the second pull of the starter cord, and Bobby pointed it upriver.

Motoring along the Ogeechee River was anticlimactic. Bobby felt like every eye was on him as he crossed the water, but he knew it was only paranoia. He passed two other boats. The first one waved, and Bobby felt a flash of anger. The second boat earned him only a scowl and an angry look, and Bobby grinned back at him. After the second boat, he didn't feel so nervous.

An hour or so later, he beached the small craft with a scrape of metal on rocks. The bluff kept him from taking the most direct route to the cave, so he had to walk cross-country until he came to the road leading upwards. Made up of broken up switchbacks, the road degraded severely the higher he went. Turnarounds were dug out in several locations, allowing more room on the turns. Before the road went bad, the turnarounds were used as parking spots for local lovers.

Several deaths occurred on or around the bluff over the years. As he trekked, Bobby wondered if The-Thing-in-the-Rock played a part in any of the deaths. Not directly, perhaps . . . but the Jenkins Mine had been unlucky for years. *That* was the effect of The-Thing-in-the-Rock: investor after investor became bankrupt after promising assays never panned out; the investors brought miners, and miners were often lost to mine accidents. As he climbed, Bobby found the activity didn't tire him out as much as before. No longer consuming the drugs, along with the strength imparted by The-Thing-in-the-Rock, he found himself almost running up the broken road.

Instead of continuing up the switchback, Bobby leapt up the earthen bank, his feet digging into the dead leaves and red mud. Bobby moved easily where he had handholds: small trees, roots, even exposed chunks of rock. He reached the lip of the switchback. Looking over the edge and down, he was hardly out of breath. He grinned to himself.

Mark's body was plumped, like the casing on a sausage heated on the grill. Where the skin was torn, a black scab covered the rip, forming a seal to hold in the essence. Bobby looked at his friend and then toward the front of the cave at the setting sun. Not much longer, and they could use the cover of darkness for one final trip.

Bobby moved deeper into the cave, following the sound of hammers on rock. The passageways narrowed, the ceiling dropping until Bobby had to squat. He found his collection of automatons clustered at the end of the mineshaft, milling around and getting in each other's way.

"Stop, stop, STOP!" Grabbing one by the shirt, he pulled him back. Rooks? The flower guy? Bobby didn't stop to glance at him. Marking the wall with a can of spray paint, he pointed. "Dig!" Bobby grabbed another automaton and did the same thing. Before long, he had them coordinated again, with two to help clear out the rock chippings that fell underfoot. They would cart them to another shaft, dump the wheel barrow, and return.

"Wait," he said, and they stopped digging. Bobby moved to the end of the shaft and put his hand on the wall. He could feel or sense something moving, deep under the rock but getting nearer. Bit by bit they were getting closer to freeing The-Thing-in-the-Rock. Bobby closed his eyes, straining to sense, hoping to find some reaction behind the rocky shelf.

He sighed and opened his eyes. Almost there. Directing his automatons, he set them to digging. He grabbed Chris by the shoulder and said, "Come up at dark."

It nodded its head. Even buried, The-Thing-in-the-Rock– and by proxy, the automatons – knew the time of day and the season of the earth. It was an old sense, almost as old as it was. To be in tune with the turn of the earth . . . Bobby smiled as he walked through the darkness.

Bobby wanted to try his newfound physical gifts and see if he could climb to the very top to the Jenkins Mine. Chris carried Mark's inflated body but despite the scabs, a little of the essence dripped on the stony ground. They walked in silence, Bobby stepping easily over obstacles in his path. Despite a sliver of the moon riding high over the river, he could see clearly. Chris stumbled at times, but kept his balance. They walked down the mountain until they came to the boat tied to the rocks, and Chris stepped into the water and lowered Mark in the bottom of the boat.

Bobby climbed in. "Push me out," he instructed, and Chris lifted the bow of the boat clear of the rocks and gave it a shove. As he was drifting, and caught by the current, Bobby said "Go back up and keep digging. We're almost there."

Chris turned and slogged through the water until he was on the bank, then climbed back up. Bobby let the nose of the boat swing downriver before he dropped the tiny prop into the water and started the engine.

He frowned at the noise of the motor. It seemed loud to him, echoing across the water, but Bobby doubted it carried very far. Night fishing was unusual, but not unknown. He pointed the nose

of the craft toward the North Bridge, and let the boat carry him
and his special delivery.

Bobby drifted close to the piling and put a bumper over the
side. A drag anchor, catching in the riprap at the bottom of the
piling, held him against the flow of the water. He could feel the
suction from the intake pipe as it inhaled water from the river,
taking it to the treatment facility several blocks inland. Just outside
the five-hundred-year-flood plain, it treated the water used by the
town and surrounding areas. He looked around him; he needed to
place Mark's essence-filled body where it couldn't drift past the
intake, but also where it couldn't be easily seen from the shore or
from the bridge above. He looked at the water. He hated getting
wet, which is one reason he never became much of a fisherman.
Sighing, he stepped off of the boat and into the water.

He could create a pocket in the riprap and tumble Mark's
body into the water. The essence could catch the current and flow
into the intake. Grunting, he moved rocks, exposing the sticky red
clay. When he had a large enough area cleared, he pulled the boat
to him, straining against the current. The spot he'd chosen was
under the bridge, but he might be seen if he slipped the anchor
and motored upstream. It wouldn't be good to be spied from the
bridge above him.

Straining, he got Mark's body to the edge of the boat.

"Little help here," he gasped, not expecting a response. But
Mark's arm moved and grabbed the edge of the boat, pulling
himself over into Bobby's arms. Bobby took two staggering steps
and dumped Mark close enough to the hole he'd created. Silt
bloomed, covering Mark, and Bobby used his foot to hold Mark
in place underwater. Breathing hard, he regained his breath and
placed rocks to hold him in place.

Each time a rock landed, a little squirt of darkness entered the
water, trailing directly toward the intake pipe.

Bobby grinned.

As he placed the last rock, something moved, and a hand
closed around his ankle, squeezing painfully. Bobby tried to

scream, but his throat closed up, holding it in. He jerked, feeling the grip loosen, and jerked again. Finally pulling free, he fell across the water, and climbed into the boat.

CHAPTER 24

THE CONVERSATION AROUND the breakfast table was even more stilted than usual. The construction workers ate in silence. Greg and Jim sat at opposite ends of the table, nothing developing between them. Cliff was shooting glances at everyone, and I saw Greg bristle as Cliff reached for the egg ladle at the same time he did. Sonja's voice floated from the kitchen, and they both looked over their shoulders before Greg chose to let go.

Cliff grinned wolfishly and ladled an extra scoop onto his plate. Bert and I exchanged a glance across the table, and he shrugged.

"Cliff, how's the barn coming?" Bert asked. I didn't think he was going to answer.

"Fine. Got it dried in, just waiting on the mechanical to be put in. Goddam HVAC assholes running behind," he said, starting to rant.

When he slowed down, Jim said, "I heard the building inspector made the framing crew fix a few things. That's what put them behind schedule."

Cliff dropped his fork and stared at Jim, who dropped his eyes at first, but then raised them defiantly. Cliff started to retort, but I interrupted.

"Think Sonja will get the pump part today?" I asked Bert. The previous day, I'd hovered behind her, waiting for an arc of electricity to send her tumbling backwards. She'd hard-wired something or the other to make the pump run long enough and top off the water heaters in each room. I'd been using bottled water to brush my teeth.

Her announcement at breakfast the morning before about the water had been greeted with silence, while I expected at least a few good-natured grumbles. But no one joshed her, they just nodded and kept eating.

"Never liked well water myself," Greg said. "I remember my daddy bleaching it once a month when I was a kid, so I always fill up my water jug in town."

"Once a month?" Bert asked. "Was it bad?"

Greg shrugged. "He said it was. We was dirt poor, on the back side of a hog farm. Said he couldn't abide pork. Always thought it ruined the water supply."

"Prob'ly right," Bert said. "But that's the best dirt you can find, some that's been under hogs." The conversation carried on about gardening until the hallway clock chimed the half hour, and everyone but Bert and I started getting up. When the table was clear, I sat back, contented.

"No rassling today," I observed.

"Near 'bout, though. Cliff and the inspector got into it th'other day. That's why Jim said it." Bert forked a last bite of eggs into his mouth.

Sonja breezed into the dining room, smiled at me, and gathered the dishes. Bert got up and headed to the porch, and I helped her gather the plates and put out the chafing dishes. The sideboard she used was battered, with drink rings and heat spots, but I wiped it down after carefully moving the paraffin tins that kept the food warm.

"So you can do more than just strum the git-tar?" she asked.

"Of course, m'lady. There's more than music in these hands. Us struggling songwriters have to be multi-talented." We were alone in the dining room, and she passed between me and the table. Since I had a hand free, I put it on her hip. She glanced toward the doorway and stepped toward me.

"I heard your song went top five," she said, moving in. A quick peck turned into a longer kiss when I wouldn't let her escape. "Congratulations," she said. We heard steps in the hallway, and she scooted away as I turned to wipe the table. Cook entered and gave us a beady-eyed stare as she collected the dishes. As she turned away, Sonja bit her lip and flushed, and I dropped her a wink. Her flush deepened, and I had to clear my throat before speaking.

"Think the pump part will be in today?"

We walked to the kitchen, and she said, "Should be. Jep usually delivers a day or so after the order."

Cook looked at both of us, letting me know we weren't as discreet as we hoped to be.

"I'm going to pull my laundry together. Isn't there a washing machine downstairs?" Sonja nodded, and Cook continued to give me the side eye. I put the dishes on the counter, and I'm not afraid to admit I got out of there as fast as I could.

"You chased him off, Cookie. Did you see that?" Sonja came close to a giggle.

"Yah," Cook said, sourly. "You carrin' on with a man who might be gone in a minute. Be a shame to see tears where that smile is now." Sonja tried to interject, but Cook hadn't finished her warning. "It's been years since our sweet Billy passed, and you deserve to be happy. But I'm telling ya," she waggled a spoon to emphasize her point. "To hang your heart on the guitar string of a sweet singing man is going to be heartbreak."

Sonja bit her tongue. Cook had been employed by Billy's parents before he was even born and she took full advantage of her position within the family, a part of the boarding house as much as the chairs on the porch or the crooked hall door on the third floor.

"Cookie, it's been seven years. I've had a handful of dates out of town so I wouldn't set tongues wagging. I didn't think yours would be one of the first." Cook gave her a withering look, and Sonja colored.

"Wagging my tongue with the advice of an older woman ain't wagging my tongue, and you know it. So do you want to try something else to explain yourself, rather than giving ol' Cook the business?" She raised a steely eyebrow in Sonja's direction, her face softening as she looked at Sonja, the lines and cares on her face deeply etched. The hands holding the spoon were chapped and red from years of washing dishes and, Sonja could admit, washing away a fair number of tears over the years.

"I don't know what's going to happen," Sonja sighed as she sat down at the table. Cook scraped dishes, and Sonja realized this was a tableau they'd repeated over the years. "I tried to slow myself down, but I don't know that I can much longer." She stared dejectedly at the table top. "Today's the third day; he would be leaving if I hadn't asked him to help me at The Dive. I don't know why he's hanging around."

"Might be for you," Cook said softly, changing her position to make Sonja think from a different angle.

"That's what I think. That's what I *want* to think," Sonja said. "But . . ."

"If he's down to his last dollar, a lady with a bidness and a boarding house is a nice set up."

The bell at the front door rang, and Sonja stood up and kissed Cook on the cheek.

"Thank you again," she said. Cook grunted and dunked her hands into the scalding water. It steamed up, and she soaped the breakfast plates and silverware. The hot water turned her skin red, but would have raised blisters on the skin of anyone else.

"Mayhap you'll listen, girlie. Wouldn't be the only thing changing around here," Cook muttered to herself.

Sonja was carrying a small box outside when I came upstairs from the laundry area. Thankfully the dryer was empty; I'd spent enough time in communal laundry rooms.

"Pump part?" I asked her. I tried to slip a hand around her waist, but she stepped back, and I was disappointed.

"Yep. We'll have fresh water in less than an hour."

Not having anything better to do, I followed her outside. She picked up a small tool bag from the table beside the back door and headed to the well house.

"I need to re-up on my stay," I said as she opened the door to expose the finicky pump.

She looked at me. "That's something we need to talk about."

Any man who hears the words 'we need to talk' right away feels a tightening in his gut and a puckering of his nether regions.

She started to speak, but I got the words out first. "I fully intend on paying my own way. I don't want your money." When I left the room earlier, I had seen the look Cook had given me. Combine that with Bert's talk the day before, and I could see which way those two were thinking.

"It's not that," she said, and my pucker factor increased.

"Then what is it?" I said, trying to keep my voice level.

"I need to know what you want," she asked.

I considered for a moment. "To get to know you better. To settle myself down. To write music," I said.

"Can you do that here?" she asked.

I shrugged. "For the most part. I've been around long enough I have a few contacts, so I'm not stuck playing the bars to pay the bills. I'd have to go back occasionally, when they have festivals or meet-and-greets. But you could come with me."

She disappeared inside the well house, and I moved over to prop the door open. At least I could help a little.

"What do you want?" I asked her.

"I have a good life. I have good customers, here and there. But I want someone to share it with."

"We've only had a few stolen kisses, but I would love to share it with you," I said. She looked up at me sharply, and I continued before she could interrupt. "But I know it needs to take its own course. No rush."

"Can you hand me the crescent wrench?" she asked. I dug it out of the bag and handed it to her.

"Are you sure?"

"About the crescent wrench, or . . ." I trailed off. "Of course, if I stay on at The Dive, I might need to change the terms of the deal."

She looked up quite sharply at that. "And how so?"

"Half priced here wouldn't help me pay my rent. I'll have to see how much cold, hard cash I can squeeze from the skinflint owner."

"Rent? Where?" She continued to install the part; closing valves, flipping breakers, and pulling out a tangle of wires.

"I'll have to find an apartment. If we're going to see where this takes us, it would probably be better if I had my own place. I'm sure I can find one pretty cheap around here."

"What about the girl in Nashville?" she asked.

"Nicole?"

She nodded.

"It's over," I said. "I think we were drifting anyway, but the last scene between us put it to rest."

"What happened?" she asked, concentrating on the disassembled well in front of her. I looked off, over the fields, remembering the last painful confrontation. The embarrassment, the shame, the hurt.

I walked out of the small room, Andrea ahead of me. I could feel the shit-eating grin on my face, but I didn't care. I knew what had happened in the room; it was the moon shot, the one in a million chance every artist is chasing. Andrea looked over her shoulder and smiled at me as she exited the corridor and slipped into the crowd. If anything, my grin grew larger, and I held the documents in my hand. I felt like my head was going to pop off, spewing art everywhere. I was on top of my craft, on top of my industry, and proud of myself and all the years I put into it.

"Adam!?" a wail came from my left, and I jumped, the grin faltering a bit. Nicole was standing there, a drink clutched in her hand, her face painted in the wounded look I knew. Uh-oh, I thought. "Who was that?" she said, and heaven help me, I glanced after Andrea. "And why were you . . ." her words ended in a wail, and people turned our way. Nicole was half drunk, a fairly normal condition for her, but now she was 'hurt.' I could see the emotion filling every pore on her face. "Who was she, Adam?" she said, and even more heads turned my way.

"Come on," I said, the good feelings almost gone. I had about ten seconds before she melted down. We'd been through this once or twice, and I knew the signs. "Look what I've got. He signed it. He's gonna—"

"Let go of me!" she wailed. "Why do you always do this?" She jerked away from me, stumbling, and tripped over her feet, even though she only had on low heels. She sat down hard, her dress compressing and showing off a good bit of leg. I, of course, could have seen much more, but it was the last place I was looking. From the ground she wailed again and threw her cup at me. Thankfully it was empty, and she didn't have good drunk-aim. It made a loud sound as it bounced across the banquet room floor. It was clearly heard

because our section of the party had gone silent, and everyone was watching. I saw the crowd shift, and Andrea peered out from the faces. Thankfully, Nicole didn't see her, or . . .

"Come on, let's go. You're drunk." I reached down and helped her up, and she cried in earnest.

"I'm not. But you're mean. Why are you so mean to me?" she said. "And walking out of rooms at a party with other women. Why would you do this to me?" Once I got her to her feet, she pulled away from me.

"Come on, let's not do this here," I said.

"Why not? Am I embarrassing you in front of your friends? Does it bother you I'm crying because of what you did?" She wiped the makeup tears from her eyes, smearing her mascara. Of course, she said the main words a little louder, just enough to keep everyone's interest. I've seen plenty of performers over the years, and Nicole was a good one.

"I know some of them, but this is an industry function, 'Cole. I'm here to meet people, not party. And not be embarrassed by my drunk girlfriend," I said, feeling the slow burn of resentment.

"Oh, so it's about you? Maybe the tramp who was in the room can make you feel better. Why don't you find her?" Nicole did a drunken pirouette, looking through the crowd that was watching both of us. Thankfully, Andrea had already stepped back; I always thought she had a sense of Nicole's insecurities. I sighed, feeling my will to fight slip away. I held up my hands.

"Nicole, this has been a night . . . a night I'll never forget. I wanted you here to share it with me, not ruin it. If you want to wallow in your insecurities, do it. But do it quietly and do it somewhere else." A few faces reacted to my words and Nicole hitched in a breath, her face trembling as my words penetrated the haze of alcohol. I turned away from her and the crowd that was watching and searched for the exit, not acknowledging anyone's commiseration or disdain. I just wanted to get outside.

"Nicole and I'd met a year or so before. We dated three, maybe four months, and then moved in together. Things were normal, but I'd noticed she could be . . . precipitous at times."

"Precipitous? That's a big word," Sonja said.

"Well, I'm a smart guy," I said. "Anyway, she would get paranoid about things. Weird shit. If the neighbors came over to borrow something. Or if the cashier took too long with her credit card. Then the focus turned to me. If I didn't make the bed just right, or I put the glasses in the wrong order. She would grumble, but the grumbles got longer. Like I said, small stuff, but taken together, it got to be a problem.

"Then it started at my shows. I've never played much to the crowd, but I had regulars. She always nattered at me if I paid too much attention to a girl in the crowd, but when she's a 50-year-old industry rep, and she's been to three straight shows, I was going to smile and be polite. The music business is about schmoozing. Everybody knows everybody, of course, and you never know who knows who."

"Like any small town," Sonja interjected. I loved being able to talk with her; she listened in the right spots and responded well with her questions and observations.

"Yep. I was trying out some newer songs. After the show I was backstage, and Andrea came up. I could tell she was in the business; there was a bit of polish about her. We swapped cards, which Nicole saw, and I agreed to send her some of my demos. When Andrea called the following week, Nicole wasn't there, and went quiet when I told her Andrea and I were going to lunch to discuss it. By then, I knew which label she was with, and the word on the street was their big act was almost done with the new record. So I knew it was a big opportunity.

"But I made a mistake. I talked it to death. Asked her what I should wear. Things like that."

"You brought more attention to it," Sonja said.

"Yes, given how she reacted to stuff, I should have known. But it was business. I was in love with Nicole, lived with her, and didn't want Andrea. Was Andrea pretty? Sure. But pretty's only part of the picture." I smacked my leg, thinking of the excitement of those days, and the impending crash just over the horizon. I should have felt it, but hindsight is always better for picking out the small details.

"So we do lunch, set up a meeting with the big dog, and I do that. He's heard the demo, I play it for him, and then I get to sit in with his band. In short, he loves the song. But the business can be slow, and I got the run around, and I don't hear anything for two weeks. I've been blown off before so I knew the signs. I also knew how close I'd come, and it bummed me out. Nicole seemed smugly happy it didn't work out, and I resented the hell out of that, but I brushed it off. Or tried to." Sonja had stopped working on the pump; she was sitting beside the machinery, her legs folded under her with her back against the wall. I was squatting on my heels, loosely holding a screwdriver, holding and twisting it as I told my story. The air in the well house was dusty, a few motes of dust floating in the beams of light flaring between the boards.

"Then I got the phone call. They were having a preview party for a handful of top label people, and she invited me. And Nicole, of course; I had a plus one. So I'm back on top of the moon."

"Uh-oh," Sonja said, picking up another tool and motioning to me. "Can you hold this?"

I held the part steady as she leaned forward and connected the copper lines.

"Exactly. So we went to the party, and Andrea and the producer pull me into a back room, and tell me which song they want to use, the details, all the good stuff. They have contracts for me to sign, a check in hand, and a thumb drive of my other songs. We shake hands, and I start signing papers. Then the producer leaves the room. After I've signed everything, Andrea and I walk out, and who's standing there?"

"Nicole," Sonja said.

"She absolutely goes ballistic. I try to get her out of sight, tell her what just happened, but she'll have none of it. The fight moves into the main room, and she's crying, half drunk; everybody is looking."

Sonja made a small noise of commiseration. I remembered the feeling of shame, the embarrassment, and the gut sinking feeling of seeing my career peak and tank in the same hour.

"So she storms out, I leave, and then I get angry. I mean, I'd never done anything. *Anything.* So we have another blowout on the sidewalk in front of our apartment. I crashed with a guy from an old band and over the next week or so, got most of my stuff out of the apartment, bought my car, –"

"I really like your car. It fits you," she said.

"And hit the road," I finished. "Nicole had this big dog, a golden retriever and beagle mix. Toward the end, he was the best thing about the relationship. When I was getting the last of my things, he knew what was going on. He sat by the door and whined the entire time. I think I miss him more than I miss her."

She dropped the wrench into the tool bag and looked up at me.

"I'm done."

I felt a moment of panic. Done? What did I do? Was I talking too much? "Sonja? What do you mean?"

She must have seen the look of panic on my face. She laughed, a high giggle, and rocked back on her heels.

"No, no, no," she said, rocking back toward me. She leaned over, supporting herself on one hand, and cupped my cheek. "I'm done with the well, silly." She planted a soft kiss on the corner of my mouth, which I closed in relief.

"You are?" I said, quite stupidly. She stood up, pulling me out the well house, and we sat in the sun.

"Yes, I am. We have all the clean water we want. About us, though." She paused, and my throat constricted. "I need to be careful with you, but I can't be afraid of loving, or reaching out. Otherwise, I'll grow old in this little town. It wouldn't be a bad life, but . . ."

"Incomplete," I supplied.

She nodded. "So we'll see where it goes. I've always thought it's better to try and fail, rather than have any questions later."

"I'll give it my best," I said, and leaned in, aiming for her cheek. The morning sun shone down on us, warming the bench beneath us and touching our skin. The wind gusted as she turned her head, catching my lips with hers. It was a gentle, little kiss, and she smiled as we moved apart. I resisted the urge to look around the yard to see if anyone was watching.

Sonja slowed at the end of Turner Farm Road where it intersected with East Riverside Drive. Instead of going straight, crossing the south bridge and continuing to The Dive, she took a left. She was almost through downtown when she realized where she was going. Downtown Tanninville was almost empty, with cars only filling every third parking space. Sonja frowned, lost in thought as her eyes skimmed the road in front of her. She took a right onto the North Bridge and was turning left to go out of town when she realized where she was headed. A tear trickled down her cheek, unnoticed, and she glared at the dark sign as it appeared in the curve. Keeping her eyes fastened on the road, she compelled herself not to look at the menacing building on the left.

After she passed it, she let out a breath of frustration. She felt the damp on her face and scrubbed away the tear track. She'd been years getting to this point, with many unanswered questions and gallons of shed tears. The pain, for so long a sharp beast gnawing away inside her, had morphed into hollow ache. It still hurt, hurt her all the way to the bone, but she was past the stage of the sharp pains. She pulled off the road at the base below the Jenkins Mine. The entrance to the switchbacks leading to the mine was somewhere up ahead, but Sonja had no need to go there.

She stepped out of her truck in a puff of dust. The rundown heels of her boots clopped on the asphalt, the only sound following her. Moving through the knee-high grass, she went to the weathered, windblown cross. Straightening it, she picked up the faded fake flowers and cleared a few handfuls of grass away from the base. She, along with the town council and about half the town, had held a memorial service for Billy in this spot a month after his death. She looked over the river.

"It's time, baby," she whispered. "I've held you as long as I could. I'd give anything for you to be here, but you're not. For whatever reason, you were taken from me, and now I have to deal with it."

She traced the name on the cross, WILLIAM K. TURNER, and with a final motion smoothed imaginary dust off the cross arm. As she walked back to her truck, she wiped away the final tears and climbed in.

Her mind drifted in the past as she guided the truck away from the bluff, going a little slower than normal along the winding road as it matched the course of the river. She knew she was leaving the bluff for the final time. As she approached the darkened sign, she looked toward the building with mistrust and a little hate. In shock, she slammed on the brakes, causing the truck to fishtail on her bald tires, leaving black exclamation points on the road. In shock, she failed to check the road behind her as she put the truck in reverse and skidded the tires in her haste. Drawing even with the parking lot, she stopped again and stared.

Bobby's car was the only vehicle in the parking lot, parked at an angle away from the doors. She looked again, closer, and put the truck in gear. If anyone had been coming, they would have broadsided her because Sonja's attention was only focused on one thing. As her truck bounced over the fresh gravel, the sound of the rocks sliding together sent chills up her back. The image of bones being ground together rose in her mind, and she shivered. She eased the truck behind Bobby's car, a faded green hatchback AMC Gremlin. A rusty bumper with a dent on the left-hand side – a gift from Derrick McGowan, a regular at The Dive – and the purple and gold tassel hanging from the rearview mirror.

It was Bobby's car. Bobby, who she hadn't seen in almost a week. Her cook had been missing this entire time, and his car . . . was here. Fear gripped her, causing her stomach to clench, and she looked around. No one knew she was here. Was there anything keeping her from disappearing, like Bobby, if someone from inside saw her? Sonja stomped on the accelerator, spinning the tires and throwing a rooster tail of gravel as she spun the truck around. A few rocks bounced off the hood of Bobby's car as she rushed out of the parking lot, still accelerating.

A man shape stood at the window, watching the truck swerve across the parking lot. As he watched, the ruts and displaced rocks from Sonja's exit trembled and pulled together, making a sound not unlike someone driving across them: grinding, popping, and sliding. The ruts filled in, and by the time Lyles turned away from the window, the parking lot was smooth once more.

CHAPTER 25

BERT WAS SQUINTING at his hand of three card poker when Sonja came roaring into the driveway, the truck fishtailing, spinning gravel and throwing dust. Bert jerked upright, sending the cards flying. I jumped as well, but kept my cards in my hands. We could see her in the driver's seat, her hair windblown and her eyes wide over the steering wheel. The seat belt caught her as she tried to get out, trapping her in the truck. I heard her grunt of frustration as she finally pried herself loose. Her face was pale under her fading summer tan as she walked toward us.

"Goda'mightydamn, woman!" Bert said, looking around for his cards.

"I knew it," she spat, stalking up to me, then swerving to pass by me as she stomped down the length of the porch. "I found it, I know I did, I knew it, but you wouldn't believe me." She raked us with her eyes, and I almost recoiled.

"What did you find?" I managed to ask. I didn't know if I should approach her, run from her, or just duck and cover.

"Bobby's car," she said, "Is outside . . . that place!"

"Who's Bobby?" I asked, at the time Bert said, "Are you sure?"

I tried to pull the name out of my memory; maybe from the first day? I couldn't, but Bert saved me.

"He's the cook," he said to me.

"Yes." Sonja seemed to settle down at Bert's acceptance. "His car is there. I saw it. I drove right up to it. And the place just stared at me." She took in a hitching breath, and I found her hand, giving it a squeeze. She squeezed me back briefly and stepped back, seeming calmer.

"I know it's Ricochet," she said, taking a seat in a rocking chair. "It has to be. Why else would his car be there? The town, the anger. It's all connected."

"Maybe he was drawn in by them," I said.

"Don't you know where he lives?" Bert reminded her. "Maybe we should go by there."

"He has roommates." Sonja said.

"Wait, wait," I said. "Shouldn't we tell Otis? Or have him do this?"

"Naw," Bert snorted. "He's too busy being an asshole."

"Could it be the drugs?" Sonja asked Bert. The conversation was going back and forth in front of me, and I was bouncing off the replies like a tennis ball on concrete.

"Not and be gone a week," Bert said.

"I think we should —" I said, but Bert continued.

"And if it was a drunk, hell, he'd have slept it off by now. He ain't never been one to lay out this long."

"I know where he lives," Sonja said.

I sighed. I didn't see any way to push her off of her course, so I pulled out my keys. "I'll drive."

We climbed into my car, Sonja beside me and Bert in back. We were delayed a few moments while Sonja insisted Bert ride up front, but chivalry prevailed. We drove through town and Sonja craned her neck as we passed empty parking spot after empty parking spot.

"Today's Monday, right?" she asked. "It looks like it's Sunday," she said.

"Lord's Supper Sund'y," Bert added from the back. "And they know the preacher ain't serving grape juice."

Heaven help me, but I grabbed a pen and paper, earning a side eyed glance from Sonja that was eerily like the one I'd received from Cook.

We turned west out of downtown, the afternoon sun throwing short shadows in front of us. We found the rougher side of town, bouncing across uneven railroad tracks. The houses crept closer together, yards filled with the scrum of hard living; unmown grass, junked cars, and crowded front porches. Sonja pointed to a white frame house, almost shrouded by overgrown privet and a dying pecan tree. Shells and nuts crunched under the tires as we pulled into the driveway where a truck sat.

"That belongs to Chris. He got on with the lumber mill after I let him go," Sonja said as I turned off the car. We opened the doors, climbing out, and walked up the overgrown walkway. The porch steps creaked as we stepped on them, and a gust of wind stirred the leaves scattered on the porch. Bert squinted down at our feet.

"Ain't nobody been on this porch," he said. "Least not since the leaves fell."

There was a pretty good number of thin, brown leaves on the front porch. It wasn't covered, but I could tell what he meant. The gust of wind also caught the milky storm door, pushing it open, and it banged back against the frame when the wind died. Sonja reached out and caught it, but only raised her fist halfway to knock.

"It's open," she said. Sure enough, the front door was cracked a few inches, revealing a dark interior. Before I could stop her she pushed it open, calling,

"Chris? Mark? Bobby? It's Sonja. Is anyone home?" She stepped into the doorway and jumped back when something thumped and rolled. I caught her, but she shrugged me off and felt inside the house for a light switch. Finding it with a click she stepped inside, calling "Hello? Anyone home?"

Bert and I followed her, discovering the source of the noise. Prepared food boxes and cans were piled beside the front door, mounded around two distinct clear spots. I followed her as she went deeper into the house.

"Someone packed up some food," I realized aloud.

I moved out of Bert's way as he said, "There's been a tusslin' in here."

I looked around the room and saw he was right. A lamp and table were knocked over, and debris on the floor had been moved around. Sonja looked in the direction of a kitchen to the right and headed left to where I assumed the bedrooms were. I followed her, looking into a bathroom while she poked her head first into the bedroom to the right then to the left.

"Someone took a shower," I said, indicating the pile of clothes beside the toilet. They were filthy, mounded up as if someone dropped them indifferently to the floor.

Sonja looked around me, and said, "That's Bobby's t-shirt. I recognize it. He was wearing it the last night I saw him."

"What was he doing to get so dirty?" I asked, but no one answered.

"No one's in the kitchen," Bert called out. "Every damn bit of food's been taken out. Must be by the door." We walked into the kitchen to find every cabinet open. The ones around the refrigerator—which I assumed had held food—were empty. The others held a mixture of mismatched plates and cups. We retreated into the living room and stood there, at a loss of what to do.

"Now do we go to Otis?" I said.

"We may have to," Bert said, and Sonja nodded unhappily.

"Look, Otis can help us. I know he jumped my shit the last time we talked, but look at the evidence. *Something* happened here. *Something's* happening in town. Maybe we can help him with it," I said.

Sonja nodded, unconvinced, and we walked outside, pulling the door shut behind us. The drive back through town was mostly silent, and I drove very slowly through town because no other cars came up behind us. Downtown was as deserted as before, with most of the shops shuttered. One car passed us, the sun reflecting over the windshield, but we saw the driver hunched over the wheel, staring at us, as we passed.

The rest of the drive was uneventful. We climbed out of the car and went inside, where Cook met us, brandishing a spoon at Sonja.

"I hope you don't mind having leftovers tonight," she said. "Nary a soul came down for breakfast this morning. A dozen eggs I cooked! Three cups of grits!" She waved the spoon in frustration. "Just so you know. I'm gonna fix a breakfast casserole tonight, and if anyone says a word, I'll give them this." She waved the spoon in the air for emphasis and marched back into the kitchen.

"I'll call Otis, have him meet us at The Dive," Sonja said, and went back to her office. I trailed after her, then reached out and caught her hand. We stopped in the doorway of her office, me holding her hand, her looking at me with a pained expression. I slipped my arm around her and held her. She didn't resist. "Maybe I should go to Nashville with you instead," she mumbled.

My heart jumped. I couldn't imagine Sonja anywhere but here, but I'd take her anywhere. "It's too soon for that," I said to her hair. "Otis will help us. He's got to see what's going on."

She pulled away from me. Sitting at her desk, she pulled out her cell phone. After dialing she leaned back, closing her eyes. "Yes, I'd . . ." she started, then frowned. I could hear a few clicks come from her phone. It rang again, and she leaned back.

"Otis, this is . . ." a garble of words came out, and she rubbed her head. "Can you meet me out at The Dive?"

I couldn't make out the short response.

"No, it's not another fight. I need . . . She did what?" She paused. "Otis, please." She paused again. "It's my people, Otis. I'm worried about them. Bobby's been missing . . . his house . . . okay, thank you."

She hung up. "Myrtle Cumberland attacked one of her neighbors this morning. He'll come once the doctor gives him an update.

"How is she?" I asked.

"Not for her; she's fine. Mr. Washington is the one in the hospital."

"She put him in the hospital? Is 'Myrtle' a biker chick's name?" I joked, but I had a feeling it was in self-defense.

"No, she's about five foot tall, with arthritis in her hips, and walks with a cane."

We looked across the desk at each other, each absorbing the wrongness of her statement and our situation.

"He'll try to get out there in a little bit. He didn't sound like himself," she finally said.

"If I hadn't met him before all of this, I wouldn't believe you. But I do." I reached across the desk and took her hand. "Let's go so we don't miss him."

Bert declined to go with us; I could tell all the excitement and movement was getting to him. I drove Sonja's truck, and we held hands. I'd written and sung about driving a pickup truck holding a beautiful girl's hand, and the feeling was everything I'd made it out to be. I was smiling to myself when Sonja said,

"What are you grinning about?"

I told her, and she gave a tired smile. But she didn't let go of my hand.

We pulled into The Dive. Even though it was midmorning, the parking lot was deserted. Sonja groaned.

"Dammit, Donald," she said.

"Was he supposed to open?"

She nodded. "He's the last person who would lay out. Dammit," she said, smacking the dash board of the truck. We climbed out, and she unlocked the front door. The bar was shrouded in shadows, a few spaced neon lights providing illumination as Sonja crossed to the wall switches. The restaurant lit up, looking as lonely as any I'd seen in my years on the circuit. There's something pitiful about an empty business, in particular one designed to serve people temporary happiness.

"What time is Otis coming?" I asked, starting to unstack the chairs turned upside down on tabletops. My years on the circuit weren't all spent performing.

"Later is all he said."

"How are we going to present it?"

"I'm not sure. Tell him about Bobby's car, the mess we found at his house, I guess," she said. She set a tray of salt and pepper shakers on the bar and went into the kitchen. In the silence, I heard the whoosh of gas. "How are you at cooking?" she called from the kitchen.

"Not bad. I won't be fast," I called back. I'd spent times on both sides of the house.

"That's fine. I —" The door opened, letting in a bar of light broken by Otis' outline.

"Don't mind," I said. "Otis," I nodded to him. He ignored me and went to the bar.

"What do you need, Sonja?" he said.

Sonja came out of the kitchen, carrying a tray of glasses. "I need to talk to you about Bobby. I found –"

"Sonja, I told you last time, I can't be looking for another drifter," Otis said.

I drifted myself, coming up to the bar beside him. He jumped a little when I leaned against the bar; I guess he didn't hear my approach.

"Now Bobby's a drifter?" she said. "He's been in town for years."

"You know what I mean. He drifts job to job, making and selling his dope. You knew he was trouble when you hired him," Otis replied.

"So just because he does a little dope, he's not worth finding?" I asked. I know I shouldn't have, but Otis' attitude was wearing thin.

"You can shut it or shit it, Nashville," he said, stepping closer to me.

"Otis, listen to me. I found his car outside that place. Ricochet. He's been there. Can you at least talk to them? Everything has changed since they got here," Sonja said.

"Are you still worried about that?" He looked around the empty restaurant. "I can see why."

"No, Donald didn't come in. Now I'm worried about him." Otis started to speak, but Sonja didn't miss a beat. "I'm worried because I've got two employees missing, half the town is different or gone, and you don't seem to give a damn!"

"I give plenty a damn!" Otis roared. "I've worked two days straight because my guys ain't right! I give a damn because even my head ain't right!"

I reached out to touch his shoulder, and he spun around at my touch. He grabbed my wrist, catching it in some kind of cop hold, and twisted. "And you! This all started when you showed up! By God, if I'da known, I'da run your ass right outta town!" He twisted my wrist, causing my arm to lock. I went up on my tip toes to relieve the pressure, and I didn't see him pull his baton from his utility belt.

"Otis, no!" Sonja screamed, coming around the bar.

I felt a massive blow to my kidney, and I forgot about the pain in my arm. I tried to fall, but his kung-fu wrist hold kept me upright. I barely saw Sonja trying to pull him off of me, and he let go of me to shove her away. We hit the tray on the bar and I heard the salt and pepper shakers bounce to the floor.

"That's enough," he rasped, pointing the baton at her. "I've got him for assaulting an officer, and you'll go too if you don't back off. I'm gonna question him about all this stuff going on while I'm at it." He straddled me, pulling my hands behind my back and efficiently cuffing me. I didn't resist. I'd seen plenty of bar arrests, and most injuries came after the cops showed up and the participants resisted.

"Sonja, it's okay," I said.

"But you didn't do anything!" she said.

"I know," I said at the same time Otis said, "We'll see about that."

Otis pulled me up, reawakening the pain in my side and arm. I walked so he wouldn't drag me, and the sunlight was painful when it hit my eyes. The last thing I remembered was Otis grabbing my collar as he opened the door to his cruiser.

"You got this coming out of the store, Sunny Jim," Otis said, and my forehead caught the top part of the cruiser's door. Everything thing went red, then faded to black, the drumbeat of a Rolling Stones songs drifting down with me.

Sonja looked at the remains of Otis and Adam's struggle; even though Adam hadn't put up much of a fight, several stools had been displaced, and the tray holding salt and pepper shakers had been flipped off the bar to spin and scatter across the floor. She trembled, trying to control the emotions that wanted to spiral out of control. Tears welled up in her eyes, but she willed them to stop. Life, especially country life, was hard at times; crops failed, banks failed, lives were lost. Living as she did, surviving the things she survived, had given her strength that she now called upon.

Slowly, she controlled her breathing. Second was the hitch in her throat. The tears were still gathered in her eyes, and she wiped them away. They didn't shame her; her father had taught her there was a time to cry, and a time to dry your tears and move on. Grabbing a broom, she swept up the spilled salt and pepper, tossing a pinch over her left shoulder. One salt shaker had shattered, but the others only had a few scuffs. She stacked them back on the tray as her mind worked through her next steps.

The stools were back into place, and Sonja looked at her work. Despite the hour, no one had come in, employees or customers. If what she'd seen in town was any indication, one more closed business day wouldn't matter.

CHAPTER 26

ELISE ELBOWED HER HUSBAND. Thirty years of snoring she could deal with, but tonight? Louder than ever.

He snorted once and said, "Bitch, what?" and went back to sleep. A minute later, he snorted again, and the sound of a rasping file filled the bedroom. Elise threw off the covers, thinking of the knife set her grandson had just sold her.

Myrtle Cumberland hitched her housecoat around her against the crisp morning. Walking to the mailbox was a chore, but the dag-burned mailman wouldn't bring it to her door. Cussed hard headed man, not wanting to take the extra fifteen steps it took to get from the street. He'd rather make an old lady walk. She grabbed her cane out of habit, even though her hips weren't hurting near as bad as they'd had last week. The front door groaned as it had since Edward had passed, and she nudged it wider with a practiced elbow.

In fact, if it weren't for the nasty dreams, she was feeling as fine as she had in years. If only that dammed mailman would . . . She heard a yip from down the street and saw that Washington man walking his little shin-grabber. The mutt was straining at the leash, looking at her, and the high-pitched yips were drilling into her head. She shook her cane at them and opened the mailbox. Nothing. Anger surged through her; had the mailman taken it? Did he have her security check? Bastard. She shut the mailbox with a clang, then spotted the dog shit on her lawn. She looked up, her anger compounding. The dog was still barking at her, and Mr. Washington was staring at her from the other side of the Cleburne's mailbox.

"Your dog shit in my yard," she screeched, and walked down the street. The cane was in front of her, waving, and she didn't hear what Mr. Washington said, but didn't need to. The look on his face was enough.

Brandishing the cane in front of her, Myrtle ran for the first time in a decade.

Jim Mitchell sat on his porch, trying to enjoy the morning sunshine. The coffee was hot, the air cool, and he knew he should be thankful for the blessings he had.

Splat.

He cocked his head at the sound. The morning was perfect; why would a tiny sound disturb it? He heard the caw of a bird, and knew it fit the morning just right. But the sound annoyed him.

Splat.

It sounded like it was coming from his driveway. He stood, the hunting and gun magazines falling to the floorboards. Nothing was in the front yard; his grey pickup truck sat in the driveway, and the bird screeched again. His eye caught the motion out of the corner of his vision.

Splat.

Bird shit. A murder of damn crows was sitting on the limb overhanging his truck. Coming from his neighbor's yard, the branch offered a perfect perch for birds to shit on his truck. He'd asked Hiller, his neighbor, to cut down the limb a few times over the last dozen years. And now, for the thousandth time, crows were using it to shit on the roof of his truck. Jim growled deep in his throat and grabbed the axe he'd been using the day before to trim some of his own trees in the back yard. He walked to his truck, not noticing the pecan shells that cut the bottoms of his feet. The birds took wing, and the escape of his truck's tormenters further enraged him. Dropping the tailgate with a bang, he climbed up, lugging the axe behind him.

I'll take care of the branch once and for all, he thought. The first cut skipped across the branch, almost pulling him off balance, but the second bit deep with a solid thunk. The third cut deeper, and his fourth stroke broke off the wedge started by the previous two cuts.

"Hey!" bellowed across the yard as Hiller came out. "The hell you doing to my tree?" A porch door slammed, but Jim took another swing. The axe bit so well, cleaving into the wood. He was lucky it was freshly sharpened.

Malcolm woke up that morning, thinking about the pump part he'd sent out to the Turner place earlier in the week. Damn shame for the woman to lose her water supply like that; like her, Malcolm's farm was on a bored well system, drilled deep to reach the aquifer as a hedge against the Georgia summers. As it was, she was a damn handy woman. Probably hard-wired the old part until she could get the new part, so her boarders should have done okay. Stirring his coffee, he thought about the day. Some sense was telling him to close the store today; for some reason, it seemed everybody downtown was out, or closed down for the last few days. He didn't understand it; everybody needed a break from time to time, but all at once? He shook his head.

He eased the cork from the bottle of bourbon, adding a splash to his coffee mug. Might as well if he wasn't going in. He could spend the day checking on his new barn; it'd been a week or so since he'd stuck his nose into it. Greg and a couple of boys from Sonja's got the water hooked up last week.

Jep came through the kitchen, his hair tousled. "Daddy, why didn't you wake me up?"

"Son, you're twenty-three. Oughta not have to wake you up."

Jep grunted, pulling down a mug for himself. "Why ain'tcha at the store?" he asked, his back to his father.

"Think I'm going to check out the barn. . . . Don't think we'll open today."

Jep clattered the spoon against the lip of the cup. "Why not?" His father had kept the hardware store open through storms and sickness.

"Just think I'll stick close to home today. Ain't had much business." Irritation crept into his father's voice.

Pounding footsteps came from the front of the house. "Daddy!" Mills called before he caught sight of his father and brother in the kitchen. "That damn Greg took out Jim with a hammer! You need to get down to the barn!" Mills' face was covered with a spray of dark red, and Malcolm's stomach dropped.

The new barn was located on the corner of their property that bordered Highway 17, which ran into town a few miles down the road. Malcolm had always loved seeing barns perched along highways, and he'd been eying the spot for years. After buying the Holloway property and expanding his soybean crop, he'd needed a place to store his equipment. He'd known Cliff for years, and Cliff had pulled together the crew that was working on the barn. Construction workers had always been a rough-and-tumble bunch, and this one was no different. But until the last week or so, the group seemed to get along and they had made remarkable progress on the barn.

All this bounced through Malcolm's mind as he and Mills bounced along the field road that led to the new barn.

"I was out there making sure the framing was ready for the inspection. They were supposed to have the cupola finished for ventilation so it would pass. So I wanted to help Cliff if I could. He was pissed at something . . . I've never seen him that ill. Jim got here late, and he and Greg were snapping at each other. Worse than two biddies, they were, and I could see Cliff getting madder and madder at them." In the distance, a siren wailed. "Finally, Cliff told Jim just to shut up or handle it. I guess Jim thought he meant handle Greg, and they started rolling around fighting. It wasn't much until Greg rolled onto a hammer one of them dropped. Greg picked it up, and caught Jim right here," Mills pointed to his cheek. "It came up, caught in the claw, and sprayed me. I was trying to get in and separate them, but Jim just dropped. As soon as Cliff saw the blood, he went after Greg." An ambulance wailed its way past the barn, slowing to make the turn. "I backed the hell up, called sheriff and ambulance, and came on up to the house." He looked at his father as their truck pulled up near the ambulance. "Why would they do that? They always seemed to get on good." Otis' patrol car turned in as the paramedics ran to the bodies lying in front of the barn. They climbed out of the truck and approached the medics, who were standing there staring at the carnage. Jim was on his back, his face caved in on one side, and another body was a dozen feet away.

"Jesus, who's that?" one of the paramedics asked. The man's head and shoulders were a bloody, pulped mess.

"Greg or Cliff," Malcolm said. "Which one, son?" he asked Mills.

"Greg," he replied, in a daze. "Cliff was wearing a red shirt."

"Christ Almighty," Otis said as he walked up. "Well, why aren't you doing something?" he said to the paramedics. Malcolm exchanged a surprised glance with Robert, the veteran paramedic.

"Otis, there isn't much to do except call the coroner," Robert said. He leaned down and picked up the medical bag at his feet. "I can check them if you want, but . . . they're done for."

"Well, shit," Otis said.

"You want me to call the coroner?" Malcolm asked.

Otis shook his head. "No, don't bother. Myrtle Cumberland went after Mike Washington, and Wash has a bad heart, and . . ."

"*Myrtle?*" Malcolm asked. Robert nodded, and Malcolm realized he'd already known. "Hell, I saw her, just . . . just . . ." Malcolm paused. "Went after him, you said?"

Otis nodded. "Over dog shit, or something. At least that's what Elaine said. She saw the entire thing. Said Myrtle went after him with her cane." The radio at his side came to life, and Otis' shoulders slumped. "What now?" he muttered as he pulled it off his belt and turned to his patrol car.

"Daddy, what . . ." Mills started to ask.

"I have no idea, son, no idea," was all Malcolm could think to say.

The feed bill gripped in his hand, Joe Kramer started his combine. Half the damn seeds hadn't even germinated, and it wasn't that far into town.

Sonja pulled up to the front porch, not driving around to the back to her usual parking spot. Bert wasn't on the rocker, but Woody was snoozing in the sunlight. The thump of her truck door caused him to open one eye, but he closed it back. From the porch railing, the house cat did the same thing. Sonja felt laughter bubble up, but she pushed it back down. It had a slightly hysterical feeling to it; if she laughed now, she might not stop until she was crying, and now wasn't the time to give in to either emotion. The dining room was empty as well, and she found Bert and Cook clustered in the kitchen, listening to the police scanner. Bert caught sight of her, waving her in.

"Damn town's going crazy," he said.

"I know." In a few short sentences, she told them what happened at The Dive.

He nodded. "Jail's probably the safest place for him. Otis is getting calls in from all over town. People going after neighbors, Greg's done hit Jim with a hammer, and Malcom and his boys had to call in help to get them separated. It sounds like everyone's lost their mind."

Cook nodded beside him. "I'm going to get my shotgun," she announced. "Any of you come after me, I'll set you down."

"Cook, no. It's not happening here," Sonja argued.

"I don't care. We ain't but two miles from the town. I was jus' talking to Bert about coming to get you."

Bert nodded, and said, "Sonja, it might be best to be prepared. What if all the crazy people get together?"

Sonja shivered. "Who's here?" she asked.

"Us three and Woody. Jim and them went off to work on Malcom's barn, but I heard them arguing before they got into his truck. I ain't seen Cliff."

"Get Woody inside. Cook, you lock all the doors. We'll figure out what to do. We can't leave Adam in town."

"Sonja, that's the best place for him!" Bert said, standing up. Cook waddled out of the kitchen.

"Where do you think they're taking the crazy people?" Sonja asked.

Bobby stood in the darkness of the cave, watching the town below him. Smoke was billowing from one end of town, but the fire department hadn't come out of the station house on Highway 520. Cars were stacked haphazardly along the streets radiating from downtown, a swath of them showing ripped and buckled metal from the blades of Joe Kramer's combine. Bobby had cackled when he saw the machine turn up the main street. A part of him cringed when he saw people fall under the blades; they were people he'd grown up with, but the sprays of blood delighted the Thing-in-the-Rock and it surged in his mind, obliterating the small twinge of consciousness. Mark's essence-filled body had done its job at the water source; the army was growing as disorder multiplied. Inside his head, Bobby could feel pinpoints of rage and lust as the others in town were consumed and turned loose by The-Thing-in-the-Rock.

Mayhem echoed in Bobby's head and he giggled. *Pings* and *dings* came from below, and Bobby thought he could feel the tools striking deep within the rock. They were so close to The-Thing-in-the-Rock; a few more hours, a day at the most, and it could ooze from below. No more small amounts; no more creeping though dead ends and cracks in the rock. In his mind's eye, Bobby could see The-Thing-in-the-Rock surging from its prison, filling the cave, and spilling out down the bluff and into the river. Everything would run, everything would die, and then they would head to old Cauthon place. Embarrassment and shame cut through his joy, and Bobby became angry. Very angry.

"We need to get there before dark," Sonja insisted. As the hours passed, news had gotten worse. Smoke billowed from the south of town, but Sonja hadn't heard the fire station respond.

"We need to sit right here," Cook declared, clutching her shotgun. "They seem to be content staying in town. Ain't anyone bothered none of us outside of town, and this is where I aim to stay."

"She's right, Sonja," Bert said. "Adam is well enough."

"If we can stop Ricochet, we can stop this! This is our town! Not his! Whatever he is!"

"Sonja . . ." Bert said, feeling helpless. They'd argued the afternoon away.

"I'm going. The only question is if one of you will go with me," she said.

Cook and Bert shared a glance. "I ain't going nowhere," Cook said. "Cook's staying holed up."

"Then I'm going," Sonja said, turning for the door.

"Damn woman," Bert said, getting up and hurrying after her.

I blinked twice, hearing an echoing conversation in the hallway. Something was holding my eye shut. When I rubbed it, two things happened; a blast of pain cleared away the cobwebs in my head and something dark flaked away, allowing my eye to open. I sat up as things came back. Otis. The Dive. Being run face-first into the patrol car door. I was in a jail cell. A little old woman sat across from me on the other bunk, and I blinked at her. Across the walkway, several men were in the opposite cell, and I looked again and recognized Cliff. He and another man were sitting on the beds and two others were curled up on the floor, asleep.

"What the hell?" I asked aloud, and the woman bared her teeth at me. The man beside Cliff actually growled and lunged across his cell at me, stopped by the bars. I didn't recognize him, but Cliff reached out. Grabbing him by the shoulder, Cliff pulled him back, growling as well, and they began to fight. They staggered around the cell, each trying to get a grip on the other.

Cliff forced him away and whacked the guy's head against the concrete floor. Going limp, Cliff rode him down to the floor, squeezing at his neck.

I watched, fascinated with dread as the man's face went from red to blue. He weakly tried to throw Cliff off of him, and even after his hands dropped to the floor, Cliff kept a strong grip on him.

"Hey," I yelled. "Cliff, what are you doing?"

Cliff was gripping him so hard his knuckles and fingers were white with the strain. I was staring at his fingers when the nails turned black, like bruises gathering. I shook my head as the black stuff dripped from Cliff's fingers and soaked into the man's neck.

As the man in Cliff cell's coughed a final time, something moved behind me and I remembered the woman who shared my cell. She was old, in what looked like a paint-spattered night dress with a robe over it. Her hair was a wild halo over her head, and I thought the splashes of red probably weren't paint. I started to say something, but nothing came out. She showed me her teeth, snarling, and I saw her thin legs tense, and I got my hands up as she leapt across the cell at me. I caught her, grabbing her by the upper arms, and spun her around. I banged painfully against the bars as she pushed me back. I saw her hands, twisted like claws, and I remembered the black stuff. I thought a bite would be as bad as her getting her hands around my neck. I didn't think I would have to be dead for it to infect me, if that's what was changing everyone around me. She snapped at my forearms and went crashing into the wall. I heard something pop inside her, and she slumped, whimpering as she hit the floor. I moved as far from her as I could as she laid in a pitiful puddle on the floor. She slowly turned her broken body toward me and reached out.

"Don't make me do this," I said to her, but the words had no impact. She was crawling toward me, her hips and legs distorted, not responding to commands from her diseased brain. "Please," I asked again. When she didn't stop, I swallowed the bitter fluid that was rising in my throat, and I kicked her as hard as I could under her chin. Even though I tried not to look, I heard the snap and crunch of delicate bones, and I couldn't control my reaction. I spewed vomit and bile, stumbling to the toilet. I heard a few scratches from the misshapen robe on the floor, and I smelled her bowels release.

When I looked up, ignoring what I'd done, I saw Cliff staring at me from across the hall. He looked from me to the lady on the floor.

"Don't look at me like that. You saw —" Cliff's head snapped to his left as we both heard the sound of a lock clang.

"Adam! Adam!" I heard a Sonja's voice, getting closer as she ran down the hallway. She came running in, a set of keys in one hand and a wooden baseball bat in the other. Bert came puffing behind her.

"Damn woman," he said, and I got the sense he'd said it a dozen times.

"Stay away from that side!" I warned as Cliff lunged for her. He caught the edge of the plaid coat she was wearing, and she turned smartly with the bat, bringing it down on his forearm. I heard the bone pop, and he howled and pulled his hand inside the bars.

"I saw him kill. I saw him kill that guy," I said, pointing. "And there's something in them, something black." I saw Bert look behind me, and Sonja unlocked the cell door.

"Jesus Christ, that's Missus Cumberland," Bert said.

"I didn't mean to," I babbled, and Sonja grabbed my arm and pulled me out of the cell. She dragged me down the hallway to a back door while Bert pulled the cell door shut. She hit the door with her shoulder, and it popped open into the twilight. I'm not ashamed to say I was babbling questions at her as Bert hurried behind us. We exited the police station into the impound lot, but Sonja led us to the back gate.

"They order food, and this is where we bring it," she said as a quick explanation. She found the right key, opened it, and looked both ways before she ran to her truck she had left parked on the street. My head was clear by then, and I helped Bert in, his face ashen and perspiring.

"You okay?" I asked.

He nodded.

"Get in," Sonja hissed as she started the truck. I climbed in after her, and she put it into gear.

"Where is Otis? What did you do?" I asked.

"Otis is dead," she said shortly. I looked to Bert, who nodded.

"How? Why?" I asked, and Sonja misunderstood me. She told me about going to The Dive, making up a fake order, and bringing it to the police station. When the deputy reached for it, she unleashed the bat, knocking him out and getting the keys.

"What if there'd been more than one?" I demanded. She shrugged.

"What's happening in town?" I asked, and she pointed. We were looking downtown, along West Riverside, and I could see a crowd milling in the distance, maybe a half mile away. Flames were coming from a few buildings, but I didn't see any red lights or firefighting equipment.

"What's going on?" I asked, as she drove away from downtown, taking a route that avoid the milling crowd.

"We're going to end this," she said, her eyes fixed on the road.

CHAPTER 27

SONJA BANDAGED THE CUT over my eye at her boarding house. She was grim, her face dirty, her shirt torn, but she was beautiful. I put my hands on her hips as she doctored me. Just touching her was reassuring.

"Are we taking the fight to them?" I asked her quietly.

She nodded as she placed the bandage over my eyebrow.

"Will we be able to stop them?" I asked.

"I don't know."

"But it's better to try and fail," I quipped at her, but she didn't smile.

"Exactly."

She stepped away from me, and I carefully probed the wound. In addition to a nice-sized egg, my skin was split. It likely should have had stitches, but we weren't venturing back into town.

"Will you go with me?" she asked, staring into the near darkness. I didn't think a night assault would be the best time to attack Ricochet, but trying to talk her out of it would be foolish. "You don't have to. This isn't your town."

"But it may be. And I'm not letting you do it alone," I said.

"Let's go, then," she said, and we walked out of the office.

"He's going," she said. I stopped in my tracks, poised between the office and the kitchen. Bert nodded glumly.

"Did you doubt it?" I asked, offended.

Cook snorted. If she'd had a braid in her hair, she would have tugged it. "At least I thought you had more sense," she said.

Bert didn't look like he felt well, so I asked, "Are you okay?"

He nodded at me, and Sonja picked up her bat and slung a shotgun over her shoulder. A small armory was laid out on the table. Several pistols, some long guns, and what looked like a bundle of dynamite.

"Will guns even work?" I asked, mostly to myself.

"We'll know shortly," she said.

Bert picked up another shotgun, and I picked up a handgun and stuck the dynamite in my back pocket. I suspected it was the building itself, not the people inside it.

Cook snorted to herself. Sonja shot her a glance, and we walked to the door.

"I think we just need to bum-rush them," I said. "Run in, and start shooting."

"Sounds like a plan," Bert said beside me.

Sonja's hand came off the gearshift and landed softly on my knee. "Adam, I'm sorry," she said. "I wanted . . . something more. But thank you for being here."

I covered her hand with mine. "I think we'll be okay. For some crazy reason, I believe we'll see the sunrise."

When Sonja hit Ricochet's driveway, she accelerated. Every light was on inside, and the building glowed. The red and blue neon from the sign flashed, bathing the parking lot and parts of the building in irregular colors. Sonja pulled up to the steps and slammed on the brakes. The gravel slid under us, making a horrible scraping noise, and she was out of the door, pulling her gun out of the truck behind her. The sun was a glow on the horizon, lighting the clouds and the smoke from town. Bert opened the door and moved out of my way, and I hurried around him, allowing him to bring up the rear guard. I wasn't surprised to hear him praying under his breath.

By the time I made it around the truck, Sonja was already up the front steps. As I cleared the steps in two jumps, she was shouldering open the door. I followed her in, seeing her pushing her way across the dance floor. Faces turned toward us, O's of surprise forming on their mouths. My eyes realized there were no townspeople inside, but I didn't connect that with the lack of cars.

She was bringing the gun up, aiming for Lyles behind the bar. A lady in a sparkly dress was sitting elegantly by the bar, and I had a millisecond to think how beautiful she was. Achingly beautiful. I thought I heard Bert rack a shell into his gun, and Lyles was looking right at us.

The beautiful lady at the bar started to shimmer and shaped into a pillar of light. There was no other way to describe it; she rippled, and out of the ripple came pure light: white and almost blinding. A glare came from beside me as someone else turned. Sonja was three-quarters of the way across the dance floor and had the butt of her gun to her shoulder. Before she could bring it level, Lyles raised his hand.

The hubbub of conversation hadn't stopped, and the music was still playing. My mind identified it as a Cat Stevens song, one of the first I'd learned. Broken Morning? Maybe the very first. No, it was 'Morning has Broken'. My mind latched onto the fact as Lyles raised both hands, one toward Sonja, one toward the pillar of light.

"Stop."

He said the word faintly, but everything froze, Sonja and myself included. The music cut off, the conversation ceased, and I could no longer move. Something wrapped me in cotton, gently, but the air around me was hard as rock. My body would no longer respond, and I had one foot in the air. Sonja had both feet on the floor, and her finger inside the trigger guard.

"Mildred, please." Lyles said, just as softly. Beside him, the pillar of light dimmed, resolving itself into the lady again. This time, she was standing beside the bar rather than sitting.

"I declare, Lyles, we simply must leave. You have not chosen well this time."

Lyles took a step and appeared between Sonja and me. He was behind the bar, then he was between us, all in the blink of an eye. He looked the same, but his eyes had a haunted cast.

"Sense them, Mildred. They are clean. Just . . . misguided."

"What are you doing to our town?" Sonja asked. I cleared my throat and discovered I could also speak. Sonja was struggling against whatever held us.

"Child, I am doing nothing. What is happening to your town has nothing to do with me or mine."

The people scattered among the dance floor drifted to the jukebox, leaving Mildred, Lyles, Sonja, and me. I assumed Bert was frozen behind us as well.

"Then how do you explain what is happening? It started when you showed up," I said.

Lyles sighed. "Do you not remember your visit here?"

We both shook our heads.

Lyles reached out and took the gun from Sonja. It came easily from her hands, and Mildred pulled the pistol from the small of Sonja's back. They approached me, doing the same, and I heard them behind me with Bert. Lyles motioned, and a table slid toward us, trailed by a few chairs. The crowd clustered by the jukebox was silent, watching us.

"Please, be seated," he said, and I found I could move.

Sonja sagged, getting ready to fall, and I caught her. "How could you do this?" she asked them.

"I am what I am, and you are what you are." Lyles replied.

Bert sat down beside me, and Sonja moved from my embrace to the chair. Lyles motioned to Mildred, and she brought drinks to us.

"I don't want anything," Sonja said petulantly. "I want you to leave. I want my town back to normal. Is that too much to ask?"

Lyles studied us. "In all of my travels, I've never quite seen anything like humanity. You occupy such a small corner of existence – much smaller than you can imagine – but you produce *so much energy*. I term this energy a 'ricochet.' I'll not bore you with the details, but let me say it like this: No other creatures, in this universe," he moved his hands in a very human gesture, indicating the room around him. "Or on this plane, can produce what you do. You offer unspeakable cruelty and unmatched compassion in one package. And you do so unintentionally. I have always found your emotions and your memories fascinating. I am able to store, for lack of a better word, this energy." A glass appeared in his hand, rotating, flipping from axis to axis.

"You trap us?" Sonja asked, her face pale.

Lyles shook his head. "Humans always think that, at first. But I offer my Regulars a chance to dance, to live, forever. They understand what I am."

"What are you?" I asked.

"I am what I am," he said simply.

"If it's not you that's causing what happening in town, then what is?" Bert asked.

"I don't know for certain," Lyles admitted. "But I have an idea." He motioned to the crowd, and they moved aside, bringing someone forward. Sonja gasped when she saw who it was.

"Tom!"

I didn't remember him very well because I'd only seen him once.

"There was another one with him. He did much the same as you – tried to challenge me – and did not find much success," Lyles said.

The man they brought forward was filthy, his clothes torn and dirty. His eyes were vacant, staring into the distance. Sonja reached for him, but her hand stopped in midair.

"You cannot touch him. He is unclean," Lyles said. Tom's hand came up, his fingers extended. The glass from Lyle's hand floated toward him and positioned itself under his fingertips. Tom's hand flattened, as if under pressure, and . . . something pushed itself out from under his fingernails to drip in the glass. Caught in the glass, it trembled, moving of its own accord. A few drops fell toward the floor, but disappeared in tiny flashes of light before they hit the floor. The glass spun and settled on the table.

"That's what I saw." I explained what I'd seen Cliff do to the guy in the jail cell, and how the old lady reacted to me.

"Can we save him?" Sonja asked.

Lyles shook his head. "He is unclean. I wish there were more I could do, but the poison is throughout his body."

"Is it a poison, or something else?" I asked. "It almost seems . . . alive."

As we watched, the drops rolled around in the glass, seeking to escape. Lyles grimaced and placed his hand over the top of the glass, and the black liquid disappeared in a tiny puff of light.

"When they first challenged me, I thought it was just a poison. But now . . . it's like an infection. I think it is alive, in a sense."

"Who challenged you?" Sonja asked.

Lyles explained what happened, and Sonja gasped.

"Bobby! It has to be him!"

"It all seems to have started with him," Bert added.

"Does Tom know Bobby?" I asked.

Bert and Sonja exchanged a glance, and Sonja shook her head. "No, I don't think so. They might have known each other from town, but they didn't *know* each other."

Lyles was watching me with a certain gleam in his eye.

Uncomfortable, I said, "So if there's no connection between them, they must have crossed paths at some point. So let's think about that." I looked at Lyles. "But I want to know about that . . . stuff. Have you ever seen it anywhere else?"

Lyles shook his head. "This particular thing? No, but I have seen its type. It is ancient on your timeline, and the only thing it thirsts for is food, or possibly fear. It can kill, control, and feed, but that's it. It has a lair somewhere, but these creatures don't do things by the half-measure. I can't imagine there was only enough to infect this man," he indicated Tom with an elegant finger, "and perhaps a few others."

Mildred had been silent, but now stepped forward. "I'm as curious about this monstrosity as anyone, but I want to know what makes these two so special." She languidly placed her hand on my neck and ran it through my hair. Chills went down my back and leg, and Sonja raised an eyebrow. Mildred smiled at her, and I suddenly felt like a bird between two cats. Two *hungry* cats. "I can do this, and I don't get much of a reaction. Beyond the physical, of course. And with her . . ." Mildred left the sentence unfinished and she crossed over to Bert. "But I can do this, and . . ." She closed her eyes and breathed deeply. "He is as open to me as a book." She opened her eyes and looked at Lyles. "Your glamour does not work on either of them. They couldn't work the jukebox on their first visit. Remember?"

Lyles looked offended. "It's not *glamour*, Mildred. We've had this discussion before. It's *reality*."

190

Mildred blew a raspberry, and said, "It may as well be glamour. Not in the fey sense, but to us girls," she winked at Sonja and me. "It's magic. You give a man—even a multidimensional man like Lyles here—the ability to control reality within a small space like he does, and he'll still claim there's nothing magical about it."

"Your identification of sex is nothing more than a label I chose, Mildred. We've had this discussion as well."

It sounded like well-traveled ground between them, but Bert spoke up. "I don't care if it's magic or mystery, I just want this pretty lady to keep reading my book."

Mildred still had her hand on the back of Bert's neck, and she threw back her head and tinkled a laugh. She jumped in place, and tittered again, and I realized Bert had goosed her. *Goosed* her. Bert was playing grab-ass with a multidimensional being capable of turning into a pillar of light.

"We've already figured it out," Bert said.

Mildred still had her hand on the back of his neck, and some of his color had returned, even if he didn't look too good.

"Adam here has a plate in his head, and Sonja got kicked by a horse as a child. So something is missing, or interferes, with this place."

Beside him, Lyles nodded. "Your reality is determined by electrical impulses within your brains. I, we, are simply able to override and extract memories, experiences, and share them as you are willing. In Adam's case, the impulses are blocked by something, and in Sonja's, there's a good chance her injury has caused her brain to work differently."

"I had to relearn how to walk. My daddy had a horse named Sugar Foot, and it got stung by a wasp as I was walking behind it. I was three, I think." I laced my hand in hers. She fingered the spill of grey above her ear. "My parents always said they were afraid I wouldn't make it."

Lyles opened his mouth to speak, but turned his head to look at the window a moment before a splash of lights came through them. He stood, and I grabbed the shotgun from the floor. Sonja was doing the same thing, and I heard a whisper of air from behind me. Looking over my shoulder, I discovered we were now

191

alone on the dance floor. All the other Regulars were gone, and Tom with them.

Footsteps pounded up the steps and across the porch and I noticed how calm Lyles looked.

CHAPTER 28

BOBBY WALKED DOWN East Riverside, savoring the sense of destruction and death around him. His automatons were still busy in the bluff, getting ever closer to The-Thing-in-the-Rock. Chaos reigned in town, the smell of smoke and blood in the air. Downtown had been partially gutted by a fire, and bodies lay here and there in the street. Even dead, they still twitched at times. As he watched, one trembled, sat up, and then began shambling toward him.

It joined the half-dozen or so that were already following him. He almost had his army; the pieces were nearly in place. He flexed his hands; they bulged, misshapen by the essence he'd drawn in before he left the cave. With Mark's body poisoning the town, he no longer needed to feed the dark ichor into the river. More by instinct than thought, he'd spent the last day absorbing as much as he could. Beckoning the closest one to him, he laid his hands on her shoulders. Looking closer, he saw that it was a former classmate of his. He laughed to the air above him.

"Betcha never thought this is how it would end, huh?" he asked what used to be Allison. His voice was scratchy, grinding in his throat, but he didn't care. He didn't need to care. She didn't respond, just stared ahead dully. He leaned forward, cupping her head in his hand, tilting her face toward his. He kissed her, forcing his tongue into her mouth. It was dry, and her lips were cold. Her tongue sat like a dead fish in her mouth, and she let out a small burp. He came away with the taste of death on his tongue, and he shivered.

"What a way to go out, huh?" She didn't blink, and he wondered what else he could tell her to do. With the added essence, she would perform her tasks more quickly and be more compliant. "Go find others. Wake them. Bring them to me."

She obediently shuffled off in the direction he pointed her. Repeating the procedure without the kiss to the others, he sent them in different directions. While waiting for them to return, he broke the plate glass window of a leather goods shop. Finding rags, solvents, and a lighter, he made an improvised Molotov cocktail and tossed it in the back of the shop. It caught, flames flaring as it found leather, wood, and paper to consume. He climbed back out the broken display window and crossed the street.

"Why use the door when you can break a window?" he asked the empty street. Climbing on the roof of a car, he sat cross-legged and watched the store burn. As the flames caught inside, he found himself sniffing the air. The burning leather had such a *nice* smell in the cool night air.

The fire had consumed the leather shop and the half of each shop on either side. Bobby could have sent more automatons to the other side of the river, but he thought the group in front of him would be enough. Each was filled with more essence than most, and they were all fairly fit. Being freshly dead, even wounded, they would put up enough fight to rid the town of the abomination beside the river.

"Find something burning or that can burn, as we walk. Follow me." He jumped off the roof and took Allison's hand. "Shall we go, my dear?"

Following Bobby, the silent mob turned and walked north.

Lyles stood beside me as something hit the front door of Ricochet. Bert was behind us, Sonja stood on the other side of Lyles, and Mildred was beside Bert. I glanced at Lyles, then at Sonja, marveling again at the beauty in her fierceness. The girl looked *good* clutching a shotgun, a determined look on her face. The front door banged again, and I could hear someone yelling.

"Let them in, Lyles. Let's get this over with."

Lyles simply raised an eyebrow at me, and the pearl earring reflected the neon. I heard the jukebox buzz behind us, and the front door opened. In tumbled the man from the hardware store, Malcolm, and two of his sons. They slammed the door behind them, looking wildly around.

"Get ready! Them crazy sons o' bitches are coming!" Malcolm said, and his sons started talking. The oldest, who I thought was Jep, saw Mildred and ran to her.

"I'm so glad you're okay, Millie," he said. He had a wound on his arm, a long scratch that had torn off part of his sleeve. Mills, his brother, nodded.

"What's happening?" Sonja asked Malcolm.

Bert moved around them, giving Jep a stony stare, and went to the front window. Mildred patted Jep on the shoulder, then recoiled and looked closer at the wound.

"We heard what was going on in town," Malcolm said to Sonja. Lyles had moved to Jep at Mildred's motion, but I got the sense he was still listening. "We saw the fire burning, and saw everybody . . . killing each other. I can't explain it any other way."

I looked for something to drink, to give it to Malcolm, and three glasses appeared on the bar. Lyles motioned to me, and I fetched them.

"They were killing each other, and no one was stopping them. I saw Otis, and he was beating on someone. Then he wandered off, and the person he was beating got up and was chasing some girl from the high school. I hate to admit it, but we turned and ran." He took the glass of water from me and gulped it down.

"I went to your place, Sonja, and Cook told us where you were. She wouldn't open the door and told us if we came in, she'd fill us full of buckshot. I told her she was crazy as hell, and we'd settle up in the morning."

"What did she say?" Sonja asked.

"She said she'd be happy to, if any of us made it that far."

"Adam," Bert called from the front door.

Lyles and Mildred were still staring at Jep's arm. He was chugging the glass of water I'd handed him. Lyles placed his hand over the wound, and light grew underneath his palm, so bright I had to squint. Jep screamed, gagging on the water, and Malcolm lunged for them. I stopped Malcolm, and Sonja caught Mills. Jep screamed again, and the light dimmed. Mildred released Jep, and he cradled the arm against his side.

"It was the antiseptic I used to clean your wound. You weren't expecting it, and it hurt more than you thought it would," Lyles said, and Malcolm and Mills quit straining against us.

"Well, shit, barkeep, you could've warned us," Malcolm grumbled.

"Adam," Bert said, a little more urgently.

"What's the matter?" I called.

"That's why we were running," Malcolm said. "A group of them is headed here. We knocked some of them down with the truck, but one broke the window and sent us into the ditch. We had to get out and run."

"I saw some of them get back up. One was crawling," Mills added, and I saw the poor boy was sixteen if he was a day old. Tears stood out at the corner of his eyes. "They just got right back up."

Bobby screamed in frustration as the truck plowed through his army. It didn't go through the center of the group, but stayed on the right-hand side of the road, plowing through a quarter or so of his automatons. They didn't make a sound as the truck rolled over them, and Bobby saw Timson Overstreet clutching the driver's side window, reaching in. The truck swerved, slipping into the ditch, and Bobby's scream turned into triumph.

Timson went flying as he was dislodged from the window, and Bobby saw three shapes climb from the truck.

"Faster, faster! Get them!" A few of the automatons ran, but the three slipped over the ditch, running for the pool of light. Bobby looked behind him; those that could get up were already on their feet, and a few were crawling, either because of shattered legs or broken backs. Bobby growled. He picked up a board with flames guttering out, and waved it to bring them back to life.

"Keep going! We're almost there!" he shouted. Pulling Allison to her feet, they moved on.

I joined Bert by the window. A crowd of shapes was advancing across the parking lot, and I heard the jukebox hum.

"What the hell?" Malcolm shouted. His eyes were wide as the Regulars emerged from the space in front of the jukebox.

Lyles sighed and said, "They've been here the whole time."

Malcolm lowered his shot gun, the fear on his face melting away. He came to join Bert and me at the window, then I walked back to Lyles.

"What was wrong with the boy?" I whispered.

"He was unclean," Lyles said.

I saw Mildred shoot him a glance from across the room. "You can heal it? Why haven't you been?"

Lyles shook his head. "A small infection like that, yes. But if someone is too far gone, there's nothing I can do. That reality won't change. It simply is."

Malcolm cursed, bringing up his shotgun, and we all approached the front doors.

"Better get your glamour ready," I said to Lyles. "Perhaps we should explain?"

"Silly boy," he said. "It's not... *glamour*." One of the Regulars approached me, a man dressed in faded buckskins with a long tangled beard. He clutched a long, thin tomahawk in his hand. When he grinned, it reminded me of a wolf. He switched the 'hawk to his left hand and clapped me on the shoulder.

Cold. Oh so cold. The arthritis burned, sinking deep into his hands, which swelled so bad he couldn't open or close them. That made it impossible to hunt, but he thought he had enough for the winter. He hated cities anyway, and wanted to die like he lived: free. He had been without food for days when he ventured from his cabin, but the blizzard was on him before he knew it. Stumbling for hours, he finally saw a light through the trees. He never thought he would be warm again.

I gasped, seeing and feeling the flood of images in seconds. The mountain man released my shoulder and stood behind the doors. Lyles gave me a sympathetic glance, and the doors opened. A tottering mass of broken and bleeding bodies were advancing up the steps. In the lead was Otis, his uniform shirt open and bloody. Long gashes ripped across his stomach, and muscle glistened as he moved.

Bobby let the crowd pass him, filling the porch with their numbers. He released Allison's hand, and she moved ahead. The doors opened, and Bobby thought they had finally given way beneath the massed weight of the automatons. A terrible cry came from within, followed by the boom of a shotgun, followed by another. Bobby saw the front row of troops disappear, falling to the floor, as they were pushed back.

"YOU ARE STILL UNCLEAN," the voice boomed, driving Bobby and the automatons back a step.

Bobby grimaced, trying to cover his ears as the sound of electronic feedback picked up. It squealed, the sound climbing higher, and Bobby felt the inside of his brain tremble. The automatons stopped, tried to push forward, and then a figure was fighting his way through the crowd. With a long, bloody beard, he fought with an axe, chopping through the skulls of his automatons, dropping them.

They bit and gouged back, finally driving the man to his knees. With a roar he became a pillar of light, consuming each automaton that had physical contact with him, the touch of the light taking them…away. More shapes came out of the doorway, and the shotguns continued blasting. Bobby screamed, rage turning to fear again, and he stumbled. The step probably saved his life because Sonja was standing on the porch and fired at point blank range. She cursed and took aim again, but the breech of the shotgun was open. With another curse, she used it as a club to knock down Allison, who was reaching for her.

"THE UNCLEAN ARE NOT ALLOWED TO FOUL THIS PLACE," the voice sounded again, and Bobby turned, stumbling away. He had not escaped unscathed; he felt the burn of a few pellets on his back, and he groaned as the skin tried to knit together, pushing the pellets out. More of his automatons were climbing the steps, but Bobby moved off to the side.

I was standing inside the building, beside the windows to the left of the door. The mountain man tore into the things on the porch like a banshee. Malcolm and Sonja both raised their shotguns, their blasts sounding like one shot. I saw the mountain man bully his way through them, chopping left and right, twisting his 'hawk free with practiced ease. He took out Otis first, and I was thankful when his ill-used body fell and didn't rise again. I raised my gun and shot, my spray pattern knocking them back. Sonja fired to the right of the doorway, creating an opening, and we all walked forward.

Mildred and Lyles hung back, but we didn't need their help. The things could be dropped with a head shot, and a shot to the chest would knock them off their feet. True, they could still grab ankles, and I'm sure the gnashing teeth would leave a mark, but we had them falling back. I saw the mountain man fall to his knees, and then he exploded in a pillar of light, evaporating those touching him and pushing back those who were close to him with a ripple of light.

In the flare of the light, I saw Sonja take aim at something off the porch. She fired, frowned, and raised the gun again. I saw the breech stuck open at the same time one of the things stumbled toward her. I started to yell, but she easily sidestepped it, reversed the gun, and batted it down.

"To the left!" We heard Malcolm yell, and all of us turned. The right side of the porch was clear, probably because that was where the mountain man ended up falling. My ears were growing numb, but I kept shooting. In the movies, gunshots are simple *pops*, but in real life, they are deafening, sounds that compresses the eardrums, numbing them. Some of the things had burning branches and sticks in their hands, and part of me realized they were trying to burn Ricochet down.

"Don't worry about the flames," Lyles said.

He was right; as soon as one landed anywhere on the porch, the flames vanished. We heard a howl of frustration, and I realized they were down. All of them. Bodies were lying all over the porch, on the ground, and not one had made it inside. We heard another scream, and Sonja stepped off the porch. I reached out, grabbed her shoulder, and held her in place.

"I see him! It's Bobby! We can end this!" she said, trying to break my grip. Mildred glided past me, catching the opposite arm, and together Sonja listened to us, and came back up the steps. "I saw Bobby," she said.

"We will only be ending part of it," she said softly.

I looked at the bodies lying around us and realized she was right. Even with their grievous wounds, they were moving again.

"What do we do about them?" I asked, bringing my gun up.

Someone stepped out of the doorway. "I'll handle this, sir," said a young man in a tan, old-fashioned uniform. Reaching down, he touched several of the struggling forms. Looking up at Mildred, he winked. "See you on the flip side, sweetheart." He turned into a flash of light, and the half dead things disappeared with him.

I managed to close my eyes right before he flashed, but it still left an afterimage on my eyes. I stepped over to Sonja as others spilled out of the doorway. A girl dressed in a grass skirt, a bundle of leis covering her chest. A boy, tragically young, in Confederate Gray. A man in a business suit that was out of date. A pair of young girls in hoop skirts. A small black and brown dog trotted out and stepped on a pair of the motionless things. Looking at over his shoulder at a boy with long hair, the dog pulsed, disappearing like the others. The boy, a teenager with a sad look followed, and after adjusting his pack, looked up at me.

"Don't let her get away. The times goes by... too fast," he said. "Always take the chance."

All of the Regulars came onto the porch and touched as many as they could and were gone in a flash of brilliance. Sonja and I staggered back, allowing the Regulars to push the hate-filled things from the porch. Malcom and his boys were standing there, eyes wide and watching the flashes of light. Sonja's hand reached out, finding mine, and she turned toward me. I pulled Sonja's head into my shoulder, and she clung to me. I buried my face into her neck, and eventually the flashes stopped. I opened my eyes, blinking, and found Sonja staring up at me.

"Well, that's two bad ideas I've followed you into. Can that be our limit?" I asked her, and as an answer she raised on her tiptoes and kissed me.

"What else did you have planned for tonight?" she asked when she stepped away.

"I could think of a few other things," I answered. I didn't mean it as innuendo, but I saw her roll her eyes.

"You couldn't get that lucky," she breathed. She gave me a quick peck, and we went back inside. All the bodies were gone, but blood and dark stains were evident on the floorboards.

CHAPTER 29

BOBBY AND THE THING within him ran for the second time, fleeing from the beacons of light flashing behind him. Some of his automatons followed, but the majority of his army lay in shambles. They tried to keep up with him, but Bobby easily outdistanced them. He panted in the cold night air and stopped running. His side burned, his throat was raw, and the essence of The-Thing-in-the-Rock bubbled and sighed inside of him.

The-Thing-in-the-Rock was the only answer now. Bobby had tried, and Bobby had failed. Whatever or whoever that place was, it was too much for him. Bobby had to make sure it was released from its rocky prison. He stopped running, waiting for his automatons to catch up.

"Did we get all of it?" I asked. Inside, Mildred was examining a vicious looking bite on Mills' arm. "Are you gonna have…"

Mildred's hand flashed, and Mills screamed. When she took her hand away, the bite mark was gone. We went back to the dining room and found drinks waiting for us on the tables. Everyone else was okay, but we were running low on ammo. Malcolm had additional shells in his truck, and we sent Jep and Mills to get them in case there was another attack.

Lyles was staring pensively at the jukebox, and the feeling unsettled me. He must have felt my eyes on him because he turned and looked at me.

"Ask the question, Adam," he said quietly.

Everyone turned and looked at me, and I felt my face redden. "We aren't any closer to finding whatever *they* are," I said. "We know Bobby has something to do with it, and so does Tom. But how did he turn the whole town on itself?"

"Bobby didn't have many friends. Him, Mark, another guy named Chris," Sonja said. "I tried to keep Mark and Chris on, but they weren't dependable. It was hard enough to get Mark to perform on the weekend, much less get them to work during the week."

"Didn't Otis suspect them of drugs?" Bert asked. "Could they have been growing or making it?"

"But that doesn't explain Tom," I said. "Where is the common factor?"

"What does – did – Tom like to do?" Mildred asked.

"The night at The Dive, he got in a fight. Maybe that's where it started," I said. "What was he doing that day?"

"Fishing," Sonja and Bert said together.

"Water," I said, getting excited. "The river. That's where Tom came in contact with it, and that's the only way they could poison the whole town." Everyone thought for a moment, and then nodded.

"It makes sense," Bert said.

"Then why didn't you come down with it?" Mildred asked.

"We're on a well," Sonja and Malcolm both answered.

"What about the fight between Greg and Jim?" I asked. Malcolm looked uncomfortable, and then said, "I had city water out at the barn I was building. It was closer to the road," he said as an explanation.

"Even if the river was the delivery method, we still don't have the source," Lyles said. "Is there anything along the river that could house something like this?"

"Could it just be pesticide runoff, or something like that? A chemical reaction?" I asked.

Lyles and Mildred both shook their head. "This is something alive, in a fashion. It has a basic intelligence. We both sensed it," Lyles said.

"Immediately," Mildred added.

"Wait, wait, wait," I said, jumping up. "When we went to Bobby's house. His clothes, by the shower. They were filthy. If Bobby's mixed up in this, or a victim of it, where would he get so dirty? Somewhere with access to the river?"

Bert and Malcolm shared a long look, understanding passing between them. Bert sighed, and looked at Sonja. To her, he said, "I'm sorry, my dear. But I think it's the Jenkins Mine."

Sonja's face fell, and I took her hand. She bowed her head, and I saw a tear fall into her lap.

Into the silence, Bert spoke. "Her husband passed up there. Others, too, over the years. It's always been a dangerous place." Sonja sniffled, and Bert picked up on his story. I looked for a napkin or something to give to Sonja, and a handkerchief appeared on the table.

"The Jenkins Mine has always been a strange place. I 'member stories my granddaddy told me about Sherman's army. They came through here on their way to Savannah, and a patrol got lost up there. Sherman blamed rebel sympathizers in the town and burned a plantation or two. But the stories started before then. Even the Indians 'round here didn't like it. They said it had bad medicine and avoided it. The Creeks and the Cherokee wouldn't even fight over it, and they would fight over anything."

"Did they actually mine anything from it?" I asked.

Bert nodded. "They got lead, feldspar, and quartz, back when that was worth something. But it seemed to be hit or miss. A company would come in, bring in a bunch of miners, and they might or might not find something. But they were always losing people. It was just a bad luck place." Bert shrugged.

"When I was a kid, we always said it was haunted," Sonja said in a small voice. "But we'd still go out there to park. Billy and I went a few times, of course; everybody did. But we never went all the way to the top. There are a dozen switchbacks along the way, and we'd just go to the first, or maybe the second. I heard the road washed away in places, and Otis blocked it. It was always dangerous, but it got even more dangerous after that."

From the far side of the restaurant, the antique map disengaged itself from the wall. It floated toward us, and I felt a sense of foreboding. Even represented on paper, the mine gave off a sense of wrongness.

As it settled on the table in front of us, I asked, "If you aren't from our dimension, can this be accurate?"

Lyles tapped his fingers on the table. "Your minds – both conscious and unconscious – have a tremendous storage capacity. You have forgotten things you don't even realize you knew. In much the same way Ricochet is able to preserve memories and a representation of your physical form, I am able to . . ." his face paused, and then a grin surfaced. "I am able to decorate as needed."

One of Malcolm's boys snorted with laughter, only to earn an elbow from his brother, who asked, "Could the thing have been calling people in? You know, like mentally, or whatever?"

"In much the same way we can influence our surroundings, it wouldn't surprise me if that happened. Humans are more sensitive then they give themselves credit for. If you would stop and listen to your senses more . . ." he trailed off.

"Billy may have listened," Sonja said suddenly. "He was always out and about, doing something. He loved this land. At one time, his family owned the land that butted up to the Jenkins Mine. The night he died . . ." she choked back a sob. "The night he died, he'd been restless all day. I could tell there was something wrong, but I thought he was just worried about the crops, or the farm, or something. I should have asked him, but I was running late to go to The Dive. I should have stopped." She sobbed for a moment.

"I was there that night," Bert picked up her story. "It was almost closing time. Helen was alive then, but I'd go when Sonja had poker games. Otis came in, and you could tell something was wrong. He went right to Sonja."

"They found him beside the highway," Sonja said. "His truck was at the barricade. They followed his tracks up to the place he slipped and fell. No one could answer why, or how." She wiped the tears off her face. "I guess I have my answer."

Malcolm spoke up. "He was a good man. One of the best." His sons nodded at his words.

"Can you help us?" I asked Lyles. "We can stop the things it creates, but can we stop the source? Or block it? Bury it?"

Lyles and Mildred exchanged a glance. "We think we can," he said finally.

"But at what cost?" Mildred asked.

"Reality is a wheel, my dear. There are no endings... or beginnings to the wheel," he said.

The answer seemed to satisfy her, and she nodded.

I bent over, examining the map. It was a cutaway version of what they called the bluff. The switchbacks were dotted lines, and the map showed two entrances, one at the very top at the end of the switchbacks, where a flat space had been created. I assumed it was for equipment or as a staging point. The mine spider-webbed from this opening, tunnels turning and twisting, leading downward into the earth. Some of the tunnels stopped, and others opened into "rooms" where more material had been excavated.

"We've always said a glacier – one of the furthest south – came grinding down, creating the valley that runs between here and east Atlanta. You can't see much of it now, except for the rivers and the river basins, but it eventually met the inland sea that once covered South Georgia and north Florida. Where the Jenkins Mine is must be the buildup of land that was scraped and pushed along, and it got left in one big lump. Over time, it solidified, and all the minerals and valuable stuff settled and condensed." Bert took a long gulp of his drink. "In most mines, the veins of minerals form when the liquid is forced into voids in the rock. In the Jenkins Mine, it's all mixed up. You can hit a pocket of lead, then a pocket of quartz, and then just granite."

Bert tapped the map. "Once they got deep enough, they made another entrance here." Out of the main collection of tunnels, another much smaller pair of lines traced to the back side of the bluff, facing away from the town. "It helped with the air flow, and could also serve as an escape tunnel if the main entrance ever got blocked."

"Like you could ever find it," Jep said at the other table. "Lookit that place. Tunnels turning every whichaway."

"My uncle said they put red arrows at every intersection, pointing the way out. A big one for the main entrance, a smaller one for the little one. The arrows were raised in case the miners didn't have a light." Bert shivered.

"They would get lost in the dark?" Jep asked, face paling. "Will we have to go in?"

"I think we need to leave someone here, in case any more of those things come back," Malcolm said, laying a hand on Jep's shoulder.

Bert nodded in agreement, and we planned late into the night. We left before dawn broke.

CHAPTER 30

WE PILED INTO SONJA'S TRUCK, Lyles flickering and reappearing in the cab. Bert handed Mildred up to the bed of the truck; she insisted on standing up so she could feel the wind in her hair as we drove. Malcolm and Bert rode in the back as well, and we drove to Malcolm's truck to reload from his supplies. We also found foul weather gear, used when Malcolm or the boys needed to feed their animals in the rain or muck. We each carried a long gun, and most of us had handguns, in addition to the dynamite.

Before he climbed into the back, I grabbed Bert's arm. "Why don't you stay here?" I asked. "We can bring Malcom's boys, and you —"

"Why? Because I'm old?" he interrupted. "This place does something. I feel better than I have in years." He looked around and lowered his voice. "Malcom's boys have a lot of years ahead of them. Me? Not so much. So I'd rather go, if you don't mind."

"We need to stop every one of those things we can," Sonja said. "Will it come back to life if we leave some of it behind?"

Lyles looked amused. Bert winked at me, and we turned to the others. "I'm afraid I'm not an encyclopedia for otherworldly life, my dear. But I would assume it would be in our best interest to remove as many as we can."

Malcolm reached into the truck bed and pulled out a long wand-like thing with a cylinder attached at the end, with a strap so it could be looped over the shoulder. As soon as Sonja saw it, she nodded. Malcolm depressed a button, and I saw a tiny electric arc. With a whoosh, a short, intense flame leapt out of the end. I jumped back.

"It's used to kill weeds, or burn off part of the fields," Malcolm explained. I expected a biting comment from Sonja, but she just smiled slightly. "It will be just perfect if we find any of those little blobs."

We climbed back into Sonja's truck. I was driving with Lyles beside me and Sonja in the passenger seat. I suggested we roll up our windows. Sonja and I couldn't fight back, trapped in the cab, and I didn't want anything to happen to us. If I crashed, our impromptu rescue party would meet a quick end. Reaching behind Lyles, she opened the glass partition in the back window. She gave instructions to Mildred's knees, and Bert and Malcolm acknowledged them.

With the windows closed, I could smell the sweat and fear that covered our bodies. Lyles had a dusty scent, the taste of dark rooms and dry books. Sonja smelled like Sonja, a slightly sweet scent that now carried a bitter undertone, but intoxicating nonetheless. I reached across Lyles and took her hand once I had the truck in fifth gear.

"Do you realize there is no other emotion in the universe like human's love?" he asked in the silence. "No other species has your specific combination of impulses. Electrical and chemical interactions like nowhere... or when. You are unique among many others."

"So there is life out there?" I asked, nodding to the stars above.

"Of course," he replied. "And over there and there," he indicated, nodding to his left and right. "There are other worlds than these, all stacked upon each other, a tower rising higher than you can imagine."

"Are you an alien?" Sonja asked.

"Alien only in the sense I'm not native to Earth. But we are not native to this dimension, either. There are many levels to reality. How many directions are there? How many universes? Dimensions are much the same."

"I'm content with this one," I said. I glanced at Sonja. "One is all I need." I saw a shape up ahead, and I turned on my bright lights, positioning the truck so Malcolm would have a clear shot. I glanced at Sonja again and saw she had her eyes closed. I realized she must have known the person it once was. We flashed by it, and I heard a gut tightening, wet splatting sound. I saw it drop in my side mirror.

Three more times I had to move the truck so Bert and Malcolm could take out the things from their higher vantage point. The second time, I had to stop in the middle of a small pack of them. Mildred helped where she could, using her tiny flashes of light.

"Do we need to help?" I asked them.

Before I could reach for the door handle Lyles said, "They are fine."

He was right; Mildred added tiny flashes of light that disorientated the creatures, allowing Malcolm and Bert to do their bloody work. A sharp smack on the roof of the truck told me it was time to drive on.

We reached the bottom of the bluff, and I remembered my drive into town. It was a little more than a week ago, but seemed like months. I remembered the feeling of cool dread that came over me as I passed under the shadow of it and shivered. The road was blocked by two telephone poles, stacked and secured atop each other, and I parked the truck. We climbed out, Lyles doing his flickering magician bit, and he was standing on the other side of the barricade.

We readjusted our weapons and started climbing. Malcolm handed the weed-burner to Mildred, who looped it over her shoulder. We formed a wedge with me at the point, Lyles and Mildred at the center, Sonja and Malcolm on the sides, and Bert bringing up the rear. We were loaded down with weapons, and I had the dynamite tucked into my back pocket. Flashlights lit our way, the beams bouncing across the rocky path. After we made the second turn, I caught the reflection of something red and blue in the brush beside the improvised road. Stopping everybody, I looked carefully before I stepped into the brush. I came out with a propane tank, a bit battered, but its weight indicated it was full.

"That may come in handy," Malcolm said. "There's a lot of boom compressed in there."

"Where did it come from, you think?" Sonja asked.

"Sometimes things are found when you most need them," Lyles said. There was a battered piece of rope attached to it, and I slung the tank over my back, keeping one hand free. We resumed walking.

They are here, Bobby thought. He sensed the whimper of The-Thing-in-the-Rock, far below, and his own fear crept in. As soon as they stepped to the other side of the barricade, Bobby and The-Thing-in-the-Rock could sense their presence. Calling down into the mineshaft, he recalled a few of his diggers. They were so close; only a few feet separated them and Bobby from the pocket containing The-Thing-in-the-Rock. So, so close.

Taking three of them, Bobby left the cave.

We were so intent on the path in front of us, we didn't think about *above* us. The first indication something was wrong was the slight rattle of pebbles. Something dropped from the dark down on top of us, and Malcolm was swept off the edge without a cry. We heard thumps, and more stones rattled down, and I cursed.

"Keep going," Sonja said, and we picked our way up the path. We craned our necks in every direction, trying to watch everywhere at once. I finally stopped the group halfway up the next switchback. We were rattled over losing Malcom so early into our trek, and we couldn't re-organize while we were moving.

"Sonja, you watch ahead. I'll watch up. Mildred, Lyles, can you watch the sides and help Sonja? Bert, you'll have to check our back." With the assignments, we moved smoothly up the hill and saw the shape a good ten seconds before it slid to a stop in front of us. Sonja and I both swiveled our guns and shot at almost the same instant.

"Damn," Sonja whispered. "That's Donny. He's a mechanic in town."

"Was," Bert said gruffly. "He was Donny."

Before we made it to the next turn, a large cascade of stones came tumbling down. We avoided most of them, but I earned a cut on one arm. Sonja clucked over it, but I allowed her to rip off a piece of my shirttail to bandage it.

"I should have let you rip your shirt," I whispered to her as she finished tying it off. "Do you know how good you'd look, carrying a scatter gun with a ripped shirt?"

She placed her hands on my exposed stomach. "Why do you think I ripped yours?"

Bert coughed in the darkness, and Mildred tinkled her laughter. Even Lyles broke a smile.

Below him, Bobby heard the laughter of a woman, and bristled at the sound. He'd used two of his automatons, but they were only down one man. Bobby gritted his teeth, and whispered, "Go get four of the diggers," to Mr. Davis, his onetime school teacher. Bobby watched the small group below him reform. Bending over, he picked up stones. It would take a minute for the old man to reach the top of the bluff, go inside the cave, and come back out. But perhaps Bobby could slow their approach.

I heard the sound of the rock whistling through the air before it hit Sonja, but I didn't have any time to yell a warning. The rock met her in the chest, and she fell backward. I retreated toward her, hearing another rock fly out of the darkness, but it fell a few feet short of me. No other rocks flew out of the darkness while I checked on her, but I expected to feel the impact at any moment. Sonja rolled over, retching, and I tried to shield her body while Bert covered us with his gun.

"Are you okay?" I asked, feeling useless. She was gasping on her hands and knees, trying to get her breath back. She nodded. I looked up at Mildred and Lyles. "Can't you do anything? Make a shield, or something?"

They exchanged a glance and whispered together. "If we do that, we limit the energy we have for later. Here, away from Ricochet, we don't have an unlimited supply," Lyles said.

I looked at Mildred. "Protect her," I said, motioning to Sonja. Mildred and Bert nodded while Sonja protested. We started back up the incline. I moved from side to side, Sonja behind me, Mildred following her, with Lyles and Bert last in line. A regular rain of rocks fell down on us, but only a few hit me, mostly off the bounces. We walked faster, assuming we'd push the rock-thrower back. As we rounded the final switchback, I let loose with a couple of blasts from the shotgun.

"Run," I whispered, just loud enough for them to hear. We started jogging, the shield breaking up and dissolving around Sonja. The rocks stopped, but as soon as we entered the clearing that held the entrance to the mine, a handful of the infected townspeople swarmed us. I yelled a warning, throwing myself to the side.

Bobby felt an itching on his skin as the group below him regrouped and started climbing. He'd gotten the bar owner a good one, right between the titties. After his second rock bounced away harmlessly, he figured out one of the two from the place of the light must have a shield or something to block the rocks. They rounded the final switchback, and to his surprise, ran up the incline. It was more of a jog, but the stranger with them fired off a couple of blasts, the shotgun spitting a tongue of flame in the darkness. Bobby ducked away from the lead pellets as they flew over his head, but it bought the group some time.

As soon as they entered the clearing near the mine's entrance, Bobby heard the shuffling footsteps of his automatons approaching. Bobby scrambled toward them and they paused at least until Bobby growled, "Get them!" with a savage finger pointed toward the group of interlopers. Bobby watched as they attacked the group, which split apart, the young guy throwing himself to the side, the bar-owner bitch bringing her gun up, and the old man dropping whatever it was he was holding. The two from Ricochet stood their ground, and the automatons split apart from them like water breaking over the rocks. Bobby raised his hands skyward as three of the four went after the bitch and the other chased the old man around the clearing.

I watched three of them go after Sonja, and the fourth chased Bert. I started to yell, but then Mildred reached out, grabbing two of them by the arm, and she . . . pulsed. She didn't bloom like the others did, but the sphere of light expanded outward from her, dissolving the two she was touching and knocking over the other. The weed burner fell to the ground with a clatter. The sphere pushed me down and knocked Bert and the other one down together. Bert gave a short scream as the shotgun boomed between them. Bert screamed again, and then everything was silent. For a moment.

The rock rumbled under Bobby, followed by a hissing sound from deep within the earth. The woman-thing's ball of light had knocked him to the ground, but it didn't matter. The-Thing-in-the-Rock was free. The muted presence in Bobby's mind exploded, roaring to life, causing him to scream again as his eardrums ruptured. Blood squirted out of his ears, flying onto the packed dirt, and *Sweetsweetessence sogood to make them scream sososo hungry.* . . .

Deep below, the The-Thing-in-the-Rock flowed over the remaining diggers. Bobby couldn't hear, but he saw the stunned looks of the attackers. He laughed as the ground trembled, a rumble deep from the earth below.

Bert climbed to his feet and grabbed the propane canister with one good arm. Something was wrong with the ground – it kept moving beneath his feet. Sonja came up to him, but he shook her off. She backed off, her eyes wide as she examined his arm. A deep gash nearly separated his scrawny bicep from the bone beneath it, but Bert found the pain wasn't that bad. *Shock,* he thought. *Gonna hurt like hell in a minute.*

Adam was climbing to his feet, and Lyles turned, easily keeping his balance as he rode the shifting earth. Their eyes met, and Bert felt the moment lock into place. He started walking toward Adam, who was approaching the Bobby-thing as it writhed on the ground. Laughing manically, blood pouring from his ears; it didn't even react as they walked up. As Adam was pointing the shotgun downward, Bert set the propane canister down. Plucking the dynamite from Adam's back pocket at the same time the gun discharged, Bert put it into his other hand.

His arm might be useless, but Bert thought he could hold it long enough. Picking up the propane canister, he started for the entrance of the mine. Lyles reached out and grabbed his elbow, keeping Bert upright, and some of the pain receded.

"Bert, no!" Sonja's anguished cry was the only thing louder than the rumbling. Adam's eyes widened as he saw what Bert carried, and he started to speak. Bert shook his head and began walking.

"Not gonna make it far, mister," he said, in a voice barley louder than a whisper. Beside him, Lyles had a small smile on his face.

"You've got miles left to go," Lyles said. Behind them, Adam caught Sonja around the waist, and she screamed again. A dawning began to break from the mouth of the cave, sunlight washing over the rattling ground. Bert blinked, looking for the sun, but realized the glow was building within Lyles. Together, they entered the mine, Lyles' light building. Step by step, they went into its depths.

"We have to go. Sonja, come on." Somehow, I found the strength to pull her, even though she was clawing my arm to get loose. I gritted my teeth as her nails cut the fabric of my shirt, then the skin below.

"Beeeeeeerrrrrtttt!" she wailed. Behind us, Lyles started to glow, and I pulled harder. I didn't know what would happen when Lyles met whatever was down there, but I didn't want to know. Bert was also carrying three sticks of dynamite and a full canister of propane; he could blow all of us off the bluff, as well as half of its top, depending how deep they went, of course.

Sonja relaxed so suddenly I almost dropped her. Then she found her feet, and thankfully, she was following me, harsh sobs coming from her mouth.

"We need to run. Come on, baby, run. We gotta go." Sonja picked up her feet, and aided by the downward angle, we were fairly flying. I'll never understand how we didn't trip and go rolling down the hill. Behind us, a miniature sun sat on top of the hill, and then blinked out. I tensed, waiting for the explosion of earth, but I realized Lyles must have gone inside.

We were halfway down before the mountain lurched beneath our feet, and then we did go flying. The mountain coughed, a tongue of flame belching out of the mouth of the cave. Rocks went flying over us, and we landed in a sprawl. I crawled over Sonja, trying to protect her from the falling debris while she curled into a ball and cried.

Eventually the ground stopped moving, and I rolled off her. A thin stream of rocks rattled around us, rolling and bouncing down the hill. By the time the rocks stopped streaming past us, her cries had dwindled to sniffles. We sat up, and I pulled her into my lap, cradling her.

"Is it over?" she asked me.

I nodded, saying, "Yes, it is."

We sat there for a while, and she looked up at me. I dabbed the tear tracks off her cheeks, brushing off the grime and grit. Her hair was wild around her head and I smoothed it away from her face.

"You ready?" I asked her.

She nodded silently and started to stand up.

I helped her up and debated picking up any of our weapons. I had Sonja in one arm and picked up someone's shotgun. Bert's?

Mine? I didn't know. Letting go of her long enough to check the load, I saw it still had shells in it. Laying it across one forearm, I slipped my other around her. "Then let's go," I said.

We started walking down the hill and made it to the first switchback. Before we turned the corner, I turned and looked back up to the mouth of the cave. Smoke was trickling out of the opening, but it still held its shape. The ground rumbled again, and I didn't think it would hold long.

"Aaaaadaaaam . . ." Mildred's voice came from around us, and we stopped. Dim light flickered, trying to coalesce.

"Mildred?" I asked. "Is that you?"

We looked around and heard a sound that could have been her, whispering.

"What was that?" Sonja asked. She seemed more alert, more together.

"I don't know. But it sounded like her." We took a few more steps, and in the path in front of us, a shape *did* pull together. Lyles was there, faintly; we could the path through him.

"Adam, I don't think we got deep enough. Adam . . ." he faded away, and I thought I saw a look of pain cross his face. He brightened for a moment, and I wondered if he was expending the last of his energy to make sure we knew.

"Adam . . . Sonja . . ." his words turned into a whisper as he faded from sight.

"What did he say?" Sonja asked, but I knew she'd heard him.

My body ached. I'd lost a good friend, and Malcolm wasn't coming back to his sons. I looked up to the opening of the mine.

"No," she whimpered beside me.

"Sonja, we have to. What if it regrows and is able to escape?"

"Dammit," she said, her voice growing stronger. "Haven't we paid enough?" She pulled her arm out of mine, but I caught her hand.

"At least we didn't get all the way to the bottom," I said, and she grunted what may have been laughter.

We walked back up, this time holding hands. When we reached the summit, we gathered all of our scattered weapons, combining the ammo and taking an inventory. We had several shattered flashlights, two fully loaded shotguns, Malcolm's weed burner, and to our surprise, found two sticks of dynamite.

"He must have dropped them," Sonja said sadly. They had blood on them, and she gently touched it. We each took one, tucking it securely into our back pockets. I switched batteries around in the light of a dying flashlight until we got one with a strong beam.

"I don't think there will be any more of those things," I said. "We just need to find any puddles of that goop." I handed her the miniature flame thrower. "You take this. I think you've used it more."

She nodded, and I held the flashlight, along with my shotgun.

"You ready?" I asked, and she nodded.

We entered the cave and found lab equipment set up after the first bend in the rock. A steel rack, with trays indiscriminately stacked. Pots sat on top of burners, and tanks like the one we found below were attached to them. "That must be where the . . . other one came from," I said. The air turned damp, and foul, chemicals and rot mixing.

"Oh my gawd," I said, covering my nose. "What is that smell?" Glass beakers, pans, and a propane burner still had . . . stuff in them.

"They were cooking meth," Sonja pointed to an arm lying up against the cave wall, "and you add in rotting bodies. It's pretty rich," she admitted, covering her nose. The flashlight beam caught a puddle of goo trailing out of the bloody end of the arm, and Sonja primed her burner. Before she depressed the button, the flashlight beam put streaks of rainbows across the oily surface. The flame shot out, burning and sizzling the material. It tried to roll away from her, but it moved sluggishly, not like it did in the glass at Ricochet.

"That's one," she said.

"How much fuel do you have in that thing?" I asked. She hefted it.

"Plenty. It's a fresh container. Malcolm was just getting ready to start overwintering his fields."

As we walked, she talked, and I let her. We moved deeper into the cave, following an ancient, narrow rail track. As we

219

walked, we passed arrows pointing in various directions. The path branched before us, and we opted to follow the rail, correctly thinking it would lead deeper. We passed a few body parts, all with the oily essence. I pretended not to see the savage satisfaction on Sonja's face as she charred the flesh and destroyed the liquid.

Pops and cracks sounded within the walls as we walked deeper. No other deep rumbles had sounded for a while, but we still glanced up and around us as the sounds continued.

"Tommyknockers. My grandfather said the sounds were the souls of lost miners, tapping to be saved."

"It's creepy as hell," I said. I knew it was just the sound of rocks rubbing together, grinding as the mine settled, but it sounded ghostly and plaintive.

"Tommyknockers, Tommyknockers, knocking at the door. I'm so afraid of the tommyknocker man," Sonja said, and I shuddered.

The rail line ended, and we found the edge of the place where Bert must have detonated the propane tank. Thankfully, there were none of his remains, but we could see where the wall was freshly scorched. The ceiling had collapsed, filling in the mine shaft, and a huge crack ran above one solid piece of granite. Looking at it, I could imagine it dropping down and crushing both of us. I didn't even want to speak in a normal tone of voice because it looked so unstable. As I watched, a small rain of grit fell down, and I heard more pops.

"Back up," I whispered. We backtracked until we were safely out of the crush zone.

"See that rock? If we can get it to fall, we can seal off the tunnel. That's where Bobby had those things working." We could see a trail of footsteps leading deeper into the mine, scuffled dirt and displaced stones. As we were studying the rock shelf, a thin stream of the evil black stuff pushed between the jumble of rocks and the mine floor. Sonja growled a curse and ignited the flamethrower as I pulled one of the sticks of dynamite out of my pocket.

Sonja was coming back to me when I heard the shuffling behind me and saw her eyes widen. I moved to my left as something grabbed my shirt, and I twisted away. I felt skin tear, and Sonja triggered the flame, thrusting it upward. I kept moving, trying to circle around and get the shotgun up at the same time. The mine filled with the smell of burning hair and roasting flesh, but the pain didn't stop the thing that was after us.

Shredded clothing, bloody arms, and hands kept reaching for us, and I dropped the dynamite as I got both hands on the shotgun. Sonja was backing up, drawing it deeper toward the cave-in. I brought the shotgun up, but I didn't have a shot.

"Sonja! Duck!" I called, and she whirled and ducked, giving me a clear shot. In the microsecond before I pulled the trigger, the thing was reaching for me. I saw the fingertips were gone, leaving grey-white bone showing through the worked-away flesh. The gun boomed, a full load of shot catching it in the chest, and flinging it back onto the pile of rocks.

Above us, the tommyknockers chattered in the walls and ceilings of the cave, and a thin rain of dust floated down. The dust turned into a trickle of stones, the sound echoed around us, and the chattering turned into a low groan.

"Are you okay?" I asked her. "Did it get you?"

She shook her head. "We need to do this and get out of here," she said.

The air in the cave moved, and we felt the mountain settle around us. I retrieved the stick of dynamite and held it, considering. My hands were trembling from the load of adrenaline dumped into my system. "A full stick or half? It looks like it wants to fall already." We looked at the crack again, and it seemed wider.

"Half. It should be scored to break it. Malcolm uses – used it to clear stumps." I found the mark and the stick of dynamite broke cleanly. Standing on my tiptoes, I wedged it into the cleft. "Hurry up, Adam."

"Do you have a lighter?" I asked. Her blank look was response enough.

We stood there staring at one another until I motioned to the weed burner. "Can you turn down the flame? Just enough to catch the fuse?"

As we were trying to figure out the flame adjustment, the beam of the flashlight started flickering. I shook the flashlight, willing the bean to strengthen. It did, but not much.

"We need to hurry," I said. She got a flame about six inches long, and I decided it was good enough.

"Move back up the tunnel. I'll light it and run," I said. She took the shotgun and flashlight from me, and I held up the flame thrower. Testing the reach of the flame, I positioned it.

"Here I come!" I yelled, and depressed the trigger. A second later, I heard the sizzle of the fuse, and scampered back up the tunnel. The flamethrower bounced in my hand, and I dropped it.

One-one thousand

I mentally started counting and caught up with Sonja. Grabbing her hand, I pulled her along with me. I tried to take the shotgun from her, but it slipped from her hand. Leaving it, we ran, the beam flickering ahead of us.

Two-one thousand

We curved around, tumbling into the wall when I stumbled. Rock tore at my shirt and shoulder, and I hissed in pain. Another tunnel joined ours, and I saw an arrow pointing up and a second pointing down.

Three-one thousand

We were panting, the heat of the mine making us sweat, pushing the dirt and grit off of us. I was wondering how long the fuse was on the stick, and I swerved just in time to avoid an old mining bucket, sticking upright between the rail track and the rough rock wall.

Four-one thous –

A massive *CRUMP* sounded behind us, and a wall of heated air rushed past us, blowing more grit and debris against our backs. We stumbled, fell, and I managed to grab her and shield her from the worst of the rocks and debris as the mountain shook around us. The flashlight flickered out in my hand. The darkness around us was absolute, but I focused on holding her. If this was the way our lives ended, I couldn't think of another thing I wanted to be doing.

The rumbles deep below continued, and the floor continued to tremble. From above us, closer to the entrance, I heard a sound I didn't realize I was dreading. A sliding, rattling sound was coming from our left, toward the surface, and the air direction changed. I felt air being pushed past us, going in the direction we'd just come from. After an unknown length of time, the rumbles stopped, but we could hear the mountain growling all around us. Sonja's breath was hot on my throat, and I reached to trace her face. Smoothing her hair back, I kissed her forehead; her head tilted up to mine, and I found her lips. They were cool in the warm air around us.

We kissed while the mine grew still.

"That's an earth shaking moment," I said when we came up for air.

She snorted laughter, and I knew she was rolling her eyes in the dark.

I felt around, finding the flashlight, and was rewarded with a dim glare. In the previous darkness, it was bright, but I had a sinking feeling. I didn't think it was going to last.

"Do we go and see what we did?" She nodded in the dust and debris, her hair wild around her shoulders, dirt covering most of her face. I wiped as much of it off as I could, thinking how beautiful she looked. I told her, and she smiled as we back-tracked down the tunnel.

The dynamite had done a better job than we thought. The entire tunnel we'd just run out of had come down, leaving a jumble of rocks spilling into the main corridor. We looked at our handiwork and grinned at each other.

"It's done," I said.

"Finally," she said, spitting on the rock pile. "Let's go. I want my life back."

We climbed back toward the surface, feeling a sort of relief, but I was afraid of what we'd find ahead. The second rumbling concerned me, but I was hoping it was one of the many side braches that had developed over the years. The mountain quieted around us until the only sound was our breathing. We followed the weakening beam of the flashlight, loosely holding hands. We walked upward, the air thickening with dust as we got closer to the entrance.

We came upon a rockslide, and my fears were confirmed. The second rumbling I heard was the sound of the opening we'd come through closing. Sonja stared at it, and I let go of her hand. Looking on the ground around us, I finally found what I was looking for. A bent nail, rusted with age, but long enough for me to grip.

"Climb up there and see if you can shift some of the rocks," I said. I squatted down, scratching in the dirt, trying to remember. She climbed up the fallen rocks and tried to roll some of the smaller rocks down. I stared at the dirt, having moved to the side, and I tried to aim the flashlight toward her. She moved some out of the way, but when I didn't hear a rattle for a few minutes, I looked up. Sonja had uncovered the top of the pile, only to find a solid slab of stone. She looked over her shoulder to look at me.

"I can't move it," she said. I climbed up to look with her.

"Do you think we can move the ones below it?" I asked, and I saw her wince as she pulled on the smaller rocks.

"What's wrong?" I asked.

"Nothing," she grunted, trying to pull the rock away, but I grabbed her hand. She tried to resist, but the rocks under our feet shifted, and I was able to turn her hand over. Her fingertips were lacerated, bleeding, and grimed with dirt. I hissed, and she looked away.

"Why didn't you tell me?" I asked, and pulled her down from the pile. "I need to look at it."

"I'm fine."

"No, you're not. But you'll be okay. Come here." I pulled off my shirt and handed it to her. She followed me over to where I was scratching in the dirt. "Clean them off as best you can, but look at this," I said, motioning to what I'd been trying to remember. She stood over my back as I talked, wincing as she blotted the blood away,

"Remember the map we saw? At Ricochet? It showed a cutaway of the mine." I pointed. "We came in here, followed it to the lowest point, but remember the vent tunnel? It could be another way out. I just have to remember what it looked like."

She laid a cool hand on my back and leaned over me.

"Do you remember anything about it?"

"I think there was another branch, somewhere along here," she said.

I tried to picture the cutaway in my mind, hoping it wasn't just an illustrator's imagination.

"If we followed it past this first side tunnel and then take a left at the next one, it should take us out."

I stood up, nodding. "I think we need to try. We aren't able to do anything else here." I took her hand from her and gently kissed her torn up fingers.

She placed her other hand on my bare chest and goosebumps prickled through my skin. I let go of her hand, cupping the back of her neck, and pulled her to me. Twining my fingers in her hair, I pulled her to me, her eyes getting bigger and pulling me in. I kissed her, slowly, deeply, and her body pressed against mine. My other hand went to the small of her back, and I fished it under her shirt, finding the skin just as soft as I'd imagined it.

We finally broke the kiss, but kept out heads together. I loved her eyes; looking into them, I felt peace. I tried to move closer, and my foot hit the flashlight. The light was dimmer than I remembered, and I squatted down to pick it up.

"You . . ." she muttered. "You pick the worst times."

"The curse of my life," I said. "We need to hurry. I don't think the light will last long."

"If we're trapped in here, I know how we'll spend our last days," she said. I shivered at the thought, either from the anticipation or the dread.

We started backtracking, heading deeper into the growing darkness. Finding an arrow, I said, "We need to remember these. When the light goes out, we'll have to find them in the dark."

We passed the first turn in the tunnel, and the flashlight dimmed yet again. I pulled Sonja's hand, stopping her. Once we were still, she pulled us to the right-hand wall. With our hands on it, I turned off the flashlight. Once again, the darkness was absolute. It pressed on us, and I had to remind myself to breathe deeply.

"See, it isn't so bad," I said. The darkness was a living thing compressing the space around us, testing all of our senses except one to the max. At the same time, the darkness took root in our minds, causing our imaginations to expand, finding every bit of stimuli and turning it into a threat.

"Bullshit." Her voice quavered, and I felt her hand squeeze mine painfully. "Let's think of the map. We went around the first turn. There should be one on the right, but it's not that one, or the one after. Third time's the charm. Ready?"

"I guess."

We took a tentative step in the dark, and then another. Tommyknockers started chattering in the darkness around us, and we froze.

I tried to sound calmer than I felt. "Same thing we heard before. No big deal," I said as soothingly as I could.

Behind me she said, "Bullshit. You're such a bullshitter."

"That's the damn truth. I'm scared shitless," I said. I wondered if we'd really killed all the things Bobby had in the mine. What if one had taken a wrong turn, sometime over the last few days, and couldn't find its way out, and was waiting for us somewhere in the darkness? I paused again, listening for any footsteps other than our own.

"Why did you stop?" Sonja asked behind me.

I was holding her hand, and she was standing to my left, with my right hand on the wall beside us. "Why don't you get behind me and hold onto my belt?" I asked her. "If we're single file, there's less chance we can trip over something."

She didn't question me, thankfully, but didn't let go of my hand until she had a good grip on my belt. At least now she'd have some warning if there was something in front of us.

I took another step forward, sliding my feet rather than picking them up. Did we see any debris, other than small rocks and such, between the rails and the rock wall? My hand hit one of the timbers supporting the rock above our heads, and I grunted.

"What?" she asked.

My thumb had been bent back, and I said, "The supports. I hit one with my hand." The darkness continued to make every little sound louder, and I heard another sound I feared. Steps were shuffling along somewhere in front of us. I stepped up against the wall, pulling her with me. Her hand was panicked as it gripped mine. All the things that happened to us were stressful and I was ready for it to be over, but I have to admit I enjoyed it when she clung to me. We were the perfect size for each other, and we held our breath together as we heard the footsteps get closer.

We smelled it as much as heard it. Rotten flesh combined with the dirt and dust of the mine, the faint metallic odor of blood, and the raw smell of intestinal gases. It moved in silence, nothing but the slow shuffle of footsteps. We couldn't even hear the thing breathing, and the silence was as creepy as the slow, dragging footsteps. I was afraid it would be able to smell us, but if it wasn't breathing it wasn't smelling, either. The thing moved past us, footsteps methodical until it continued up the tunnel.

"And to think I thought this was a quiet place to stay for the night," I whispered to Sonja. She shook under me, and I realized she was laughing. I brought my hand up, cupping her chin, and she raised her mouth to mine. She kissed me frantically between huffs of laughter, and our skin grew slippery around our mouths. If I'd known stress made her this forward, I would have done it earlier. Finally we stilled, but I could feel her heart beating against my chest.

"Ok, you ready? I think we're getting closer," I whispered.

She nodded against me, and I started back down the corridor. My hand was on the right, Sonja was holding my belt, and I was taking small, steady steps. I stumbled over small rocks in my path, and one time I kicked some type of metal implement. It dinged off the rail, and both of us froze.

"What was that?" Sonja whispered to me.

"I don't know. Some type of tool," I answered.

"Should we grab it?" she asked.

I started to decline, but thought better of it. I bent over, feeling around, and found what I thought was a broken pickaxe. It was curved, with a blunt end, and a pointed tip. A wooden handle extended from the center and ended in a shattered wooden handle. "I found it."

We continued our shuffle steps, kicking the occasional rock and pausing every few steps to listen. A tiny gust of air pressed against us, then reversed motion to flow past us.

"Adam," Sonja said, "did you feel that?"

"Yes, I did." A new smell replaced the fetid stink of the mine. Fresh air was ahead of us, somewhere, and I had to stop myself from running. "We're getting close."

The push of air got stronger, and we ran into another obstacle. A wire grate covered the exit from the mine. Beyond it, we could see the shine of stars and the thin daylight of dawn through the overgrowth. We were on the opposite slope from the entrance, and I looked for a way to dig out of the wire. It was pitted and rusted, anchored in concrete ages old. Instead of trying to dig, I simply took the pickaxe and used it to torque the wire until it broke. I was halfway through the bottom row when we both heard the sound of slow steps behind us. We turned, and in the growing light could see something approaching us. His clothes were black with dust, his skin grey and in tatters. Literally falling apart, the person's bones showed through in places where the skin had been had been ripped off.

Sonja went to one side of the tunnel and I went to the other. The creature paused, trying to decide which of us to attack, and turned toward Sonja. It moved slowly, and Sonja had no problem fending it off while I brought the pickaxe down, straight into the back of its head. It shuddered once and was still.

"Easiest one of the night," I said, grabbing its ankles and dragging it away from us.

Sonja wrenched the pickaxe out and was working on the barrier when I got back. She figured out an easier way to snap the thin wires and started moving up the side as I watched. I marveled at her toughness and the single-mindedness of her attention.

As she worked, I peeled back the wire until we had a corner of it exposed. "Try it," I said, and she dropped the pick axe and wriggled on her belly until she was through the wire. I got down on my stomach, scraping it on the rock, and followed her.

EPILOGUE

Dawn was rising before us as we came down from the mountain. The truck was where we left it, and it started as soon as I turned the key. Sonja slumped in the seat, exhausted, bloody, and filthy, except for tear tracks that cleaned a path down her cheeks. I tried to execute a three point turn. I failed miserably, because I could barely turn my head, but I got the truck pointed to the road. As we turned the first switchback, we saw the town laid out before us. Someone from outside had finally noticed what was going on; lights pulsed from the tops of ambulances, fire trucks, and police cars of every color.

"The cavalry has arrived," I said. "About time."

"Will it still be there?" she asked.

"I don't know. Without Lyles . . ." I let the words trail off.

"Why did Bert do it?" she asked.

"He had to," I said, the first thing that came to mind. I thought back to our conversation before we climbed into the truck before driving up the bluff. "I think he knew."

We topped the last rise before town, Ricochet coming up in the next curve, and I was transported back to my drive into town, before I met Otis, before I met Sonja, when the only thing I had on my mind was my thirst and the need for a smoke. The gas station I stopped at was now a burned-out shell, and we zipped past it without stopping. The rack holding cookware and fishing poles was knocked over and scattered, but I saw the bench was undamaged. For a brief second, I considered stopping and throwing it into the back of the truck

.

Instead, I pushed down on the gas, wanting to see what lay ahead. The road angled downward, curving, and I had to hit the brake. We saw the edge of a sign, and then breathed a sigh of relief. It wasn't lit, but I was expecting to see the weed-choked parking lot I'd seen the week before. The parking lot did have a few weeds in it, and the building itself looked dingy and windblown. Each of the signs on the exterior of the building had a fine, thin film of dust and spots of rust.

"Please, no," Sonja moaned.

I stopped the truck. We were the only car in the parking lot with the exception of Bobby's car. But it now sat on four flats, and every window was a starburst of broken glass. The paint, already faded, was flaking, with rust showing through in spots.

"Let's go inside," I said.

"Don't we need to go see the police or something?" she asked.

I walked around the truck, feeling every bump and bruise from the last twenty-four hours. "Maybe. No. I don't know. We need to rest first, maybe get cleaned up," I said.

We walked up the steps, which creaked under our weight. Our footsteps sounded hollow, and when I touched the front door, it groaned open like a bad horror movie. The floor was covered in a thin film of dust, as if it had been abandoned for years.

Sonja let out a sigh, and I barely caught her before she fell. Scooping her up, I wobbled before I caught my balance. The thick, fancy drapes were now dumped in a pile on the floor. I tottered over, feeling the last of my strength dissolving. I fell to my knees, clutching Sonja to my chest. I half lowered, half dropped her into the pile of fabric, holding my breath against the expected explosion of dust.

Hope flickered inside me when the fresh scent of cotton floated up, but everything faded to black around me. I fell over myself, getting one arm around Sonja, and then we slept. Or maybe we died; to this day, I'm still not sure. I guess we won't know until the juke drops the next record.

My mind picked up the sound first. I hazily identified it as a
steel guitar, realizing it was a twelve string; no six string can make
such a full, warm tone. I moved, and pain shot through my back,
reminding me of the night before. I felt a tingle in my hand and
winced when I realized my arm was no more than a piece of
cordwood, numb from the shoulder down. I felt a hand shake my
shoulder.

"Come on, boy, you can't lie around all night," a deep voice
said. I cracked one eye open, and against the brightness, a face
appeared. Young and familiar, I tried to place it. "Of course, if I
was lying with that pretty thing, you couldn't get me up either." A
laugh tinkled somewhere behind the face, and *it* was maddeningly
familiar.

"Sonja," I croaked. "Baby, wake up." Sonja didn't move, and
I placed my hand against her face. It was cold to my touch, and
my heart lurched. She finally murmured and cracked open an eye.

"Adam?" she whispered, her voice hoarse.

"Drinks! Drinks for the sleeping couple!" The voice above
me said, and I tried to will my eyes open. I felt strong hands grip
my chin, and a glass a few degrees above freezing was placed on
my lips. Something delicious slipped past my lips, coating my
throat. I saw feminine hands pull Sonja off my shoulder, and I
tried to pull her back to me. I was easily manhandled, and I settled
for gripping her hand. The warm burn of alcohol replaced the
soothing cold, and I felt it flow to my stomach. Another sip
tickled on the way down, and I felt the rush of blood along my
limbs.

"Sonja," I said, my voice stronger.

"She's here, just give it a second. Gawdamighty, Millie, you
ever hear such carrying on?"

The voice and the fuzzy face finally clicked. My eyes opened
wide at the same time as Sonja's.

"Bert?" I asked the young man in front of me, but Sonja was already ahead of me. She leaned clumsily forward, wrapping him in a hug as she began to cry.

"Better believe it, sonny boy," he said. He patted his chest. "How do I look? I can always be the grumpy old me, but..." he grinned, his cheeks folding into a dimple. "It turns out I have miles left to go."

I looked at the older woman beside me who had been helping Sonja. "Mildred?" I asked. Several decades older, she was still beautiful. Fine lines were etched around her face and crow's feet were carefully carved into the corners of her eyes, but the smile and the eyes were the same. "What happened?" I asked, rather stupidly.

"Three plays for a dime," Bert said. "I guess that was just one of mine."

"All you need for a good time," Mildred finished for him.

"But I saw you go into the cave," I insisted. "And Ricochet . . . it was deserted. And run down." As I looked around me, my eyes took in the lie. Ricochet was back in its glory, light bright, wood shining, with an older man behind the bar. A *much* older man. When he saw me looking, he carefully raised a glass in a hand that trembled slightly. "Lyles?" I asked, and Mildred sighed.

"He gave a lot of himself, this time. I wish he'd learn. He'll heal, eventually, but it will take time and energy. He may not be able to. . . . We may be here for a while."

Sonja disengaged from Bert, saw me, and cried again. She leaned into me, and I took her into my arms. "That's not a bad thing," I said. "This place . . . . grows on you, after a time."

"We'll have time enough, I'm sure. That's the one thing we have plenty of. At least here," she said.

CPSIA information can be obtained
at www.ICGtesting.com
Printed in the USA
LVOW10s0058060917
547685LV00009B/190/P